STACKED

MARS FITNESS
BOOK 2

LINDEN BELL

STACKED

When the person you desire is so close, and yet so far.

SAWYER

I've been in love with my best friend and roommate since the first day of boarding school over a decade ago. But Preston has always been oblivious, obsessed with his PhD research, and more importantly, straight.

When the new, sexy grad student walks into my gym, I have to wonder... is it time for me to move on?

PRESTON

Some guy is trying to steal my best friend. I won't let him. Sawyer's mine.

Maybe I haven't appreciated Sawyer enough over the years, but that's going to change now. I'll do whatever it takes to keep him by my side. Even if it means kissing him.

Stacked is a best friends to lovers, bi-awakening, nerd/jock MM romance between possessive, protective, and co-dependent room-mates. Expect the most tender caretaking, slipping into each other's beds in the middle of the night, and adorable clinginess.

It is the second book in the Mars Fitness series and can be read as a standalone.

CONTENTS

SAWYER

Westbourne Academy, on the outskirts of Boston, Massachusetts, looks like it was plucked from the set of a Harry Potter movie. With water-stained beige stone walls, arched stained glass windows, and actual freaking towers, the building feels more like a castle than an expensive boarding school for New England's wealthiest families.

But then, I wouldn't be surprised if it *is* actually a castle that they've turned into a high school.

"You really didn't need to come in with me," I mutter to Mom as we pass another student giving us curious looks in the hallway. Enrolling mid-semester as a poor kid on an athletic scholarship is mortifying enough on its own. The last thing I want is Mom drawing more attention to me.

Besides, I only have one suitcase. I could've found my room without her help.

"But I want to see where you'll be living!" Mom doesn't even try to keep her voice down.

"Shh!"

"What? This place is beautiful! When will I ever get a chance to see the inside?" She stares at the soaring arches lining the hallway that leads to the boys' residence. She couldn't look more like a tourist if she tried. All she needs now is to pull out her phone and start taking pictures.

Oh, crap. I spoke too soon.

"Sawyer, wait, turn around!" Mom pushes me in front of her and takes a few steps back before lifting her phone and pointing it at me.

"Oh my god, Mom! Stop!" I hiss at her, turning away, and curling in on myself.

She just smiles smugly at me and ruffles my hair like I'm some child. Ugh. She knows exactly what she's doing and she's not afraid to embarrass the hell out of me in front of my new classmates.

"Come on!" She strides ahead of me. "I think it's this way!"

I duck my head and hurry after her. The sooner we find my room, the sooner I can get rid of her and figure out how to make friends with these rich kids.

The boy's residence is through a set of heavy double doors that open up into a long wide hallway. Off to one side is a set of stairs that lead up to the second floor but my room should be somewhere down here. Bronze numbers screwed into each door sit above plaques with elaborately engraved names.

Thomas McClelland.

Emory Williamson.

Josiah Perkings.

Francis Redman.

Jeez. Rich people have weird names. Why do they all sound so old?

"Here we are." Mom stops in front of room 130. It's at the very end of the hall. The plaque on the door reads *Preston Boyer.* Guess they haven't got around to putting my name up there yet. Or maybe the scholarship students don't get plaques.

Mom tries the door handle and jiggles it back and forth.

"Shouldn't you knock first?" I ask.

She shrugs. "It's your room. Are you going to knock every time you go in?"

"I don't know," I mutter, then hand her the key. My student card is supposed to open most doors at the school —anything with a scanner. But here in the residence, they still use keys that slot into locks on the door handle.

Mom takes it and unlocks the door. She pushes the door open an inch and shoots me a pointed look before knocking. "Hello? Anyone home?"

Silence.

"See?" She scoffs. "Nothing to worry about!"

I roll my eyes. Why does she have to be such a mom?

Inside, the dorm room doesn't look nearly as Harry Potter-ish as the rest of the school. It's got the wrought iron windows and hardwood floors, but all the furniture is modern. There are two beds and two desks, but the guy already living here—*Preston Boyer*—has taken over the entire room. There are clothes strewn over every available surface and paper and textbooks sit in stacks on the floor. The computer setup is impressive. Three screens are mounted in a curve on the wall and I recognize the expensive gaming keyboard and mouse on the desk. The gaming chair sitting in the middle of the room is expensive too.

"Wow." Mom plants her hands on her hips as she surveys the mess.

I can already imagine the speech she's reciting in her head. If this was my room at home, I would get a nice long lecture. I hope whoever Preston Boyer is doesn't show up while she's still here. She's not above parenting other people's children.

"I guess this side is mine?" I inch toward the side where there's slightly less stuff, wondering how the hell I'm going to move it all. I didn't bring that much with me, but I'll still need *some* space. You know, a mattress to sleep on and all that.

"Who the hell are you?"

Mom and I spin around at the new voice.

In the doorway is another boy, shorter than me and scrawny. The school uniform he's wearing is wrinkled, one pant leg is caught in a sock, and the tie is loose and off-center. He's got a mop of black hair and thick black-framed glasses, but what really catches my attention are his eyes.

They're blue. Like the ocean. Like the sky. And they're zeroed in on me with such intensity that my lungs stop working. My brain stops working. The only response I've got is *whoa* and *cool*.

Beside me, Mom clears her throat and steps forward. She puts on her mom voice when she speaks. "This is Sawyer and I'm his mom, Ms. Paige. He's moving into this room today. And you are?"

The mom voice works because the boy shrinks back

and clutches the textbook he's holding closer to his chest. "Preston Boyer," he says, eyeing Mom warily.

"So nice to meet you, Preston." Then she hooks her thumb over to my side of the room. "Would all this be yours?"

Preston's eyes dart from Mom to the bed, piled high with clothes, to me. There's a little furrow in his brow like he's trying to think of a response and drawing a blank. Like maybe all this stuff isn't actually his.

Then he blurts out, "You're not my roommate."

Mom's in front of me, so I can't see her face, but I know exactly what it looks like. Her eyebrows are halfway up her forehead and her lips are pursed into her "What did you just say?" expression.

Oh shit. Preston's in trouble.

"As a matter of fact, he is. Sawyer's enrolling as a student at Westbourne and he's been assigned to this double room. So your choices are to become friends and get along or find another room to sleep in. Either way, you need to move your things. Now."

With each word coming out of Mom's mouth, Preston shrinks into himself even further. I kind of feel bad for him, even if he's being a jerk. Getting on Mom's bad side is never a good idea.

"Hey, Pres. What's taking so long?" A pretty blond girl wearing a cheerleading uniform materializes behind Preston. It takes a second for her to notice me and Mom in the room. "Oh! Hi! You must be Sawyer."

She squeezes past Preston and approaches Mom with a big smile plastered on her face. The girl is brave. "I'm Madison. Preston's girlfriend." She extends a hand for Mom to shake, then does the same with me.

"Mads!" Preston hisses like Madison is consorting with the enemy. "What are you doing?"

Madison glances back at him. "I'm welcoming them. Come on, Pres, don't be a jerk. You knew you were getting a roommate."

"No, I didn't!" Preston shuffles into the room, staying behind Madison like she can protect him from Mom. Madison looks like she can hold her own, but no one can stand in Mom's way if she's determined.

"Yes, you did." She rolls her eyes and turns to the mess on Preston's desk. "The Residence Office sent you a letter, remember?"

She shuffles through his things, tossing them around as Preston's expression grows pained. He's probably one of those people who has some weird ass filing system that only makes sense to them.

"Here it is!" Triumphantly, Madison holds a crumpled piece of paper high in the air. It's the same thick cream-colored stuff that my acceptance letter was printed on. "Sawyer Paige. Moving in September twentieth. Please clear away any personal items that have been stored on the other side of the room."

As one, we all stare at the personal items that have definitely not been cleared away.

Silence stretches for long moments before Madison breaks it. "No worries! I can help! It shouldn't take too long." She marches over with a big grin and grabs a stack of books off the desk.

"No! Wait!" Preston drops the textbook he's holding and reaches for the ones in Madison's hands. "You can't just move stuff around! I have a system!"

Ha. Called it. This guy is strange. Living with him is

going to be a drag, but at least I don't have to worry about being the token loner.

"Fine, here, I'll hand you the stuff and you put it wherever you want, okay?" Madison takes him by the shoulders and spins him around so he's facing his side of the room again. "Just keep it all over there."

Did she say she was his girlfriend? How the hell did a confident, pretty cheerleader end up with this disaster of a guy? I exchange a look with Mom, who has to be thinking exactly the same thing.

Then she sighs and pats me on the shoulder. "Looks like you're all going to get along just fine."

It's going to be a long year.

SAWYER

I cue up the latest dance mix I've curated for the gym I work at and do a quick spin as Duo Lipa sings about dancing the night away. *clap clap*

As the front desk manager for Mars Fitness, I hold the reins to the gym's sound system. It's a part of my job that I take very seriously—good music is as key to an effective workout as pre- and post-stretches.

Across the lobby, behind the juice bar, Logan's head starts bobbing along with the beat. When the chorus comes around again, we both lift our hands up and double-clap at the same time. He points at me and cups his mouth with his other hand.

"Woo!" he yells, and I "Woo!" right back at him.

"And these two lives of the party are Sawyer—" Beau, one of the gym's owners, nods at me, then over toward the juice bar, "—and Logan."

Beau is our default tour guide and he's got funny anecdotes for every feature of our facility—including the bowls of lube and condoms we stock in the locker rooms. "As long as everyone is a consenting adult," is our motto, and we pay very selective attention to what goes on in the showers and steam room.

Beau gestures to the guy who came in earlier asking about memberships. "This is Fitz. He's new to the city and wants to join Mars."

"Awesome!" I reach over the counter and hold my hand up for a high-five. "Welcome to Mars!"

Fitz laughs and slaps his palm against mine. "Thanks."

He looks a little shell-shocked. Behind his trendy glasses, bluish-gray eyes dart between all of us like he doesn't know who to focus on. It's a typical response for newcomers to Mars. We can be a lot to absorb at first, but once a member settles in, we pride ourselves on creating a safe and inclusive community.

"I'll leave you in Sawyer's capable hands." Beau shakes Fitz's hand, then turns away.

Meanwhile, I grab a tablet and pull up the registration forms. "How long have you been in the city, Fitz?"

He smiles widely, eyes sparkling as he peers at me through his glasses and a deep dimple forms in his left cheek. Damn. A dimple. So freaking cute.

"Just got in yesterday."

I hold the tablet toward him and Fitz reaches out to grab it. But he doesn't take it, and I don't let go either. We're connected across the counter by the tablet and suddenly the music and constant clang of the gym dims just a little.

"And looking for a gym to join already," I say, my voice pitched a little lower.

"What else is a gay supposed to do in a new city?" he responds, sounding a little breathless.

"In that case, you've come to the right place."

Fitz's eyes travel lazily down my body and up again. "I think you might be right."

I hold his gaze for a moment before nodding to the tablet we're both still holding. "Just need you to fill out all the forms—there are quite a few—and bring it back whenever you're done."

I nudge the tablet in his direction and he takes it, holding it to his chest like I've given him a precious gift.

"You can grab a seat at one of the tables." I gesture to the cafe-sized tables that dot the lobby between the front desk and the juice bar.

"Thanks," Fitz murmurs coyly as he turns away.

I watch as he walks to the closest empty table. He's wearing pastel-green shorts that end just above his knee, but are tight enough to reveal a well-rounded bubble butt and strong thighs. Below them are nicely defined calves, and when he turns around, his shins are dusted with a thin layer of dark hair. The front of his shorts isn't tented or anything, but there's a fullness there that hints at a decently sized package. His stomach and chest are obscured by his close-fitting polo, but based on the way his shoulders fill out the shirt, they'll be just as pleasing to the eye.

I meet Fitz's gaze as he stands beside the table, watching me checking him out. Oops. Caught me. I flash him a quick smile, and ooo, there's that dimple on his cheek again. Cute.

"New member?"

I drag my attention away from Fitz to find Connor

standing off to the side, gym bag slung over his shoulder. Connor's been a regular at Mars for a while now, especially after he started dating Donnie, our spin instructor. He looks pointedly at Fitz, whose head is bowed as he taps on the tablet, then back at me.

"Or should I say, "fresh meat"?" Connor bites back a laugh at his own humor.

"Yeah, fresh meat." I wiggle my eyebrows as I play into his innuendo.

"You show him the showers yet?"

"Not yet," I say with a bit of a laugh in my voice. "Beau did the tour, but I'm sure there are some things he forgot to show him."

"Right." Connor nods. "Gotta make sure he knows where the condoms and lube are."

"Yeah, and you know, which shower head has the best water pressure. That sort of thing." My imagination provides a helpful image of me on my knees in front of Fitz, showing him just how much pressure a head can give.

"I'm guessing yours?" Connor snickers.

"Something like that."

"Hi… I'm done."

We both turn to find Fitz a step away, holding up the tablet. How much of that exchange did he hear? From the way he's looking at me with heat in his eyes, probably the important parts.

I take the tablet from him, purposefully closing my hand over his before letting him slip his hand out from under mine. The touch was brief but more than enough to send pleasant little tingles up my arm.

"Awesome."

"I'm Connor, by the way."

Fitz breaks eye contact at Connor's interruption, and his smile grows from sultry to sheepish, and whew, that's pretty cute too. "Hi, I'm Fitz."

"Welcome to Mars. If you're into cycling, you should definitely try out a spin class. My boyfriend's the best instructor in the city."

Fitz nods at the suggestion, but the dimple doesn't make an appearance. It doesn't mean anything, but there's a tiny seed of satisfaction at the revelation. Dimples don't come out when Fitz is being polite. They come out when he's flirting.

"I'll keep that in mind. Thanks."

"Speaking of which—" I glance at the big clock behind the desk, then at Connor. "Aren't you late?"

"Yup!" Connor gives the counter a light tap and a knowing smile. "See you around, Fitz."

Once Connor's out of earshot, Fitz leans against the counter, resting his forearms across the top. It brings him a little closer to where I'm standing on the other side. "Everyone's so friendly here."

"Uh huh, we're all about the community."

Fitz dips his head an inch and even through his glasses, I can see him peering at me through his thick, dark lashes. "Fresh meat?"

Oh yeah. He definitely overheard my conversation with Connor. Oops. At least he doesn't seem bothered by it. If anything, he looks even more interested.

"Fresh meat," I repeat, tacitly confirming his implied question.

There's another moment of us gazing into each other's eyes before an especially loud clang from the main floor breaks through our little bubble. I clear my throat and wake up the tablet to check the forms Fitz filled out.

Mars has a reputation in the city's LGBTQ community as a prime hook-up location for queer men. It's understandable when we have a steady stream of guys coming through, each one more muscle-bound than the last. I'm the first to admit that I've sampled the wares—not all the time, but every once in a while when someone catches my eye. Someone cute with dark hair and light eyes, perhaps with a dash of nerdy. Someone like Fitz.

A scan of Fitz's forms doesn't turn up any glaring omissions. I wave him down toward the computer at the end of the desk. "Everything looks good. Let me print out a membership card for you."

Once I've double-checked all the info on the card, I click print.

"You also get one free session with our personal trainers," I ask as I crouch down under the desk to grab a new member gym bag filled with Mars swag. "Would you like to book that now?"

"Can I book the session with you?"

I surge to my feet. Or at least, I try to. I don't quite clear the edge of the desk and bang my head on the way up. "Ow, fuck."

"Oh shit! Are you okay?" Fitz's eyes are wide as he stands on his tiptoes. His hands are planted on the top of the counter like he's going to hoist himself over it. "Come here. Let me see." He waves me toward him.

I rub at the tender spot. "It's fine. I didn't hit it that

hard." Still, I bend my head and turn away from Fitz to present him with my booboo.

Gentle fingers brush through my hair, too softly for any real assessment, but even then, I lean into the touch. "Hmm. I think you'll be fine." The fingers glide down my neck and across my shoulder before dropping away.

When I turn to face him again, his expression of concern has turned into something more heated.

"I can give you a more thorough examination, though. I know a thing or two about brains."

Like how to suck them out of my dick?

I don't say that out loud, of course. I'm a gentleman. "Perhaps when my shift ends? I'm here till closing, unfortunately."

Fitz checks the time on his phone. "I can make that work," he says, dimple coming out to play.

Can someone develop a Pavlovian response to a dimple? Because I wouldn't be averse to trying.

Someone else comes up to the counter. "Hey, can I grab a towel, please?"

I reluctantly move away from Fitz to pluck a freshly laundered towel from the stack behind me. "Here you go."

"Thanks, buddy."

I turn back to Fitz. "Uh, where were we?" I ask, distracted by the dimple that's still visible on his cheek.

"Personal training session?" The dimple deepens.

"Oh yeah, right. Um, you asked if you could book a session with me. No, sorry, I'm not a personal trainer, unfortunately."

The disappointment in his eyes is palpable. "That's too bad."

"But we've got some of the best guys in the city." I click

a few buttons on the computer to pull up the gym's personal training schedule. "They'll really put you through your paces."

Fitz lets out an exaggerated sigh. "Okay, I guess I'll have to settle for someone else."

Laughter bubbles up through my chest, light and fizzy. "I can always help with cool down, if I'm free," I say, my voice teasing.

"I'll hold you to that."

Chuckling, I scan through our schedule to find the next available appointment. "I can get you in for a session this Saturday. How's that sound?"

"You'll be here on Saturday?"

"Yup." I pop the "p."

"Then book me in."

"Awesome." It takes a few more clicks to finish up Fitz's registration and training appointment. Then I slide his new membership card and gym bag across the counter. "These are yours."

"Thanks, Sawyer." He takes them, then glances back with a question in his eyes. "I'll come back to check for signs of brain injury in a few hours?"

I smile and my skin tingles in anticipation. "I'm looking forward to the examination."

It's late by the time I make it home to the loft apartment I share with Preston. It's one of those converted warehouse things with rustic brick walls, concrete floors polished by decades of foot traffic, and soaring ceilings with exposed ductwork. With three bedrooms, each with its own bathroom, an open plan kitchen/living room, and a generous patio, it's way more space than the two of us need.

But it was a graduation gift from Preston's parents, so we moved in the summer after senior year of high school. Preston lets me live here rent-free, which is the only way I can afford such a nice place in Brooklyn while also paying for tuition. I might be Mars's front desk manager, but I don't do full-time hours in order to work slowly toward my undergraduate degree.

I'm still buzzing from my post-work stress relief session with Fitz when I let myself in. It's quiet and most of the lights are off, but that doesn't mean no one's home. A half-empty takeout container sits on the kitchen counter and I let out a quick sigh of relief.

Good. He ate. He usually doesn't unless I remind him.

I pack up the remaining food and stash it in our fridge before going in search of Preston. I find him exactly where I expect him to be: in the third bedroom that we've converted into an office.

His fancy mechanical keyboard is pushed off to one side and he's face down on the desk, drool pooling under his cheek. My heart twinges at the sight. I need to wake him up and drag him to bed. His neck will be sore in the morning.

Still, I let myself study him a moment. His black hair is stuck up in all directions like he hasn't brushed it in days. One tail of his shirt hangs out over his pants while the other one is still tucked in. There are stains on his pant leg that look like he spilled coffee on himself. And he's wearing two mismatched socks.

He's a disaster.

And I love him.

I think I've loved him from that first day at Westbourne when he walked in on me and Mom, all confused, yet indignant. I still remember the way he looked at me, startling blue eyes, so full of intensity, so sure I was intruding on his space.

Preston's given me a lot of looks since that day. Happy ones, sad ones, angry ones, excited ones. We've been through quite a bit during our four years of high school in New England, and then another eight in New York. But that first time we locked eyes will always be seared into my memory.

Preston is scatterbrained and a klutz. He's not great in social settings and generally not good with new people at all. He can be too blunt, miss social cues, and sometimes end up offending others unintentionally. He once told me his parents got him tested for autism when he was a kid, but they didn't like the results, so the diagnosis was never mentioned again.

Despite all that, he's a genius. A legit, off-the-charts IQ prodigy who's completing his PhD in neuroscience. He should be set to graduate this coming spring.

Most importantly, he's my best friend. I can't imagine life without him and I don't want to.

I set my hand carefully on his shoulder so I don't startle him. "Hey, Pres."

"Huh?" He sits bolt upright, eyes blurry, a line of spit dribbling down his chin. "Oh, Sawyer. When did you get home?"

He drags the back of his hand over his mouth, and I snatch a tissue out of the box on his desk to wipe up the spot he missed.

"Just now." I comb my fingers through his hair, trying

unsuccessfully to tame the unruly tresses. Each touch settles the adrenaline I've accumulated from a busy shift at the gym. Each caress sends a comforting warmth through me until I breathe a sigh of relief.

"Is it late?" Preston asks.

"Yeah, it is." I rub his back. "Come on. Let's get you to bed."

Preston stumbles out of his chair and leans on me as I guide him to his bedroom at the end of the hall. He flops down on his king-sized bed, looking small and delicate against the dark bedspread.

I remove his socks, then tug him back up to his feet to get the rest of his clothes. He's minimally cooperative, lifting limbs when I need him to, but otherwise, he lets me do the work.

We've done this hundreds of times before and it feels almost like a ritual—I undress him, revealing his body one item of clothing at a time. His pale skin is dusted with dark body hair. His muscles hug his bones, giving him a long, lean silhouette. He sways as I move around him, always toward me, always seeking me out. And even though I know it's just so he doesn't have to support his own weight, a part of me thrills at the idea of Preston wanting to rest his body against mine.

When he's down to his briefs, I lift up the covers and he crawls in under them. He immediately turns on his side, curling into a ball and I carefully tuck the covers around him. He's out before I can turn the lights off. But I know he won't stay that way for long.

I pad to my room and get ready for bed with an ear attuned to any sounds from the hallway. I shouldn't. Just like I shouldn't keep my door cracked open when I climb into bed. Just like I shouldn't feel a thrill of happiness when minutes later Preston slips into my room, then into my bed.

Just like I shouldn't feel a deep-seated joy when his warm body scoots up behind me, back-to-back, and we both fall asleep.

PRESTON

My lungs burn as I run up the stairs to Professor Graves's office on the fifth floor of the science building on the Grantham University campus. My meeting with him was supposed to start ten minutes ago, but I got distracted by… I don't remember now. Must not have been important.

I skid to a stop a couple steps short and brace a hand on the wall as I catch my breath. Stairs really aren't my friends. Any kind of physical activity, really. The only sports I have any interest in are the ones played on a computer screen.

When I'm confident I won't pass out on Professor Graves's floor, I push away from the wall, grab the doorknob, and let myself in. Only to stop short—there's already someone here with him. Someone I don't recognize. I can't be that late, can I? He hasn't moved on to his next meeting, has he?

"Preston, come in." Professor Graves waves me in. "I

want you to meet Fitzgerald Green." He gestures to the guy sitting in a chair in front of Professor Graves's desk—the chair *I* normally sit in.

"Oh, it's just Fitz. Fitzgerald sounds so pretentious. Hey, nice to meet you!"

Just-Fitz holds out his hand and I stare at it for a moment before my body clues in on what it's supposed to do. I take it—squeeze it firmly, only one pump, exactly the way Dad taught me to do years ago. It's supposed to communicate confidence, assertiveness, and leadership, he said, even if I don't have any of those qualities.

Just-Fitz's handshake is also firm, with only one pump. And the way he leans back in the chair, smiling casually, makes him appear equally confident, assertive, and leader-like.

"Take a seat, Preston."

I sink uncomfortably into the second, empty chair. It's facing the wrong direction. The seat cushion is lumpy in a different way from the chair I'm used to. Why couldn't Just-Fitz have taken this one instead?

"I've heard a lot about you, Preston. I'm really excited to get to work with you this year."

I do a double-take because why is he talking to me? That's not what I'm here for. Then my head snaps just as quickly to Professor Graves. What does he mean, "work with me this year?"

"What?" I practically spit out.

Professor Graves has that look on his face, the one he gets when he has to tell me something I'm not going to like.

"Fitz is the new grad student in our department. I

announced he was transferring in during our meeting last week."

I don't remember that, but I tend to not remember things I have no interest in, so it's possible Professor Graves mentioned it and I just forgot.

"What does that have to do with me?" As the question leaves my mouth, I get a sinking feeling. The only reason he would have for introducing us, the only way I would end up working with Just-Fitz, is if I'm assigned as his mentor.

"Because you're his mentor—"

"No." The objection flies out before I can stop it.

Professor Graves closes his eyes for a second like he's gathering his wits. "You're his mentor, Preston. And Fitz will be assisting you in the lab."

Another objection hangs from the tip of my tongue, but I manage to swallow it down when Professor Graves lifts a hand to stop me.

"I know this is difficult for you. You prefer working alone. But being a mentor is a requirement for graduation, remember?"

Which is what I need to discuss with him. "About that." I shift to the front of my seat. "I—" I cut myself off this time when I realize Just-Fitz is still in the office with us.

Professor Graves takes advantage of my hesitation and continues on. "Fitz will help you with the last of the experiments you've got planned before you defend your dissertation in the spring. In return, you'll supervise his literature review."

"Can't you assign someone else? Everyone knows I'm not

a good mentor." The department tried to sic me with a mentee last year and it was a disaster. The guy didn't know what the hell he was doing in the lab and he didn't understand a single thing I tried to explain. I ended up ignoring every email he sent me and he eventually requested a new mentor. Good riddance. I don't even remember his name now.

Professor Graves shakes his head. "No, we can't. Everyone else has been paired up. Some of your colleagues have two mentees. Besides, Fitz did his undergraduate thesis on Stable Diffusion, so not only are you the last person available, but you're also the most obvious choice."

"I've read the papers you've published," Just-Fitz jumps in. "Your work is really fascinating. It's exactly the type of research I want to do."

My research has evolved over the years, but it generally involves the use of artificial intelligence to further understand how the human brain works. The development of Stable Diffusion, an advanced artificial intelligence model, has really pushed my work forward by leaps and bounds.

But if Just-Fitz thinks he's going to impress me because he read a couple journal articles about the AI program, he's got another thing coming. I've got better things to do than babysit someone who can't keep up.

"See? It's a perfect match." Professor Graves sets both hands down on the table with a finality that hits me with dread. "It's settled then. Preston, make sure you do an orientation with Fitz and get him up and running by the end of the week."

He turns back to his computer as if the meeting is over. But I haven't even told him my problem yet.

"Wait. No. I. But—" My tongue can't decide which

words it wants to form, and Professor Graves and Just-Fitz stare at me in confusion.

Finally, Professor Graves glances at Just-Fitz. "Why don't you get settled in the grad student office, Fitz. Preston will catch up with you later."

Just-Fitz nods, utters some meaningless pleasantry, and lets himself out.

About time. I take back my chair, collapsing into it as the air caught in my lungs pours out in one long *whoosh*.

Professor Graves leans forward, arms folding across his desk. He gives me a few seconds to gather myself before he levels his gaze at me. "What's the matter, Preston?"

I breathe in experimentally and when my lungs don't seize, I forcefully slow my thoughts so the words don't get jumbled up as I speak them.

"I don't need to mentor anyone because I'm not graduating this year."

Professor Graves's mouth opens, then shuts. He tilts his head like he didn't hear me correctly. "Why aren't you graduating this year?"

"I'm not ready." My research isn't anywhere near complete. I still have so much to do and not enough time to do it. But most importantly, the thought of graduating chills me to the bones. "I can't."

Professor Graves sits back in his seat, his chair squeaking under the movement, and he reaches up to adjust his glasses. "I don't understand. You were on track at our last check-in. Has something changed since then?"

"No..." Nothing's changed, per se. It's just that the closer graduation gets, the less I can ignore the reality that's looming in the distance. I don't want to join the family company. I don't want to take over Boyer Pharmaceuticals. I never have.

"So why would there be a delay in our timeline?"

"I just— I don't— there's not enough time!" My lungs feel tight again as I try to suck in a breath.

I don't want to graduate. I don't want to leave academia. It's the only place I'm remotely useful. It's the only place where I know what I'm doing and won't fuck something up. I can't be trusted anywhere else, or doing anything else.

Just ask Sawyer and Madison how many times they've had to rescue me when I've unwittingly dug myself into a hole. Or had to physically drag me away from my desk because I've become so engrossed in my work that I forget about everything else. The only way I survive the society functions my parents drag me to is because Madison usually comes with me. The only way I don't die of starvation or thirst is because Sawyer is there to feed me and make me drink water.

I'm good at what I do. My research is important. I'm going to be one of the best neuroscientists in the world. Why would anyone want to make me do anything else? That's a question only Dad can answer.

Professor Graves furrows his brow. "There's still eight months until your defense. That's plenty of time to complete the rest of your research. Plus, now you have Fitz to help you."

I shake my head. He doesn't understand. "I don't want help. I don't need help. I just need more time."

His expression turns grim and sympathetic. "I'm not sure I'm seeing the whole picture here, Preston. But unless there's an unexpected setback with your research, we don't have a legitimate reason for pushing back your defense."

He raises his hand again when I try to stammer my way through another objection.

"Either way, it's too early to be postponing anything. Let's get through this semester and re-evaluate your time-line in January. If the timing appears too tight, we'll deal with it then."

That doesn't resolve my problem, but I've known Professor Graves long enough to know when he's done putting up with my shit.

"Is there anything else?" he asks with a warning in his voice that my answer better be "no."

"No," I mutter dutifully. If there's one social behavior I'm good at, it's backing down in the face of authority.

"Great. Make sure you schedule that orientation with Fitz. I expect it done by the end of the week. That means you've got less than three days."

I nod and listlessly push to my feet.

"Shut the door behind you, please," Professor Graves says, eyes already glued to his computer screen, fingers flying over the keyboard.

I manage to get halfway down the hall before I slump against the wall. If there weren't so many people from my department in this part of the building, I'd slide all the way down to the floor and curl up in a ball.

That did not go as planned. But then, what had I expected? Professor Graves is young for a tenured professor—only a handful of years older than I am—and he's got a reputation for being the "cool advisor" in our department. But that doesn't mean he's a pushover. The chances that he would have let me delay my defense just because I wanted to were slim to begin with.

Something buzzes against my thigh, the vibrations magnified by contact with the wall. I jump and scramble for my phone, almost dropping it in my haste.

When I manage to unlock it, there's a message on the screen from Sawyer.

SAWYER

> Remember we're having lunch today. I'm in the quad, but if I don't see you in five minutes, I'm coming to get you.

Oh, shit. Sawyer. Lunch. I totally forgot. Today is Sawyer's day on campus and we usually try to eat together before he goes to work at the gym.

The quad is on the other side of campus and it'll take me at least five minutes to get there unless I run. My poor legs. My poor lungs. They've already been overtaxed today.

Still, I rush down the stairs, not bothering to wait for the world's slowest elevator. I have to squeeze my way through a group of undergrads loitering in the doorway and then do my version of a sprint—which is more like a fast walk with some hopping every few steps—across campus. I only let myself slow down when I see Sawyer's silhouette in the distance.

Oh, good. I haven't missed him.

His back is to me. Wide shoulders fill out his fitted long-sleeve t-shirt. The sleeves are pulled up to his elbows, leaving his forearms exposed. His jeans are faded and worn, but they accentuate how long his legs are. Legs that are much more used to running than mine are—legs he put to good use on our high school rugby team.

Sawyer throws his head back and his laugh rings through the air. I would recognize that sound anywhere. Hearing it always makes me feel better. No matter how shitty my day has been, no matter what I'm worried about, it'll all get worked out once Sawyer's here.

My lips start curling into a smile but then freeze halfway when Sawyer shifts to the side. I didn't notice that he was talking to someone. The smaller person was hidden behind Sawyer's tall frame. But now that I'm closer and our relative positions have changed, I can see who Sawyer's talking to. Laughing with.

Just-Fitz.

My attempt at a smile melts off my face as irritation scratches at me. Just-Fitz has already ruined my meeting with Professor Graves, and now he wants to ruin my lunch with Sawyer? Who the hell is this guy anyway? Where the hell did he come from?

Just-Fitz's gaze shifts over Sawyer's shoulder as I stalk toward them. I see the moment he recognizes me, followed immediately by a look of wariness.

Sawyer notices and follows his gaze, turning halfway until he spots me. The smile that lights up his face fills me with gratification, and it grows when he starts walking in my direction, leaving Just-Fitz trailing after him.

SAWYER

The spark that lights up in me whenever I set eyes on Preston is completely irrational and totally unfounded. I've known him for over a decade. I've lived with him the entire time. He's never shown an iota of interest in me and if it hasn't happened by now, it never will. And yet, there's still a tiny piece of my heart that continues to hold out hope. It doesn't make sense, but no matter how many times I've tried to get over Preston, I always keep coming back to him.

My feet eat up the distance between us like my body can't stand to be any farther away from him than necessary. It's only after a few steps that I notice he's not looking at me. In fact, he's glaring at something behind me —at Fitz.

I reach for Preston, placing my hand on his shoulder, and he automatically leans into the touch. He's still glaring at Fitz, though.

"What are you doing here?" Preston can be a little too

direct for his own good sometimes, but there's something more in his voice than mere bluntness. There's an edge that I don't often see in him.

I glance quickly at Fitz who is hanging back and wearing a nervous smile. "This is Fitz," I say as I gently nudge Preston in his direction. "He's new in town and just signed up for a gym membership at Mars the other day."

We also got fairly well acquainted, but I'm not about to mention that to Preston.

"I know who he is." Preston inches forward. Almost like he wants to face off with Fitz, and I tug him back a little.

"You know each other?"

Fitz lets out a stilted sound that I think is supposed to be a laugh. "Yeah, we're in the same department."

"He's in *my* department." Preston corrects him.

Ah. That's what's happening here. Preston isn't good with change and September is full of change in academia. He always bristles when new students join his department and suddenly there are a bunch of unfamiliar faces around. He'll get over it, though, he always does. It just takes a bit for him to adjust.

"Cool!" I try to infuse extra enthusiasm into my voice. Maybe Preston will feel better if I show him that Fitz is a friend, not a foe. "You study neuroscience too, huh? No wonder you know a thing or two about brains."

Fitz's laugh is genuine this time as I mention the "examination" he gave me after I hit my head. A little twinkle appears in his eyes and my libido perks up at the possibility of a repeat performance.

Preston snaps his head around and now his glare is focused on me. The disapproval in it effectively demolishes whatever interest my dick was cultivating in Fitz and guilt trickles in instead.

That's the thing about my one-sided love affair with Preston. My heart belongs to him, but my body wants things he can't give me. There's nothing technically wrong with fulfilling that need elsewhere. Preston and I are best friends; we haven't signed a chastity pledge or anything. And yet, whenever I'm reminded of this disparity, I feel like I've let him down, like I've failed him, betrayed him.

"Um…" I shift uncomfortably and adjust the strap of my bag over my shoulder. "Preston and I are going to get lunch," I say and watch as the twinkle fades from Fitz's eyes. Crap. Fitz is genuinely a nice guy, and despite my inner turmoil, I still want to make him feel welcome in this new city. "Have you eaten? Want to join us?"

I catch Preston's deepening scowl out of the corner of my eye, but Fitz lights up again at the invitation.

"I'd love to! If I'm not intruding, that is."

"Nope, not at all," I respond before Preston can mutter something that's accidentally rude. "There's a noodle shop nearby that we always go to. You're going to love it. It's really popular with students."

I lead the way out of the quad, Fitz on my right and Preston on my left. An awkward silence settles around us as we walk. Am I imagining that Preston sticks a little closer to my side than usual?

We turn left when we get to the sidewalk and encounter a group of students coming from the other direction. The sidewalk isn't wide enough to accommodate all of us and Preston is forced to fall behind me and Fitz. I swear I can feel the heat of his glare on my back.

"Are you sure it's okay if I join you? I don't want to butt in or anything," Fitz whispers to me quietly.

"No! Not at all," I whisper back at him, and then scramble for an explanation. "Preston just gets moody when he's hungry."

"Hangry." Fitz chuckles. "I know the feeling."

"Exactly. He'll be fine once I get some food in him."

Fitz makes an agreeing sound, but there's still a hint of tension in his expression like he doesn't believe me.

We get to the restaurant and I pull open the door, holding it for Fitz, then Preston, to pass through.

Fitz shoots me a flirty smile, complete with a dimple sighting, and a quietly murmured "thanks."

Preston, on the other hand, still has that scowl firmly etched into his face. The urge to take him in my arms and hug him until the scowl melts away is almost too strong to resist. I don't like that he's upset. I want to fix it for him. But I can't really bundle him up in my lap and cuddle him in public.

I settle for taking his shoulders in my hands and stepping in close enough to peer at him over his shoulder. "How about you grab that empty table for us?" I suggest.

Preston glances up at me and for a split second, I'm distracted by the sight of bright blue through long dark lashes. My chest aches with want and I unconsciously drag him up against me. The back of his head touches my shoulder and if circumstances had been different—if Preston and I were who I want us to be instead of who we actually are—I would've dipped my chin an inch and covered his lips with mine.

But I don't do that. I draw on the self-control I've

honed over the years and force myself to set him away from me. "Go on. I'll get your usual for you."

Preston shoots Fitz a suspicious look, then shuffles away, sulking. My hands stay on his shoulders until he's out of my reach. I watch until he pulls out a chair and sits down.

"So, you and Preston are…?"

I drag my gaze away from Preston to find Fitz watching me with confusion. "We're best friends. And roommates."

He nods but the confusion doesn't budge. "For a moment there it seemed like you were… more."

I chuckle, or at least try to. "No, no, we're just friends. Preston's kind of a touchy guy and I've sort of picked up on it over the years." It's not a complete lie. Preston is much more tactile than anyone else I know, but my need to touch him back is all my own.

"Right."

"Anyway, let's order. Everything on the menu is amazing."

The restaurant isn't huge. It's one of those order at the counter and bus your own tables kind of places. But the portions are big and the prices are low—two key requirements for any business catering to students.

The roaring gas fire and the clanging of metal utensils against metal woks bounces off the walls and the scent of garlic and fish sauce fills the heated air. We're a little early for lunch, so there are only two people ahead of us. If we wait twenty minutes, the line will start spilling out the door.

I order the wide noodles with beef for myself and the crunchy noodles with seafood for Preston. Fitz goes with something called Singaporean noodles that I've never tried before.

"How long have you guys been roommates?" Fitz asks.

"Since high school." A happy fluttering feeling dances in my chest at the memories of us in that room together. Me forcing Preston to turn the lights off so we can sleep. Preston helping me study for exams. "We went to Westbourne Academy. It's a boarding school up in Massachusetts. And then we moved to Brooklyn together for college."

Fitz's expression goes a bit wistful. "Must've been nice having someone to get to know the city with."

"You don't know anyone in New York?"

He shakes his head. "Nope. My parents weren't thrilled with the idea of me moving all by myself. But I needed a change of scenery and the program at Grantham is really good."

"Will you be working with Preston at all?"

Fitz winces and sneaks a glance at Preston who's slumped in his chair. "That's the plan. Although, he doesn't seem to like me much."

"Preston's not great with change," I say with my voice lowered. "He'll come around."

"I don't know about that. I get the sense he's not easy to win over." He smiles at me, left cheek dented with that dimple. "Maybe you can put in a good word for me?"

"Sure thing. I'll tell him to go easy on the new kid." I bump his shoulder with mine and Fitz's dimple deepens.

"Order twenty-seven! Twenty-eight!"

We grab our trays from the counter and carry them to the table where Preston's waiting for us. I set Preston's plate down, then break apart a pair of disposable wooden chopsticks for him. He takes them and fiddles with them for a bit before poking at his food.

After a minute or two of this, I lean over and whisper quietly in the small space I've created between us. "Is everything okay?"

It's not like him not to devour his food. He forgets to eat so often he's usually perpetually hungry without realizing it. All I need to do is present him with something edible and he'll gobble it down.

Preston's gaze flits from his plate to Fitz, then back again. He gives me a stiff nod before stabbing his noodles with the chopsticks and stuffing his mouth. There's definitely something going on with him, but it'll have to wait until we're home tonight before I can work out what.

Meanwhile, Fitz is watching us again, or more like observing us with a keen awareness I want to discourage. I don't want him to get a bad impression of Preston. Preston could use more friends, especially ones he can connect with over his research.

"You mentioned you'll be working with Preston?" I ask. "You know, I've never been able to understand what the hell Preston's research is about. Something to do with brains and computers?"

Fitz straightens and lights up, kind of like the way Preston does when he gets to geek out over science.

"Yeah, it's super cool." Fitz sets his utensils down, noodles forgotten. "We're using the latest developments in artificial intelligence to study how the brain works. The experiment that Preston's been running is focused on visual processing. Basically, we scan someone's brain while they're looking at a photo. Then we feed the data into the AI algorithm and it tries to regenerate the image based on the data. It's incredible. You wanna see?"

He's already pulling out his phone and cueing up the photos. I take the phone when he hands it to me.

"The original images are on the left," Fitz explains. "And the AI-generated ones are on the right. You can see the AI images aren't perfect reproductions, but the resemblance is close!"

On the left side of the screen is a picture of a stuffed teddy bear and next to it is… well, it looks like a badly decorated cookie where all the different colors of icing have melted into each other. But I can still make out the ears, the mangled face, and the bow that's tied around the bear's neck.

I tilt the phone toward Preston so he can see the screen too.

He barely glances at it before turning back to his food. "I've seen those before. They aren't new."

Ouch. I flash Fitz an apologetic smile, then flip through a few more examples on my own.

There's a clock tower that AI has turned into an impressionist painting. It's a hodgepodge of colors, but they're about the right ones, and the silhouette is the same. The next example of an airplane in flight is similar.

"Wow, that is cool."

"Right?" Fitz is nearly bouncing in his seat. "If we can get AI to mimic the functioning of the brain, then we can better understand how the brain works."

"It's more complicated than that," Preston mutters under his breath.

I reach over and rub the top of his back. "I'm sure it is,

but hey, I'm just a jock. You've gotta dumb things down for me."

Fitz's dimple appears again. "Jocks can be smart."

Under the table, a foot bumps into mine. I'm about to pull my foot back and apologize, but then Fitz catches my gaze. There's an unspoken question there, a check-in to see if he's okay to continue. His foot moves slowly, sliding forward so his ankle drags up my calf.

My body reacts physically to Fitz's come-on, but my brain misfires as it tries to reconcile my response with the fact that Preston is sitting right next to me. I want and I don't want at the same time. I'm stuck in between, pulled in opposite directions.

A cough breaks me out of my stupor. "Don't you have to get to work?" Preston asks. His voice is laced with annoyance and… hurt?

My heart stutters at the possibility that Preston would be bothered by me hanging out with Fitz. That he would care. That he would be jealous. But that's ridiculous. Our relationship isn't like that. I make no secret of having slept with other people. I've brought people back to our apartment, and I've even dated a bit. He's never objected, never shown any signs he was upset.

It must be my imagination superimposing my own feelings onto him. At most, Preston's merely frustrated with having to adjust to a new person in his life.

"Are we keeping you?" Fitz asks.

"Uh…" I check the time on my phone. I'm not late yet, but there are a couple errands I want to run before my shift starts. "I should get going."

"You haven't finished your noodles." Fitz points to my plate.

"No worries. I'll grab a to-go box." I slip out of my seat to request one from the restaurant staff. When I get back, Preston's staring daggers at Fitz, while Fitz has his head bowed, pretending not to notice.

Note to self: it's too early to leave Preston alone with Fitz. Good thing I grabbed a second container for him.

"What time do you work till today?" Fitz asks as I dump my food into a box and then do the same with Preston's.

"Till close. Will I see you there?"

He nods. "I'm planning on going in after my class this afternoon."

"Awesome!" I rise to my feet, tugging Preston along with me. "I'll see you later, then!"

With one last smile to Fitz, I push Preston out the door. Through the front windows of the restaurant, I spot Fitz following our progress down the sidewalk. He waves at me and I wave back. Then, with a burst of surprise, I realize I'm genuinely looking forward to seeing him again.

CHAPTER
FOUR

PRESTON

It's been an hour since Sawyer walked me back to the office I share with the other grad students in my program. He kept going on and on about how nice Fitz is and isn't it great that I'll have help with my research now.

No, it's not great. I don't want help. I certainly don't want help from Fitz.

God, he was so annoying. All that smiling. All that laughing. Throwing himself at Sawyer like that. What does he think he'll accomplish by sucking up to my best friend?

Look at me, boo hoo, moving to New York all by myself. Look at me, I'm so smart, I can explain how artificial neural networks work. Look at me, I'm a smart jock, I'll see you at the gym later.

Well, fuck Fitz. Sawyer's a smart jock too. Just because he doesn't study neuroscience doesn't mean he's not smart. He got into Westbourne on an athletic scholarship and he was the captain of the rugby team. He also kept a 3.9 GPA the whole time. The only reason he hasn't gotten his bachelor's degree yet is because he's working so much at the gym.

I'm still fuming silently at my computer screen when a loud buzz makes me jump. My phone is vibrating with an incoming call from my mom and I'm sorely tempted to ignore it. Nothing good ever comes from a call from my mom. She always wants me to do something I don't want to do or go somewhere I don't want to go.

But even as I'm staring at my phone, a message pops up from Madison.

MADISON

Your mom's calling you. Answer the phone.

Ugh. I can ignore Mom, but I can't ignore Madison. She won't hesitate to hunt me down and berate me into compliance.

I pick up my phone and tap on the accept button. "Hi, Mom."

"Hello, Preston. How is school?"

I spin around in my chair, leaning back so I can stare up at the ceiling. "It's fine, Mom."

"That's lovely. Listen, The Art Society is holding a fundraising dinner, and your father and I bought out a table. We expect you to be there."

I stifle a groan. I hate it when they summon me like this. It makes me feel like I'm some sort of thoroughbred they're trotting out for their friends to inspect. "I'm really busy. I have a lot of work to do."

Mom sighs as if she's the one being put upon. "Your name is already on the guest list, and it's for a good cause—"

Everything my parents do is "for a good cause," but is it really? These high society events are full of snobby, rich people bragging to each other about how much money they've donated. Do they actually care about "the cause"? Most of the time, they don't even know what the cause is. All they're concerned with is maintaining the right image for their supposed friends.

What I've never been able to understand is why my parents want me at these things. I don't know how to make small talk or butter people up and lavish them with false praise. I don't know how to work the room or network or any of that. In fact, I'm more of a liability than anything else. I can never be trusted not to stuff my foot in my mouth.

"—you don't have to do anything—"

Which is a blatant lie. If I didn't have to do anything, then why do I need to be there? They want me to smile and shake hands with people I don't know. They want me to pretend I'm the son they've always wished I was, the one who will take the company over from Dad someday and be some powerful pharma CEO.

"—Madison will collect you on the day of, make sure you're dressed appropriately, and accompany you to the dinner—"

Chaperone me is more like it.

"—all you need to do is be there and smile—"

I don't smile. Not the way they want me to.

"—the flight is already scheduled—"

"Flight?" I cut in. "The dinner is in Boston?"

"Of course, it's in Boston." Mom scoffs and I try to remember if she mentioned that already. I don't think she has. "Where else would it be?"

"I don't know," I respond in resignation. Annoyed, I push my foot against the floor and my chair goes flying down the narrow space between the rows of desks. It crashes into the wall before I manage to stop it and my phone slips out of my hand. When I pick it up again, Mom's still talking.

"—Madison and Sawyer and they've both confirmed that you don't have anything else scheduled for that evening—"

I want to counter with something like, "They're not the bosses of me." But the truth is, they are. They know my schedule better than I do. If they say I'm free, then I am.

"—we don't ask much of you, Preston. Your father has already pushed back his own plans by years to let you complete your studies. The least you can do is show your face every once in a while."

It's not as simple as that, and she knows it. She and Dad talk about my academic career as if they've been *so* lenient with me. Like this is some wild, youthful adventure they've allowed me to go on and eventually I'll need to settle down and grow up.

They don't understand that this is who I am. I'm a neuroscientist. It's what I'm good at. It's what I want to do with my life. What's so wrong with scientific inquiry? How is it reckless to want to understand the human brain?

"—don't want you to give Madison a hard time. She's being very kind to escort you here and back."

Madison's always been the model child. My parents probably wish she was their kid instead of me. It's why they pushed us to be together for so long. Madison went along with it until we graduated from high school because her parents loved the idea as much as my parents did. But then she decided she didn't want to be saddled with me for the rest of her life. I don't blame her.

"I'm not going to give—"

"It's settled then. I've got to go. Goodbye."

The dial tone rings in my ear before I can finish my sentence. "Bye," I say to the empty room.

I spin my chair around in a circle as I pull up the text message thread with Madison.

PRESTON

I don't want to go to the fundraiser.

MADISON

Neither do I.

So why do we have to go?

Because mommy and daddy pay for everything, so when they say jump, we say how high.

I shuffle my chair back to my desk and toss my phone on top. My parents do pay for everything, but not because I've asked them to. I have a trust fund my grandparents left me. My parents don't control it and there's more than enough in it to live off of. I don't need their money. But they insist, and as with almost everything else in my life, I don't really push back.

MADISON

It won't be so bad. Just one evening. There and back in no time.

Ugh. I push against the floor again, sending my chair

back-first down the row toward the door of the office. There's plenty of room, but I'm stopped by something—no, someone—sooner than I should have.

I look up to find Fitz looking down at me with an awkwardly nervous expression. He's holding the back of my chair.

"Hey, am I interrupting?"

I jump up and spin around, putting some space between us. What the hell is he doing here? Doesn't he have class? Isn't he supposed to go find Sawyer at the gym?

"What do you want?"

Fitz flinches like I'd physically slapped him. "I wanted to ask you about the orientation Professor Graves mentioned. Do you have time in the next few days?"

I tighten the grip on the phone in my hand. I want to spit out, "No, I don't have time," but I manage to swallow it down.

I can put him off and tell him to come back some other time. I'm busy and I haven't gotten any work done today. I glance at the dark screen of my computer. But *am* I going to get any work done? Not if Fitz and Mom keep circling around me, asking me for things I don't want to give.

"Let's just do it now." I stomp back to my desk, grabbing my chair from Fitz along the way.

"Now?" Fitz glances at his phone. "How long do you think it'll take? I wanted to get to the gym."

The gym. He means Sawyer's gym. My hackles rise at the reminder and I throw my phone into my bag a little too forcefully.

"It won't take long," I say, except it will. It'll take as

long as I can possibly drag it out for. Without waiting for an answer, I shoulder my way past him. "Lab's this way."

Fitz manages to catch up and fall into step with me with barely a huff. "I really am interested in your research, you know."

I try to hurry my steps, but Fitz doesn't seem to have any trouble keeping up.

"I'm excited to help you with it. I'm sure I'll learn tons."

I'm not always very adept at reading people. I tend to miss subtle shifts in tone, the micro changes in facial muscles, and the way the same words can mean multiple things. But Fitz seems genuine in his enthusiasm—he certainly gave that impression when he was gushing all about *my* research during lunch with Sawyer.

"But, uh, I don't want to step on any toes or anything, if you know what I mean." He doesn't elaborate, which makes me think he might be saying more than I'm hearing.

"Okay."

"You can tell me to back off, I won't be offended or anything."

Can I? I'd love to. But Professor Graves wouldn't be too happy about it. "Okay."

There's a pause before Fitz speaks again. "Anyway, the sentiment stands. You know, for whenever."

What the hell is he talking about? If I can foist him off on some other grad student, I'll do it in a heartbeat. But Professor Graves was clear this morning—I'm stuck with him. "Just follow instructions and don't do anything stupid."

Fitz flicks his eyes sideways toward me in surprise, but he wisely shuts his mouth and nods. "Got it."

We walk the rest of the way to the lab in silence, thank god. I reach for my ID badge and—wait, where is it? I pat my pockets and only find crumpled napkins and pieces of scrap paper. I dig through my bag—phone, notebooks, textbooks, journal articles… where the hell is my badge?

"Here, I've got mine." Fitz holds up his own school ID. The colors on it are clear and bright, and his picture shows him smiling with that annoying dimple on his face. It's newly printed, crisp and fresh, unlike the faded, scratched-up, peeling card I can't find.

He holds it against the black rectangle next to the laboratory door. It beeps once, the little light turns green, and the door unlocks.

"Thanks," I mutter under my breath as he lets me enter first.

The neuroscience lab is a series of rooms in the basement of the science building. A couple rooms are for testing, where subjects come in and put on a brain scanning cap so we can capture their brain activity. The rest of the rooms are filled with diagnostic equipment that enables us to process and analyze the data we've collected.

Fitz lets out excited exclamations at every piece of equipment I point to, asking dozens of questions, one after another. It's annoying the first few times he interrupts, but then his enthusiasm starts rubbing off on me. I've been working in this lab for years now, and even though I love my research, the novelty of seeing state-of-the-art equipment like this has worn off.

It's all still shiny and new to Fitz, though, who can't seem to stop himself from touching everything. He examines the caps and puts one on his own head. I boot up some programs and show him the different types of scans we perform.

He asks to see the latest data I'm working with and despite myself, I do.

"Wow. That is so cool!" he exclaims, not for the first time since we set foot in the lab. "How did you get Static Diffusion to do that? I thought it didn't have that capability yet." He points to the newest tweak I've made to the model.

So I explain, falling deeper and deeper into my research with every question he asks. He's got an endless supply of them and most of them are good. I almost forget who he is and why I don't like him when he sits up abruptly and grabs his phone.

"Oh, shit. I told Sawyer I'd meet him at Mars in half an hour." He looks sheepishly at me. "Can we pick this up later? This is really cool stuff and I want to see the rest of it."

The happy, giddy feeling I get when I'm engrossed in my research crashes and burns around me. He's meeting Sawyer. At the gym. So they can do jock things together.

"I'm so sorry." Fitz pulls the cap off his head and stands, pulling his bag over his shoulder. "I'm super excited to work with you, though. Thanks so much, Preston!"

He rushes out of the lab, leaving me sitting there at a computer terminal all alone—fluorescent lights bouncing off the white walls, the hum of the computer the only sound breaking the silence.

I shove to my feet, the wheeled office chair shooting out behind me, and clench my hands into fists. Something tight and twisted and uncomfortable lodges itself in the middle of my chest. It grows and expands until it feels like it's eating me from the inside out.

What was I thinking, letting my guard down around Fitz? He's not my friend. I'm not supposed to like him or get along with him. I have to work with him and that's it. I need to remember that the next time he tries to worm his way in. I need to remember he's the enemy.

SAWYER

Lizzo's About Damn Time plays through the gym's speakers and I sing along to the lyrics as I grab a fluffy white towel from the laundry cart. It's still warm from the dryer and when I shake it out, the air fills with that freshly laundered scent.

"So…" Logan from the juice bar skips up to the front desk and taps excitedly on the counter with both hands. "Last night was date number three!"

I smile at the unfiltered excitement rolling off him. "With the new guy?"

"His name is Jay." Logan gets a dreamy look in his eyes. "Isn't that a great name? Jay. So strong. So masculine. Oh, sorry!"

Logan steps back so a member can reach the card scanner.

"Thanks!" I wave the guy through and grab another towel. "Sounds like it's going well."

Logan leans over the counter and squeals, "He stayed over last night!"

I lift my hand to give Logan a high five. "Nice! Good score!"

Logan slaps my hand but rolls his eyes. "It's not a score. I think he might be the one." He props his chin in his hand, elbow on the counter.

"The one?" The words come out a little garbled as I use my chin to pin a towel to my chest and fold it in half.

"You know, "The One". My true love. My soulmate. The love of my life."

I have to laugh. "You've been on three dates! You don't even know the guy!"

"I know him!" Logan's all indignant now.

"Really?" I shoot him a skeptical look and he huffs.

"Sometimes you just know, okay?"

I shouldn't be surprised. Logan's a hopeless romantic. He falls in love with a new guy every other month, and even though his relationships never work out, his enthusiasm never dims. He's always certain this next guy will be it, his Prince Charming, and he'll get swept off his feet. It hasn't happened yet. We're all still waiting.

"How is this guy different from the last guy, what was his name again? K-something?"

Logan reaches over the counter to snag a folded towel for a member. "Here you go! You're welcome!" Then he turns back to me, waving his hand dismissively. "The last guy was a dud. Jay's no dud. He's the one."

"Is that even a thing?" I ask, replacing the towel Logan snatched with a fresh one.

"Of course, it's a thing!" Logan gasps, looking legit offended. "You don't believe you have A One?"

My heart aches in my chest and I suck in a deep breath to release the pressure. Do I have A One? I have no idea. I know who I want to be my "one". Except, can he be the one when he doesn't return my feelings?

Logan points over his shoulder in the direction of the gym's main floor. "Are you going to tell me that Beau and Gavin weren't destined to be together? What about Christian and Sebastian? Donnie and Connor?"

My heart does that uncomfortable squeezing thing again as Logan lists off all the happy couples at the gym. I discreetly rub my chest as I reach for another towel.

I can't deny there's something appealing about the relationships they have. The love radiating off them, the intimacy that wraps around them like a cloak. It's impossible not to notice the looks they exchange with each other, the silent, coded messages that only their other half can understand.

A gym member wanders over to the juice bar, squinting at the menu.

"Oh! Gotta go!" Logan rushes back to his station and a moment later, the industrial-sized blender starts up.

The whir of the blades, mixed with Lizzo from the speakers and banging equipment from the main floor, leaves me strangely isolated with my own thoughts.

Do I want a relationship like the ones my friends have? Sure, why not? I wouldn't say no if it came waltzing through the door. But am I going to find it? I don't know and I don't really want to think too much about it.

I've dated my share of people—guys and girls. I've always had a good time and enjoyed their company, but I never seriously considered a long-term relationship with any of them.

Maybe because I'm already in a long-term relationship with someone—a one-sided one.

We've never talked about it, but if I had to guess, Preston's probably asexual and aromantic. He dated Madison in high school, but they always had a lopsided dynamic.

Madison was the driving force and Preston just went along with it. When Madison finally broke it off after we graduated, Preston wasn't all that upset. He's never shown interest in anyone since then. He's certainly never shown that kind of interest in me. All he cares about is his research.

"See ya guys later!" I wave to a group heading out of the gym together. The last person holds the door open for someone to come in.

Dark hair, slim build—for a second I think I've conjured up Preston with nothing but my thoughts. But it isn't Preston. It's Fitz.

Of course, it's not Preston. He never comes here. What would he even do in a gym? I shake my head at my own ridiculousness.

"Hey, Fitz!" I call out as he approaches the front desk.

His hair is windblown and his cheeks are a little rosy. His eyes are bright behind his glasses and that dimple appears on his left cheek when he smiles at me. He really is super cute and I find myself leaning over the counter more than I usually do.

"Hey, Sawyer!" Fitz rests his forearms on the counter-top, making no move to take out his membership card.

"How was your class this afternoon?" I ask. "What did you say it was? Research ethics?"

He nods. "Yeah, it's pretty basic stuff, but it's mandatory, so…" he shrugs. "Preston showed me around the lab, though. That was really cool."

The mention of Preston sends a trickle of guilt winding through me and I rock backward a little. "Nice. I've been in there a couple times. No clue what any of that stuff does."

Fitz laughs, the sound clear and bright, and his face lights up. "It's amazing. I can't wait to get into the research." His excitement for nerdy stuff reminds me of Preston and I'm not sure how I'm supposed to feel about that. On the one hand, Fitz's obvious passion for brain stuff is super attractive. But on the other—Preston.

"You headed in for a workout?" I ask, pointing toward the locker rooms. "I've gotta make my rounds so I can walk with you."

"Sure!" Fitz fishes out his membership card and sticks it under the scanner.

"Logan!" I shout across the lobby. "Watch the desk for me!"

I wait for the thumbs-up from Logan before slipping out from behind the counter.

"I know I asked this already, but…" Fitz says with his voice lowered and when he hesitates, I glance questioningly at him.

"But?"

"You two seem really close." He puts extra emphasis on that last word, enough that there's no doubt what he's asking.

I chuckle, but the sound is more stilted than I intended. "I mean, we are, but—" I stoop down to pick up a wet wipe abandoned on the floor and walk it over to the trash bin.

Fitz's giving me a wary look when I turn around again.

"But. We're just friends." When Fitz's expression doesn't change, I hasten to add, "Preston's straight."

"He is?" Fitz furrows his brow.

"Yeah, he's never looked at a guy before." He's never looked at a girl before either, but that's not something I need to share.

I gesture Fitz into the locker room before me and follow him to a bank of lockers. He picks one at random and pauses with s hand on the metal door.

"That's surprising."

"What is?"

"That Preston's straight. My gaydar definitely pings around him and I'm rarely wrong."

Fitz is for sure wrong. If anyone knows, it would be me. Preston hasn't shown interest in guys, ever. Even so, Fitz's statement sparks a tiny flame of hope that I'm reluctant to extinguish. Nothing will come of it—no amount of hope would be enough. But still, the idea that Preston might feel even a fraction of what I feel… I can't help but cling to it.

Fitz rushes on when I don't respond. "I don't mean to argue with you. I mean, obviously, you know him better than I do. I just don't want to trespass or anything."

I force myself to smile. "Nope, no trespassing." Although the idea that I belong to Preston is fuel for the doomed hope flickering in me. "No walls or fences or anything. I'm public property." I wave my arms down my body to present myself to him.

Fitz laughs and it echoes off the metal lockers around us, off the raised ceiling above us. The dimple winks at me and his glasses magnify the blue-gray of his eyes. It's hard not to be drawn in by the combination, to be enticed. My body reacts, despite the objections of my heart.

"Okay, good." Fitz's smile turns sultry and his eyes grow heated.

I take a step closer, pushing aside any doubts that might be lurking. I said I'm public property—and I am. No one has any claim on me, no matter how much I wish that weren't the case. I'm free to do whatever I want, with whoever I want.

Fitz trails a single finger down the middle of my chest. "I want to use the steam room after my workout, but I don't remember how to work the controls." He dips his chin and peers up at me. "Can you show me again?"

He settles his hand on my waist and the warmth of his palm travels through the thin fabric of my t-shirt to my skin.

"Hmm, yeah, it can be a little tricky. The system is pretty sensitive." I crowd him against the lockers a bit.

He nods. "I wouldn't want to break anything."

"No, we wouldn't want that."

"So… in about an hour?"

I glance at the clock on the wall. "Gym closes in an hour and a half?"

He smiles. "Works for me."

Suddenly, the sound of running water cuts out and a couple guys come in from the shower. I step away from Fitz to give them room to get around us.

"An hour and a half," I repeat as I continue backing away.

"An hour and a half," he confirms. He holds my gaze for a lingering moment before turning to his gym bag and unzipping it.

I hurry to finish my sweep of the locker room, the showers, and the steam room to make sure there's nothing I need to take care of and make my way back to the front desk.

Logan's behind the desk, chatting with Donnie, our spin instructor. The moment Logan spots me, he jumps and lets out an excited shriek.

"O! M! G! Sawyer! You've been holding out on me. Who is that hottie?"

I struggle to fight back the smile tugging at my lips. "Who?"

Logan points an accusing finger toward the locker rooms. "You know who! You don't normally escort gym members to their lockers."

"Oh, Fitz?" I shrug nonchalantly as I slip behind the desk and grab the last towel in the laundry cart. "You've met him before. He joined earlier this week."

"No, I didn't!" Logan gives me a light shove on the shoulder. "I was behind the bar. I barely saw the guy."

"I didn't meet him," Donnie says, pulling his reading glasses off his nose. "Who is he?"

"He's a member. You know." I direct the last words at Donnie whose boyfriend, Connor, was also a member when they started dating.

Donnie glances back at Logan. "That's it?"

I should keep my mouth shut. They don't need to know that extra bit with Preston. But Logan's giving me ridiculous puppy dog eyes and Donnie's basically the wisest person on the planet, so if I don't tell them, who am I going to tell?

"No, that's not it. He's also a grad student at Grantham. In the same department as Preston."

Logan gasps like this is the juiciest piece of gossip to ever pass through the Mars grapevine. "You mean your co-dependent roommate and best friend, Preston?"

I bristle a little at the description, except it's not an inaccurate one. "Yeah, I only know one Preston."

"Uh huh. And what does Preston think of Fitz?" Logan asks, poking right at the sore spot.

"Preston doesn't like him." I hold up my hands before Logan can go on. "But only because Fitz is new. Preston's not good with change. He'll adjust. It'll be fine."

Logan narrows his eyes and crosses his arms. "Sure, it'll be fine. Your co-dependent roommate and best friend will adjust to your attention being diverted by someone else."

"That is not what's going on." I object, turning to Donnie with a silent plea for him to back me up.

He winces with a slight head shake, then mouths a "sorry" as he slips his reading glasses back on.

"See? Even Donnie agrees with me." Logan bumps me with his shoulder before ducking out from behind the front desk and sauntering back to his juice bar.

"You're wrong!" I shout at him. I wish Preston was jealous, but that would be too good to be true.

PRESTON

The apartment is dark when I push open the front door. I pause for a moment, wondering whether I've accidentally broken into someone else's unit.

It's late. Way past midnight. Sawyer should be here. Unless he's on his way to the lab to find me—it wouldn't be the first time I've fallen asleep in the lab only to have Sawyer show up and drag me home.

I pull my phone out and check for messages from Sawyer. There are usually at least a few before he escalates to physical measures. But there aren't any. Weird.

I drop my bag on the floor and shrug out of my jacket, letting it drop on top of the bag. I move through the kitchen and into the living room, not bothering to turn on lights as I go.

There's a big couch that fills our living room, one of those three-sided, U-shaped things with an equally large ottoman in the middle. On the opposite wall is a huge TV surrounded by bookshelves. They hold my textbooks, the thrillers Sawyer sometimes likes to read, and random stuff Madison's found for us over the years. The only illumination comes from the city lights filtering in through the windows.

I sink down into a corner of the couch, pulling my feet up and stuffing a pillow between my knees and chest to rest my chin on. I wrap an arm around my shins while my other hand holds my phone, screen on, the time in big white numbers. No messages. No notifications.

The apartment is so quiet. Sirens from emergency vehicles blare in the distance, but here it's eerily still. No footsteps, no sound of someone else moving around. Is it always like this? How come I've never noticed it before? I sink a little deeper into the couch and curl a little harder into myself.

Suddenly this place feels so big, so empty. It's never felt that way before, even when I'm home by myself, even late at night. Why does it feel so echo-y now?

Where's Sawyer? The apartment won't feel so creepy if he's here with me. I check my phone again—nothing.

Maybe he went out with the guys at the gym and forgot to tell me? He doesn't usually forget things like that, though.

Or maybe he's out with Fitz.

The mere thought sends my heart racing and makes my stomach twist violently. I know Fitz went to the gym today. I know his plan was to meet Sawyer there. Are they still there now? What are they doing together? Are they working out? Getting drinks? Or something else?

I blink as my frontal lobe goes static-y for a second,

struggling to compute options and probabilities I don't want to acknowledge. Could they be having sex together? It's not outside the realm of possibility.

Sawyer has sex all the time. He's brought guys and girls back to the apartment before. He's told me about the people he's had casual sex with.

Fitz is friendly and outgoing. They obviously get along. He seems like a likely candidate for Sawyer to have sex with. Could that be what they're doing?

I squeeze my eyes shut as my brain sends out error messages. No, that's wrong. Sawyer can't be having sex with Fitz. Not Fitz, of all people. Anyone but him. I don't like Fitz. He's an interloper. He's annoyingly happy and frustratingly smart. I don't want Sawyer to have sex with Fitz. I don't want Sawyer to have anything to do with Fitz.

I tap on the screen of my phone to check for notifications again, even though I've been holding it this whole time and wouldn't have missed it buzzing in my palm. Still nothing. Where the hell is Sawyer? Why hasn't he messaged me? Why hasn't he called?

Maybe he's hurt? Maybe he's not with Fitz but he's just hurt somewhere. In the hospital or something. They would call his emergency contact, wouldn't they? Except he's my emergency contact, but I'm not his. Madison is.

Madison! She would know if something happened to him. I unlock my phone.

PRESTON

What happened to Sawyer?

MADISON

How should I know?

> You didn't get a call?

> No, should I have? What's going on?

> I don't know! Sawyer's not home.

Three dots bounce up and down as Madison types her response. Then they disappear. Then reappear. Then disappear again. Then suddenly my phone starts ringing.

Madison doesn't wait for me to say hello. The second the call connects, she's speaking.

"What the hell's going on, Pres? Why do you think something happened to Sawyer?"

"He's not home!"

"So?"

"He should be home by now." I'm practically wailing.

Madison hesitates before sighing. "Did he say he'd be home by now?" She's using her placating-Preston voice. The one that sounds like she's talking to a five-year-old.

"No," I mumble into the pillow in my lap.

"Did you come home to an empty apartment?"

I press my face into the pillow, feeling silly and miserable at the same time. I know I'm overreacting. I'm blowing things out of proportion. Sawyer's allowed to have a life. He doesn't need to be at my beck and call at all hours of the day.

It's just that he's usually here! I was expecting him to be here! He's supposed to force me to eat dinner, then make me take a shower and go to bed. Then he'll go to bed and leave his door open for me to sneak in. It always happens this way. It's our routine.

And now he's not here. He's most likely with *Fitz*. And I'm all alone.

"Preston?"

I sniffle before answering. "Yeah?"

"Did you call him?"

"No…"

Madison's eye roll is so loud I can hear it through the phone. "Maybe you should do that. Or message him. Let him know you're worried. I'm sure there's a very simple explanation."

"Okay." It's the rational, grown-up thing to do. But Sawyer's the one who messages me. Not the other way around.

"He's probably on his way home right now."

"Okay."

"God, you sound miserable," she mutters, which she probably didn't mean for me to hear.

But she's right. I am miserable. Miserable and alone.

"Do you want me to stay on the phone with you until he gets home?" Madison offers, and even though I know she doesn't really want to, I jump at it.

"Yes, can you?"

She sighs. "Yes, of course, I can." There's movement on her side of the line, shuffling and clattering sounds like she's doing stuff while talking to me. "How's your research going?"

"It's… um…" On a normal day, I can go on and on until Madison has to interrupt to stop me. Right now, not only can I not form any words, but I can't even tell you what my research is about. That's how fried my brain is from trying to process the idea of Sawyer with Fitz.

"Wow. Tongue-tied about your research." Madison laughs softly. "Oh, Preston, it's going to be okay! Sawyer's just late, that's all. People are late all the time!"

"I know…" But knowing doesn't make it any easier to wait through. In fact, it might be worse because now I can't stop wondering *why* he's late and *who* he's with.

"Anyway, I'm doing well. Thanks so much for ask—"

A key slots into the front door and I flip around on the couch, holding my breath as I listen for the lock to flip, then the knob to turn, and finally the door opens.

Sawyer walks in and pauses at the entrance the same way I did.

Elation rushes through me as I try to jump up from the couch. But I'm too uncoordinated and get tangled in the pillows around me.

By the door, Sawyer mutters, "Shit, he's still at the lab," then he hits the lights.

I wince and squeeze my eyes shut at the sudden flood of illumination, sinking back down into the cushions of the couch.

"Preston?" Footsteps—familiar, comforting footsteps—walk across the apartment, toward me. "You're home. Why are you sitting in the dark?"

I blink my eyes open to find Sawyer behind the couch, squatting down so he's at eye level with me.

"I…" I'm not sure why I didn't turn the light on when I got home. It hadn't felt necessary at the time. I was focused on more important things.

"Hello? HELLO?!" A muffled voice comes from under one of the pillows and I feel around until I find my phone. Oh. Madison. Oops. I dropped the phone in my excitement over Sawyer getting home.

"He's home now," I say as I bring the phone to my ear.

"Oh good. Glad you forgot about me now that Sawyer's there." Madison's voice is heavy with sarcasm.

"Sorry." I do kind of feel bad for taking up her time, but I honestly didn't know what else to do.

"Is that Madison?" Sawyer holds out his hand and I pass him the phone.

"Mads?" He stands and takes several steps away so I can't hear the other side of the conversation. "Yeah, I'm here now. Sorry about that… No, nothing's wrong. Just out with a friend… Yeah, I know, I will… Okay, thanks again, Mads. See you soon. Bye."

Sawyer turns back to me, hands on hips. His eyebrows are pulled high and together like he wants to scold me but he's not sure if it's worth it.

I duck my chin and whisper a sheepish, "Sorry?"

Sawyer shakes his head and drops his arms with a sigh. "Come on. You haven't eaten yet tonight, have you?"

Just then, my stomach grumbles loudly in agreement.

Sawyer waves his hand, gesturing me to come out from around the couch. I untangle myself and rush to catch up with him in the kitchen.

"*I'm* sorry I was late and didn't let you know," Sawyer says as he opens the fridge and pulls out a container of food. It's one of the prepared meals our housekeeper/cook makes up. There are always a couple in the fridge in case it's too late for takeout and Sawyer doesn't want to cook.

He dumps the food onto a plate and pops it into the microwave. Then he braces his hands on the kitchen island, opposite me. "You okay?"

I grip the edge of the counter, feeling both embarrassed and indignant. "I was alone."

Sawyer doesn't respond, leaving space for me to elaborate. I hate it when he does that, making me figure out how to say out loud the thoughts that are racing through my mind.

"I was alone, and… you weren't here, and… I didn't know where you were."

Sawyer's lips quirk to one side. "You were worried?"

"Yes." The admission melts away some of the heaviness and tightness that seized me when I came home to an empty apartment.

"You missed me?"

"Yes." More of it falls away, and I slump in on myself.

"Come here." Sawyer comes around the end of the island and I hurry to meet him halfway.

He pulls me into a hug and I sigh at the familiarity of it, the safety and comfort. All the pieces that have been rattling around inside me for the past hour finally fit themselves back together.

"Where were you?" I whisper into the crook of Sawyer's neck, even though I'm not sure I want to know the answer.

Sawyer takes a breath before answering. "Getting drinks with Fitz."

I stiffen, I can't help it. I was right. Sawyer was with Fitz. My worst fear come true.

The microwave dings and Sawyer gives me a quick rub on my back before setting me on my feet. He grabs the food and places it in front of a stool at the island.

"He's kind of scared of you, you know. Actually, I think he's a bit starstruck. He's read every single paper you've published." He grabs a fork and holds it out to me.

I take it and only then realize how hungry I am. I'm not even sure what I'm eating. Some sort of rice dish, but it smells wonderful. I barely taste it as I shovel it down my throat. My stomach appreciates it and so does my brain, because if I'm busy eating, I don't have to respond to Sawyer's comments about Fitz.

Sawyer comes to sit on the stool next to me, turning around so he can lean back against the edge of the island. "Fitz is a good guy. You should give him a chance."

I hum something noncommittal. Giving Fitz anything, including a chance, is the last thing I want to do.

"I'm going to show him around a bit since he's new to the city. I hope you don't mind."

A rogue piece of rice tries to slip down my trachea and my cough reflex sends the rest of the food in my mouth flying across the island. Sawyer's hand is immediately on my back, rubbing circles.

"Whoa, slow down. Chew before swallowing." He hands me a glass of water that seems to materialize out of nowhere.

It takes me several minutes to stop coughing and breathe normally again. My cheeks are wet with tears and my throat feels raw. Sawyer stays beside me, rubbing my back the entire time.

"Better?" he asks as he presses a napkin into my hand. I have no idea where he got that either.

I wipe up my face and nod.

"Want to keep eating?"

I shake my head.

Sawyer chuckles. "Didn't think so." He gives me another quick rub on the back before taking the plate and packing up the leftovers.

His words from a moment ago echo in my ears. *I'm going to show him around a bit since he's new to the city. I hope you don't mind.*

I do mind. I mind a lot. But how do I say that without sounding like more of a jerk than I already am? He knows I don't like Fitz. Fitz knows I don't like Fitz. Yet they're still hanging out and getting drinks. The more they spend time together, the higher the chances they're having sex.

I don't know why I care—I shouldn't. It's none of my business who Sawyer has sex with, and yet that idea lodges itself in the middle of my brain's limbic system, irritating and uncomfortable, refusing to be ignored.

I want to ask whether they've had sex, but I'm not sure I want the confirmation. If I don't ask, I can keep assuming they're not. Regardless, I can't bring myself to say I'm okay with them becoming friends.

Food stored, counter wiped, and dishes in the dishwasher, Sawyer turns back to me. "Ready for bed?"

I nod and let Sawyer lead me down the hall to my bedroom. Once there, he stands in the doorway.

"Need anything else?"

Yes. Lots. You.

But I shake my head no.

"Cool." He smiles tiredly. "Good night, Pres."

"Good night," I mutter to the door he shuts behind him. I mope as I use the bathroom, washing my face and brushing my teeth. I change into pajamas, then stare at the bed. It's so big, way too big for me. I always feel like I'm drowning in it, like I'll get lost in all the sheets and never find my way back out.

I walk past the bed, not bothering to pull back the covers, and open my door to tip-toe down the hall. Sawyer's bedroom door is cracked open and I slip through.

The lights are already off and there's a familiar lump

on Sawyer's side of the bed. I sneak under the covers on my side and scoot backward until my back is pressed against him.

"Good night, Pres," Sawyer whispers again.

"Good night, Sawyer," I whisper back just before unconsciousness takes me.

SAWYER

The wind is brisk when Fitz and I get off the subway on the Manhattan side of the Brooklyn Bridge. I looked up some touristy—but not too touristy—things to do in the city, and walking across the pedestrian footpath of the bridge was one suggestion I haven't done myself yet. Might as well cross off items on both our bucket lists.

We're not the only ones with this idea, though, so it's easy to follow the stream of people meandering toward the bridge.

"This is so cool!" Fitz is bright-eyed, smiling a mile wide.

His enthusiasm is contagious and I find myself laughing into the wind for no particular reason.

"Thanks for bringing me here. With all the moving, finding a place to live, getting everything sorted out at school, this is the first time I've actually done anything fun since I got to New York."

"Really?" I bump him with my shoulder and wiggle my eyebrows. "You haven't done *anything* fun?"

He shoots me a flirty, coy smile. "I haven't done anything fun… outdoors."

"That's better," I tease. "I have a fragile ego, you know. I need constant affirmation."

"Ha! Fragile ego?" Fitz laughs out loud. "I don't believe that for a second!"

"Hey! I can be sensitive." I put a hand to my chest, acting offended.

Fitz loops his arm through mine and leans in to speak in a lowered voice. "I'll just have to keep stroking your ego then."

"You can definitely keep stroking something," I respond quietly.

As we make our way up the inclined walkway to the pedestrian footpath, the wind picks up, blowing off the water. It whips at our cheeks, our hair, our clothes, strong enough that we have to lean into it as we stumble along. Despite the sun shining high in the sky, it's still chilly, the perfect temperature to cuddle in close so we can keep each other warm.

When we get to the main boardwalk, Fitz finds an empty spot along the steel railing and leans over the wide beam to peer down at the cars below. "Whoa! We're so close!"

I stand next to him and watch car after car roll by, almost close enough to touch.

Fitz turns to me with such joy in his smile. His glasses magnify the gray-blue of his eyes, making them look even wider than they already are. His dimple is on full display today, and I can't help but reach out and cup his cheek. I graze my thumb across the soft indent and Fitz turns his face into my palm. He plants a quick kiss before taking my hand into his.

Together, we turn our faces up, letting the sun shine down on us while the wind washes over us. I've got goosebumps across both arms, but I don't think it's from the weather.

"Come on," Fitz says after a minute, pulling me farther onto the bridge. "I need to take pictures for my folks!"

He hands me his phone and I snap a few shots of him with the tower of the Brooklyn Bridge behind him. He's a natural on camera, striking poses and making cute faces. I don't do anything but point the phone at him and tap the button, and even then, his image jumps off the screen.

"Do you want a picture with your boyfriend?" I turn to find an older woman with her hand extended, wearing a friendly smile. I'm about to correct her, to tell her that Fitz isn't my boyfriend, but the words die on my tongue.

He *isn't* my boyfriend, we're nowhere near anything so official after a couple blowjobs and this sort-of date. But could he be? Maybe? One day? Logan's words trickle through my brain. Is he the one? Am I even looking for the one?

"Sure," I say, handing Fitz's phone over. My musings about Fitz and what we could become are left unsaid in my mind, and instead, I join him to pose for the camera.

We stand with my arm around him while he hugs my waist. His head rests on my shoulder and my cheek rests on his head. When the woman returns the phone, we huddle together, blocking out the sun with our bodies to examine the photos she took.

We're both smiling. We look happy, comfortable with

each other, and intimate. We look like we're in love, and the realization is jarring—I want that and it makes me feel guilty as hell.

Halfway between Manhattan and Brooklyn, the thick cables that hold the bridge together descend below the footpath, giving us uninterrupted views up and down the East River. Fitz finds us another empty spot and we lean against the railing, gazing out on the rippling water, the towering buildings on the Manhattan side, and the slightly lower ones in Brooklyn.

Fitz's arm is pressed against mine and a part of me wants to draw him closer into my side. It wants to hold him and kiss him and be the couple that the woman and the photo claim we are.

But another part of me, a deeper part, feels a little sick at the prospect. What about Preston? What about my love for him? My commitment to him? How can I claim to love him when I'm out on a sort-of date with someone else? When I'm contemplating a relationship with someone else?

How is it possible to want two conflicting things at the same time? I don't know.

Fitz grabs the railing for leverage and leans away from it, tilting his head back to face the sky. "Whoa!" he shouts and the wind picks up the sound, carrying it away.

He's so full of life, so vibrant. Quick to smile and always ready with a laugh. I haven't known him long, but I can't deny how easy it is to be with him. We have a similar sense of humor and similar interests, but we're not so similar that it's boring. He's smart, athletic, cute. He's fun to be around and also considerate and thoughtful and kind. He's a great catch.

I should be thrilled with Fitz, and I am… mostly. I should be eager to lock things down with him, and I am… somewhat. If only…

I shake my head. There's no point in entertaining "if onlys". If things are going to happen between me and Preston, they would've happened by now. But they haven't, so I need to let go of the past and figure out what I want for my future. If that future includes Fitz, then I should count myself lucky.

Fitz rights himself and smiles at me. An especially strong gust of wind blows up the river, pushing Fitz off his feet. I catch him with my whole body, chest to chest, stomach to stomach, thighs to thighs. His mouth is an inch from mine and his breath is warm as he laughs out loud.

My gaze drops to his mouth and his tongue sneaks out to wet his lips. His chin inches upward and mine bows lower. When we make contact, Fitz sighs and relaxes into my embrace. His arms snake around my waist, holding us closer together, and my body responds, heat pooling in my groin.

When we pull apart, there's some extra color on Fitz's cheeks. His eyes are a tad darker and his breathing is a bit faster. His hands have slipped under the hem of my jacket, fisting my shirt at the small of my back. He smiles, dimple flashing, and I smile back.

This thing between us is good. It has potential. I want it —I think.

Fitz nestles his hand in mine as we continue across the bridge toward Brooklyn, walking closer than we were before. When a cyclist zooms by, I pull over, putting my hand on the small of his back to keep him out of the way. Then we fall into step again, side-by-side, hand-in-hand.

"I hear there's a great ice cream place under the bridge," Fitz says as we get to the downward-sloping path at the end.

"You did, did you?"

"You're not the only one who can search the internet for things to do in New York." He bumps my shoulder and swings our clasped hands.

"Okay, then, Mr. I-can-run-internet-searches. Take us to the ice cream place!"

In the park under the bridge, we each grab a cone— Rocky Road for Fitz, chocolate chip cookie dough for me. Then we wander the paths that wind along the water's edge.

"The guys at Mars seem really cool," Fitz says as we stroll.

"They are! Logan's hilarious. He's always falling in love and getting his heart broken. He just started seeing a new guy and he's convinced they're soulmates." I lick a wide strip up my double-scooped cone.

"Soulmates, huh? Do you believe in those?" Fitz has taken a bite out of his ice cream, leaving a crater in the top scoop.

"I don't know." I shrug and suddenly it feels like I'm in the middle of a workout, my heart thudding in overdrive to keep up. "You?"

"It's a nice idea," Fitz says, seeming nowhere near as affected as I am. "But sounds too farfetched for me. What does it even mean to have a soulmate? What are the requirements? The qualifications? It's not something you can put parameters around and test."

I smile despite the tightening in my chest. That's such a Preston thing to say I can actually hear it in his voice.

"On the other hand…"

I meet Fitz's gaze.

"Just because there's no way to test something doesn't mean it's not true. Science just hasn't caught up yet."

That's *not* something Preston would say, but the sentiment doesn't ease the constriction around my lungs. Instead, it makes me yearn for something I can't have.

I lick another strip of ice cream, then clear my throat before speaking again.

"You've met Beau," I continue, desperate to leave the subject of soulmates behind.

"He did my tour." Fitz nods.

"Yup. He's married to Gavin. They grew up together."

"Aw, childhood sweethearts?"

I let out a choked laugh. "Not quite. Best friends, but Beau didn't know he was into guys until after he got married *and* divorced."

"Hmm." Fitz flicks his eyes toward me. "The straight best friend, huh?"

I'm not so oblivious that I miss the insinuation in his voice. But again, not something I want to dwell on at the moment. "Then there's Donnie and Connor. And Christian and Sebastian. Donnie's our spin instructor and Christian's a personal trainer. Connor and Sebastian are both members."

"I see. So what you're saying is Mars Fitness staff have a habit of falling for gym members."

I force out a chuckle at Fitz's teasing, though it's getting increasingly difficult to draw a full breath. "Yeah, it appears we do."

We're at the north end of the park, where there's a fancy carousel and benches with views of the Brooklyn and the Manhattan bridges. We take a seat on the bench, watching the carousel turn as the horses float up and down.

"Um…" Fitz breaks the silence after a moment, pointing at the ice cream cone in my hand.

"Oh shit." I forgot I was still holding it and now it's half melted with sticky sweetness running in rivers down my hand. I try to lick it up, but I only make more of a mess, getting ice cream all over my face. "How come yours didn't do this?"

Fitz laughs. "I ate mine faster."

He offers me his napkin, which is still pristine without a spot of ice cream on it. But it's too little, too late. There's too much liquid ice cream to mop up and I rush over to the nearest trash bin to toss what remains of the cone.

"Here." With one hand holding my chin, Fitz dabs at my nose and my cheek with his clean napkin. Then he leans in and licks up the smears on my chin and my lips. "Mmm, delicious."

It's so cheesy and cute that we both dissolve into giggles and gradually the tightness in my chest floats away.

Fitz catches my gaze as the giggles fade. His eyes twinkle behind his glasses, their natural brightness made brighter by the mid-day sun. His cheeks are ruddy and his lips are sweet from the ice cream.

"I think I'm good with the bridge," he says with a head tilt and an eyebrow raise. He trails his hand down my front and settles it on my hip. The unspoken question hovers between us.

Despite myself, my body reacts, dick stirring and limbs

growing heavy at the prospect of getting off. There's no reason for me to say no. There's no reason to deny myself.

I bow my head and plant another quick kiss on his lips. Then I take his hand in mine. "Yeah, I'm done with the bridge too. How about I show you my place?"

"I thought you'd never ask."

PRESTON

The latest batch of images generated by Stable Diffusion is not what I expected. In fact, they're measurably worse than the last batch. Which makes no sense. The tweaks I made to the model should've worked. The images should be more defined and the colors a closer match.

"Pres!"

A hand grabs my arm and yanks me backward. If I hadn't been clutching my tablet so tightly, it would've flown out of my hand and landed on the sidewalk.

"Jesus, Pres. You've got to pay attention when you're crossing the road."

I glance around and it takes me a moment to realize where I am: across the street from my building, and I was about to walk into oncoming traffic. Oops.

"Sorry, I've been trying to figure out this adjustment I made to my model. Do I need to revert back to what I had before? Or maybe the adjustment wasn't big enough. Yeah, maybe I need to turn it up even more." My feet start moving in the direction of school, but Madison stops me with a hand on my arm.

"Ah ah, no way. I've already dragged you out of your lab once today. I'm not doing it again. We're going to be late as it is. Light's changed. Here we go." She marches forward and I have no choice but to scramble along beside her.

"I have so much work to do!" I whine, even though it won't do any good. Madison's been tasked with getting me to that fundraising dinner in Boston and she never fails at her job.

"Yeah, Pres, so do I. But here we are." She holds out her hand, palm up. "Keys."

I reach into my pocket and they're not there. Huh, maybe in my bag? Madison has to hold my tablet and a couple textbooks for me before I find the keys at the bottom. I pass them to her and she gets us through the front door and up to my apartment.

I've got my head bent over my tablet again, studying the code, when I walk straight into Madison's back.

"Sorry!" I say automatically, then look up and see what made her stop in her tracks.

In the middle of my apartment, halfway between the kitchen and the living room is Fitz. Naked.

Okay, not entirely naked. He's wearing a pair of boxer briefs, but that's all. If there's any doubt around whether Fitz works out, this is definitive proof. Toned muscles under evenly tanned skin. Smooth chest and a thin line of hair down the middle of his stomach. With his hair all mussed, he looks like he just stepped out of an underwear ad.

Something hot and violent roils around in my stomach

at the sight of him. I want to charge at him, tackle him to the ground and pummel him. I want to throw something, anything—even my tablet—at him, and scream at the top of my lungs. Who the hell does he think he is, waltzing around in *my* apartment like he owns the place?

My feet try to carry me forward, fueled by the raging inferno erupting inside me. But Madison's a brick wall and won't move out of the way.

"Oh, hello!" Madison gives him a very deliberate once-over. "And who might you be?"

Fitz has the decency to realize that he's—basically—naked in someone else's home. He shuffles to hide his immodesty behind the kitchen island.

"Hi! I'm Fitz. I, uh, I'm the new grad student in Preston's lab."

Madison slowly turns to regard me over her shoulder. She's got a million questions running through her head, and she shoots every single one at me with a single look. "Is that so? How interesting. Unfortunately, Preston's never mentioned you to me before. And since we've just arrived, you're here before we are because…?"

Fitz swallows visibly, his Adam's apple bobbing. His gaze darts down the hall toward the bedrooms. That's when I hear the sound of a bathroom fan—or rather, I notice the lack of noise when it suddenly gets cut off. A door opens and footsteps echo, growing louder as they get closer.

Sawyer appears a moment later, wearing boxers that show off his thick thighs and a tight Mars Fitness t-shirt that stretches across his broad chest and muscled shoulders. His blond hair is a shade darker than normal, wet from the shower he must've just taken.

He pauses when he spots Madison and me in the doorway. "Oh, hey, guys. I didn't realize you were home."

"We just got here, actually!" Madison sounds cheerful, but there's a sharp edge in her voice. She turns back to Fitz. "And we're introducing ourselves to Fitz. I'm Madison, by the way. Think of me as the third musketeer."

"Hi, Madison," Fitz squeaks.

"Fitz joined the gym recently," Sawyer says, his gaze sliding from Madison to me. "I was showing him the Brooklyn Bridge earlier."

There's something in his eyes as we look at each other, something that makes my heart lurch and my lungs contract. I want to go to him and claim him and hold him to me. I want to press myself against him, feel his arms around me, and stay that way until our breaths fall into sync. But I can't because Madison's still standing in my way, and I can't because Fitz is edging his way in.

"I'm pretty sure I know what's going on here, so Preston and I are going to sneak right past you and get ready for tonight's event in his room." She grabs me by both shoulders and physically hauls me forward as she skirts around Sawyer and Fitz. Under her breath, she whispers to me, "Come on, keep going. One foot in front of the other."

I don't consciously move my feet, but by the time we get to my room, my legs no longer want to hold me up. I sink onto my bed and Madison shuts the door behind us.

My fingers dig into the covers and my stomach feels like it's turning itself inside out. I can't get the image of Fitz out of my head, standing there, in the middle of *my* home, wearing absolutely nothing.

I know I'm not the most observant person. I don't put

two and two together very well in most cases. But even I'm not so oblivious that I don't know what he's doing here. He's having sex with Sawyer. Sawyer's having sex with him. They're not just friends anymore if they ever were to begin with. They're friends with benefits… or maybe more.

After a moment of silence, Madison asks softly, "You okay, Pres?"

I jerk upright at Madison's question. Gone is her overly cheerful expression. Her eyes are gentle with concern and her mouth is slightly downturned in a worried frown.

No, is the first answer that pops into my head. But what reason do I have to be not okay?

I don't like Fitz—fine. But I've never put limitations on who Sawyer can be friends with, who he has sex with, who he sees. He's dated a bunch of people in the past. He's brought those dates home before. I've seen them here —men and women—and tried to have awkward conversations with them. I've never felt so viscerally irritated by anyone else in Sawyer's life.

So why Fitz? What is it about him that triggers this kind of response?

Madison pushes away from the door. "Alright, enough of that. Let's get you in the shower. You'll feel better afterward, promise."

I let Madison take my bag and my jacket, and then she pushes me into the bathroom. "I'll pick out your 'fit for the night and hang it inside the door."

I move robotically through my shower, then mindlessly change into the shirt and pants Madison slipped inside. When I step out, she hands me a belt, socks, shoes. She holds up the suit jacket for me and slips it over my shoulders, smoothing the fabric down my back and adjusting the lapels to lay flat against my chest.

"Nice." Then she grabs two tie options from the bed. She holds one up to my chest, then the other, squinting with her head tilted to the side. "Hmm, hold on."

My bedroom door is standing open now and Madison steps back so she can shout through it. "Sawyer! Need your help in here!"

Immediately, footsteps start heading in our direction.

"What's up?" Sawyer pokes his head in. He stills when his eyes land on me and they take a slow, roving path from my head down to my feet and up again.

Heat rushes through me—probably a delayed reaction from the shower or something—and I tug at the fitted collar of my shirt.

Sawyer clears his throat. "Sorry, what did you need me for?"

Madison smirks and holds up the two ties. "Which one?" She moves to stand behind me, reaching around to place each tie against my chest. "Option one? Option two?"

He thinks about it for an awfully long time. I don't know anything about fashion—he must be making a dozen different considerations about colors and patterns and stuff.

"Just pick one, damn it!" Madison finally starts losing her patience.

"Option two," he says, his voice rough for some reason. He coughs and mutters a "sorry," before rushing out to the kitchen, probably to grab some water.

"God, the two of you." Madison shakes her head as she loops the tie around my neck and flips the two ends over each other in a complicated knot. When she tightens the tie, she yanks it up so high, she nearly strangles me.

"Ow." I tug at it, loosening it enough so I can breathe.

Madison rolls her eyes with a sigh. "Okay, good enough. Come on, the plane's waiting for us."

She passes me my phone, wallet, and keys. I stare longingly at my tablet, wondering whether I can bring it with me. But Madison pushes it out of my reach and directs me out of the room. When we pass Sawyer's bedroom, the door is closed and the murmured voices inside are barely audible. I slow to a stop, straining to hear what they're saying—what are they talking about? Are they talking about me?

"Oh, no, you don't." Madison backtracks to grab my arm and drags me out of the apartment. She doesn't let go until the town car pulls up and she pushes me into the back seat.

The second the car pulls away from the curb, she turns to me. "Okay, spill. What's the deal with Half-Naked Guy?"

I chew on the inside of my lip, not sure how to explain Fitz, or rather, my reaction to Fitz. I know it's irrational. I don't understand the basis for it.

"He's the new grad student in my lab," I say, starting with what Madison already knows.

"Uh huh, and?"

"And he joined Sawyer's gym."

"Yes, I've got that much already. Tell me something I don't know."

"He's new to the city and Sawyer's showing him around."

Madison pins me with a threatening glare. "Pres."

I slump down into the back seat. "I don't like him," I say in a small voice.

When I don't continue, Madison heaves a sigh. "How come? Did he say something? Do something?"

"No…" I peek sideways at Madison when she makes a frustrated noise. "Yes?"

"Which one is it?" she practically growls.

"Both?" It's not anything he's said or done, it's everything he says and does. It's all of him, everything.

"Jesus fucking Christ."

"I don't know, okay? I just don't like him!" I cross my arms and glue my chin to my chest. I'm not proud of how I feel about Fitz, but my resentment runs deep and I get a perverse satisfaction from stewing in it.

He's too damn happy, too smiley. He's smart, athletic, and charming. He's got everything. He's so *perfect*, how could I not find him annoying? The better question is, why doesn't anyone else find him irritating?

"Pres?" Madison reaches across the back seat and places a gentle hand on my elbow. "Do you think you might be jealous?"

Jealous? I let the word roll around in my amygdala, testing it against my emotions. I've never been jealous before, at least not consciously. I don't know what it feels like. Is that what these feelings are? Am I jealous of Fitz?

But how? I don't want to be Fitz. I don't want to be all smiley and happy all the time. I don't care about getting along with other people. I've got my research. I've got Madison and Sawyer. That's all I've ever needed.

"I don't know," I finally concede. "Maybe."

I sulk the rest of the way to the airport and keep sulking when we board the plane my parents chartered for us. As soon as the small jet takes off, Madison disappears to get ready, leaving me to pout by myself.

I really wish I brought my tablet now, I could distract myself with work. Instead, I'm running the code by memory while trying not to get sidetracked by thoughts of Fitz and Sawyer in our apartment, by the possibility that I could be jealous of Fitz.

"You better be smiling by the time we get to dinner," Madison warns as the plane touches down on the tarmac in Boston and taxis toward the terminal. "I'm not answering to your mom if she complains about how much you're scowling."

"I'm not scowling," I object with a scowl.

"Uh huh, sure."

The ride to the event venue is thankfully short and by the time we pull up in front of the hotel, I've managed to school my face into a more neutral expression.

Madison examines me while waiting for the valet to open her door. "It's not a delightful grin, but it'll have to do." She pats my shoulder. "Come on. The sooner we get in there and show our faces, the sooner we can leave."

Mom spots us the second we step inside. "Madison! Preston!"

With her hand in the crook of my elbow, Madison directs me farther into the ballroom.

"Mrs. Boyer!" Madison leans in to give Mom a couple air kisses. "You look stunning!"

"Oh, please, no need to flatter an old woman," Mom says as she pats her hair and smooths her hand down the front of her dress. "You look spectacular as well. Love the hair and the dress. You two make a lovely couple. You always have."

Beside me, Madison stiffens and her grip on my elbow tightens. She hates it when our parents bring up our old relationship. It's an open secret that our parents still want us to get married and unite the two families. It was the only reason we dated in high school at all. Back then, we were too young—and in my case, too oblivious—to have our own opinions on the matter. But then we grew up, and Madison had enough of their meddling and my weirdness. Neither of us was very brokenhearted after she broke up with me, but that hasn't stopped our parents from trying to get us back together.

Madison makes a laughing sound, measured and polite. "Preston will always be my childhood sweetheart. Won't you, Pres? But we all have to grow up someday."

"Yes, well," Mom looks at me. "Some more than others, I suppose."

"Is that Preston?" A booming voice carries over the din of conversation in the ballroom and I fight the urge to duck and run.

Madison gives my elbow an encouraging squeeze and Mom cocks an eyebrow, telling me to behave. She moves behind me, putting a hand in the middle of my back and I straighten my posture at her unspoken instructions.

"Preston!" Dad, tall and intimidating, marches across the room toward me. The crowd of people milling about part to let him through like he's got an invisible bow breaking the water in front of him. Behind him, a slew of men in dark suits follow in his wake.

"My boy!" He claps me on the shoulder hard enough that I can't help but flinch. I try to wrest myself out of his grasp, but his grip is iron-clad. "How's school, son? On track to defend your dissertation in the spring?"

"Actually, not really—"

Dad turns away from me to address the entourage forming a semi-circle behind him. "Preston's doing his PhD in neuroscience. Really cutting-edge stuff with artificial intelligence and brain mapping. It's going to revolutionize how we treat brain-related trauma."

"No, my research isn't about—" I don't know why I bother. He doesn't hear me—no one does. Dad plows on with his business associates while I stand next to him like the puppet he wants me to be.

"Preston's all set to head up our new AI research division. He's going to be a great asset to Boyer Pharmaceuticals."

He pushes me in front of him and starts rattling off names. All I can do is shake hands and try to smile while chewing on my inner lip.

I don't want to join Boyer Pharmaceuticals. My research has nothing to do with the treatment of traumatic brain injuries. I don't know how to head up divisions or be an asset, and I have no interest in either.

But none of that matters to Dad. He inherited the company from Grandpa, so I have to inherit it from him. In his mind, that's the only option, and he's determined to see it through.

SAWYER

I double-check the weights are properly secured to the barbell before swinging around to the front of the power rack.

"Never used one of these before?" I ask Fitz as he secures the weights on the other end of the barbell.

"Nope. It's intimidating as hell," he says with a wide smile on his face. "I've only ever used the ones where the bar runs up and down on a track."

I nod. "We've got Smith machines too. But I prefer the power rack because it gives you a full range of motion and you'll build better core strength for stability."

Fitz moves into position, arranging himself with the bar across the back of his shoulders.

I tap his foot with mine. "Feet a bit wider apart."

He adjusts. "Like that?"

"Yup. Looking good. Go ahead whenever you're ready."

Fitz takes a deep breath before lifting the bar off the J-hooks. I rest my hands gently on his sides to guide him as he lowers himself. Under the thin fabric of his t-shirt, his muscles contract and shift as he moves. His shorts pull tight across his ass when he reaches the bottom of his squat. There are tiny tremors in his legs as he pushes himself back to standing.

I spot him through a set of twelve before helping him rack the barbell again.

"Woo!" Fitz exclaims shaking out his legs. His face is flushed a pretty pink and his eyes are bright behind his glasses.

"Awesome job!" I hold my hand up for a high-five and do a little shimmy to the beat of Used to Know Me by Charli XCX streaming through the gym's speakers. "How's it feel?"

Fitz bounces on his toes. "Amazing! A little scary at first when I was finding my balance, but it helped having you right there." He puts his hands on my sides, mimicking the way I spotted him moments ago. "I thought you said you weren't a personal trainer."

I rest my arms on his shoulders—they're the perfect height—and we sway side to side to the music. "Oh you know, working at a gym, I've picked up things."

Fitz sways a little closer to me. "You're welcome to pick me up anytime you want."

"Don't worry. I'm planning on it." And even as the words leave my mouth, there's a little niggle of doubt at the back of my mind.

Preston got back late from his fundraiser thing in Boston that day. I was already in bed, trying to sleep, but mostly thinking about how Preston looked in the suit Madison picked out for him.

It surprises no one that Preston isn't a suit-and-tie type of guy. But damn if he doesn't wear them well. His trim physique is exactly the body type clothing designers dream of, and Madison always makes sure everything in his closet is perfectly tailored to his size.

"Alright, set two." I take Fitz's hand from my side, spin him around like we're ballroom dancing, and twirl him back to the power rack. He steps into position and steadies his breathing. I place my hands lightly on his sides as he works through another twelve squats.

I was still awake that night when Preston got back from Boston. I'd left my bedroom door cracked open as usual. Preston's shadow darkened the doorway for a moment before he moved down the hall to his own room. I kept waiting for him to come back, straining to hear sounds of him moving around. But he didn't.

A part of me had been tempted to get up and go to him —just to see how his evening had gone and make sure he was okay after seeing his parents. Dealing with them always drains him and puts him in a bad mood. But another part of me remembered what I'd just done with Fitz that afternoon, the cute date we'd shared, the dirty sheets still sitting in the laundry hamper.

I'm hung up on Preston, and it's not healthy, I know. Here is the perfect opportunity for me to get over him and move on. We'll always be best friends, but maybe it's time we stopped being so co-dependent. Maybe it's time I found someone who can return my feelings.

That was one of the worst nights of sleep I've had in a long time.

The jolt of the barbell landing on the J-hooks jerks me back to the present, to Mars and Fitz. He turns around, an amused and questioning look in his eyes. "You okay? You zoned out there for a sec."

I shake my head, clearing away thoughts of Preston. "Sorry, got distracted."

"Ouch, should I be offended?" Fitz crosses his arms in mock anger, a teasing smile still grazing his lips.

"No, sorry. I'm sorry."

His expression softens, then grows reserved. "Would the distraction have anything to do with Preston?"

My attention snaps into sharp focus at the sound of Preston's name. "Why? Is something wrong? Did something happen in the lab?"

"No," Fitz says, a tightness appearing around the edges of his smile. "But he hasn't been in the best mood. Or so I've been told. I don't think I've ever seen him in a genuinely good mood."

My brow furrows at Fitz's confirmation of my worries. Preston hasn't been the same since that trip to Boston. He's quieter than usual, crankier than normal. He's snapped at me a couple times, which isn't typical for him. He hasn't even been sleeping in my bed every night.

"Is he okay?" Fitz asks.

I shake my head. "I don't know."

"Hey, Sawyer. You guys done with the power rack?" Everest, one of our newer trainers asks me.

"We've got one more set. Give us a minute," I respond as Fitz gets himself back into position.

"Sure thing."

I spot Fitz through his last set, then grab some wet cloths to wipe everything down.

"Do you think it's me?" Fitz asks as we move to the open mat area to wrap up our workout with stretches.

We grab onto each other's shoulders, then kick up our heels to stretch out our quads.

"What do you mean?"

"Preston. I know he doesn't like me, and we've been spending a lot of time together. Am I the reason he's been so grouchy lately?"

I scoff even as my heart aches at the thought. The only reason Preston would be upset about Fitz spending time with me is if he's jealous or something. But I'm still doing all the things I've always done for Preston, so what is there to be jealous about?

"No," I say, shaking my head. "It's not you, promise."

Fitz's face shines with a smile, complete with the dimple on his left cheek.

We hit the showers and steam room, deliberately taking our time. When I get home, I'm loose and languid, endorphins running high.

I find Preston in the third bedroom office, hunched over his keyboard, face inches away from the screen. He doesn't notice me right away; he's so engrossed in whatever he's working on.

I take a moment to watch him, the furrow in his brow, the way he chews his lip. He doesn't wear glasses anymore after his parents insisted he get laser eye surgery. But if he still wore them, they'd be halfway down his nose. His chin sticks out as if he's trying to peer through invisible glasses as they dangle halfway off his face. His posture is awful—like a turtle with his head stretched out too far from his shell. He's going to strain his neck if he keeps sitting like that.

And yet, despite everything, my heart swells at the

sight of him, so much so that I have to forcefully suck in a breath around the tightness in my chest.

I push myself away from the door. "Hey."

Preston starts, his head snapping around right before he cringes and his hand goes to his neck. "Ow."

Called it. I always do when it comes to Preston. I have since the first day we met.

I step behind his chair and push his hands away. "You need to sit properly," I chide him as my fingers find all the knots in his neck and gently apply pressure. "What's the point in having this fancy gaming chair if you just hunch over in a ball?"

Preston hisses in pain when I hit a particularly tight spot.

"You need to stand up every once in a while. Walk around, change positions."

"I do," he mumbles, and in the reflection of his computer screen, I can see his pout.

I shake my head and resist the urge to bundle him up in a hug. Boundaries. I'm supposed to be creating boundaries. "Have you had dinner?"

Preston looks up at me with his big puppy eyes.

"Of course you haven't." I pull his chair away from his desk. "Come on, then. Let's get some food in you."

I direct him out to the kitchen with my hands on his shoulders to make sure he doesn't slip back into the office.

Like the rest of the apartment, our kitchen has an industrial flare with dark distressed cabinets and copper hardware. The large island in the middle also houses the sink and a big gas stove sits against the wall. It's not often we get to use our kitchen for actual cooking. Our housekeeper uses it more than we do. But every once in a while, it's nice to putz around and make something from scratch.

"You're going to help me make dinner," I say.

"But I don't know how to cook," Preston responds, slumping against the edge of the kitchen counter.

"You don't have to know how to cook." I open the fridge and pull out a meal kit I ordered a couple days ago. "You only have to read the instructions to me." I hand him the two-page recipe and he squints at it.

"It looks complicated."

I pull ingredients out of the insulated bag the kit came in. "It's not, promise. What's the first step?"

Preston flips to the first page. "Bring five cups of water to a boil."

"Five cups of water. Got it." I pull out a pot from the cabinet and fill it at the sink.

Preston leans over to peer inside. "Shouldn't you measure it? How do you know it's five cups?"

I shrug. "I just eyeball it."

His brow furrows and I know exactly what his objection will be.

"That's not very exact," he says, right as I counter with—

"It doesn't have to be exact. Cooking isn't science, Pres."

He looks disgruntled as I set the pot on the burner and turn on the heat.

"Technically, it is. You're adding heat to materials and thereby changing their properties. You mix acids and bases together to create compound solutions. That's all chemistry."

I chuckle and drag him in for a sideways one-armed

hug. "Yes, okay, fine. It's not an exact science then, it's okay to throw in some creative flair."

Preston twists his lips up. "I'm not very creative."

The self-condemnation makes my heart twinge. I give him a squeeze and a shake with the arm that's slung around his shoulder. "You're plenty creative. Don't ever doubt that. Now, what's the next step?" I tap on the recipe Preston's holding.

He scans the page before reading. "Dice the onions."

"Dice the onions." I pull out the chopping board and a knife. I'm by no means a chef, but I've learned enough in the years we've lived on our own to keep from cutting my fingers off.

I peel back the skin and dice the onions as uniformly as I can. A smile curls on my lips from the simple joy of standing with Preston in the kitchen. Neither of us speaks, there's no awkward rush to fill the silence. When my chopping board gets full, Preston rushes to grab a bowl without me asking.

"Thanks," I murmur as I scoop up the onions and slide them into the bowl.

"Welcome," he murmurs back. Then he sniffles. And he sniffles again. "Ow, my eyes."

I glance over to see them shimmering with tears, a few escaping down his cheek. "Oh, it must be the onions."

He raises a hand to rub them and I grab his wrist before he makes contact.

"No, don't rub your eyes. You've got onion juice on your hands."

Preston lets out an anguished sound and holds his hands out as far as his arms will allow.

Laughter bubbles from the very core of my being, from

the deepest place where all my secret longings are hidden. It tickles as it rises through my stomach, my chest, bursting out as I throw my head back with unabashed delight.

"Don't laugh! Help!"

Only Preston would need rescuing when his eyes are watering and his hands are covered in onion juice. He wasn't even the one chopping them!

"Oh my god, Pres, I love you." The words slip out before I consciously think them.

My heart thuds against the inside of my ribs, but Preston doesn't seem to notice, or if he does, he doesn't read into them. Instead, he whines and waves his hands in the air.

I take him by the wrist and drag him to the sink, then stick his hands under the water. "Wash, then dry." I grab the roll of paper towels and rip one off for him.

"This is why I don't cook," he mutters, pressing the clean paper towel to his eyes.

"Because your eyes water at the mere mention of onions?"

"Raw ones, yes," he pouts and peers out above the paper towels.

His eyes are such a striking blue, framed with black lashes, and my breath catches in my chest. God, they're so pretty. So intense even when he's being all mopey. I could stare into them for ages and never get bored. I could get lost them in and never want to be found again.

My body moves of its own accord. I step into Preston's space, wrap my arms around him, and pull him to me. He snakes his arms around my waist and gazes up at me. Our faces are so close, and for a second, I let myself imagine.

What if I bent my head and pressed my lips to his? What if he sighed and returned the kiss?

The moment ends when he presses his face into my neck, but the damage is done. My chest aches with unfulfilled longing. His cheek is cool from the recent tears, and the light scent of lavender on his laundered clothes fills my senses. I can't help but bury my nose into his hair, breathing him in.

Preston hums softly and melts into me, his arms tightening around my waist. He fits so perfectly against me, his bumps and dips matching up with mine as if we were two puzzle pieces made for each other.

My eyes drift shut as I savor the moment, trying to imprint it in my memory. The way he feels in my arms, the weight of his body resting against me, the light puff of his breath on the sensitive skin of my neck. It feels so fucking good to hold him like this it should be illegal.

I want to stay here forever. Hit pause on time so I can keep holding him and never let go. I want it so badly, it feels like I might die. I want him. I need him. I love him. But I can't have him—not the way I want to.

The water on the stove starts boiling and the lid on the pot rattles to life. It takes all the self-control I possess to let Preston go, to set him away from me and step back. When my hands fall away, the loss of him feels like a knife stabbing me through the chest.

PRESTON

I like shrimp, but peeling their shells off is slimy and gross. I can barely suppress a shudder as I grab the soft slippery body and pull on the stiff cartilage of the tail. But peeling shrimp doesn't seem to bother Sawyer, so I don't want it to bother me either.

I know I'm not a practical person. I don't know how to cook or clean or do my own laundry. I've never needed to do any of that before, and I probably never will. But having Sawyer next to me, showing me what to do, doing it with me—it makes me feel a little less useless than I actually am.

"You good with doing the rest of these?" Sawyer nods to the remaining shrimp in the bowl. "I'm going to start the next step."

I nod and determinedly pick up another shrimp.

Sawyer pulls out a second pot from a cupboard and sets it on the stovetop before peering at the instructions

I've left on the counter. "A drizzle of oil and two table-spoons of butter on medium-high. Then sauté onions."

He floats as he moves around the kitchen, grabbing ingredients and utensils from drawers and cupboards I've never looked inside of before. His shoulder grazes mine as he brushes past. His hand goes to the small of my back when he reaches around me to grab the bowl of onions. It's mesmerizing to watch him dance through the space in one long fluid motion.

After Boston, I'd tried to stay away from Sawyer, tried not to be as needy and dependent on him as I usually am. He's seeing Fitz, and despite how much that bothers me, Sawyer has the right to date whoever he wants.

It's hard, though. I don't sleep well in the big bed by myself. I've been more tired than normal, more distracted. Every change I make to my AI model seems to generate worse results than the last. I hate it. Everything's awful. I want to go back to the way things were before Fitz came waltzing uninvited into our lives.

I miss Sawyer. I miss him a lot.

I yank the tail off the last shrimp and hold up the bowl. "I'm done."

"Awesome! Good job!" Sawyer flashes me a smile. It's sure and confident.

I bask in it. It chases away my insecurities and replaces them with Sawyer's unwavering belief in me. He used to smile at me like that all the time and now I realize how much I've taken it for granted.

Sawyer takes the bowl of shrimp and sets it on the counter by the stove. "What's next in the recipe?"

I wipe my hands clean and pick up the instructions. "Add orzo, squash, and spices. Salt and pepper to taste."

Sawyer rips open the packaging on each of the ingredients, naming them out loud as he dumps them into the pot. "Orzo, squash, spices. Salt and pepper. Got it. Next?"

"Sauté for two to three minutes, until the orzo is toasted."

"Two to three minutes, cool." He holds up the wooden spoon and offers it to me. "Want to stir?"

"Me?" My voice squeaks.

Sawyer chuckles, low and warm, rumbling and soothing. "Yes, you. Who else would I be asking?"

"I've never stirred anything before."

"It's easy. I'll be right here." Sawyer extends his hand toward me.

I take the spoon, closing my hand over his. He doesn't pull away, leaving us both holding the spoon at the same time. Our eyes meet and something happens.

I don't know how to describe it. Neither of us speaks, neither of us moves, but it feels like an invisible energy is drawing us together. It reaches from the center of my chest to the center of his, then winds around both of us, wrapping us in a cocoon.

Sawyer's eyes are a captivating mix of blue and green, shifting between the colors like a rotating kaleidoscope. I inch closer. He smells of soap, citrusy and fresh, the way he usually does after he's showered at the gym. He's so warm, radiating heat like a cozy blanket I want to cuddle up in.

He hugged me earlier, after the onion incident. It's been a while since we've hugged like that—at least two weeks. I never want to go that long without a Sawyer-hug again. Just standing there, leaning on him, all the tiredness from my sleepless nights simply melted away.

A few minutes in his arms and I feel more like myself again.

How is that possible? How does he do that? I don't know, but he's the only one who can.

I shuffle forward and my toes bump into his. An inch of air separates us and suddenly I loathe that inch of air with every fiber of my being. I want to be in his arms again. I want to burrow myself into him and smother myself with him. I want to live surrounded by Sawyer and never ever have to leave.

I tilt my head back to gaze up at him. There's a small bump on his nose where he broke it playing rugby in high school. He was upset when it happened, but I kind of like it. It makes him look more rugged, tough, capable. He's got some scruff along his jaw and on his chin, the blond hairs only visible when he lets them grow out a bit. They catch in my hair sometimes, when we hug and he hasn't shaved in a few days. The curve of his lips is so elegant, subtle yet complex. I want to trace the contours of them, to feel the way they arch and dip so perfectly.

Suddenly, Sawyer blinks and steps away from me. He pushes the spoon toward me and pulls his hand out from mine. He clears his throat and nods toward the pot. "Go ahead."

No. Wait. I wasn't done yet. I haven't had enough. I want more.

But Sawyer is already busying himself with tidying the kitchen, gathering up the discarded packaging and food scraps.

I go to the stove and carefully lower the spoon into the pot. Sawyer is right. It's not hard. The scent of onions and toasting orzo fills the kitchen and I breathe it in. My stomach rumbles in response, reminding me just how hungry I am.

Sawyer comes up behind me, the heat from his body warming my back. "I think we can add the water now."

He takes the boiled water and carefully pours it over the food.

I'm not sure what happens next. I must move the wrong way, change the angle of the wooden spoon still sticking out of the pot, or something. But the water splashes onto my hand.

It's hot. Scalding. I yelp as I pull my hand away and the wooden spoon comes with me, clattering to the floor, taking some squash and orzo with it.

"I'm sorry!" I cry out, cradling my hand to my chest, staring dumbstruck at our dinner all over the kitchen floor.

Sawyer moves fast, turning off the stove. "Are you okay? Let me see."

He steps over the mess on the floor and reaches for my hand. I give it to him and he guides me to the sink to run it under cold water.

"Doesn't look burned," he murmurs, turning my hand around to examine it. "Does it hurt?"

I shake my head, feeling silly and stupid. It was only a few drops of hot water. My skin isn't even red. Why did I make such a big deal out of nothing? "No, I'm okay."

Sawyer snags a dish towel and pats my hand dry. "I'm sorry. I should've told you to move your hand out of the way before I started pouring."

"No, *I'm* sorry. I should've known to take the spoon out first. Now our dinner is ruined." I stare forlornly at the floor.

Sawyer smiles and I feel all fluttery inside. "It's not

ruined. The squash can be salvaged and we don't need every single grain of orzo."

He presses my hand, still wrapped in the towel, to my chest, and then magically cleans up the stuff I spilled on the floor. I don't know how he manages to do it so fast. A few wipes and in a minute there's no evidence that the floor was ever dirty in the first place.

I tiptoe to the stove and peek into the pot again. There's still plenty of food in there, more than enough for both of us.

"See? Sawyer says, stirring the pot a few times before placing a lid on it. "All good."

I must look extra pathetic because Sawyer takes pity on me and pulls me into a hug. I'm nowhere near proud enough to resist the comfort that only Sawyer can offer.

If there's one thing I've figured out in the past couple weeks, it's that I need Sawyer. Physically. Psychologically. Even the little bit of distance I've tried to create between us is too much. Life is miserable when he's not in the center of it. I can't function if Sawyer isn't at my side every step of the way.

I don't want to pull away from Sawyer again. It's selfish of me, I know, but if it's a choice between me and Fitz, I want Sawyer to choose me. We've been best friends for so long. We've been happy like this. Why do things have to change?

I'm not sure how much time passes while we hold each other in the kitchen. Eventually, Sawyer rubs his hand on my back a few times. "Gotta check on the food," he murmurs and I reluctantly let him go.

I stick close though, standing behind him, hands on his waist, head on his shoulder, as he finishes cooking. He adds the shrimp I helped peel, along with bunches of spinach. A few minutes later, he starts dishing the shrimp orzo with spinach and squash onto two plates.

"Wanna watch a movie while we eat?" he asks.

I nod and we bring our plates and silverware to the living room. Sawyer sits in the middle of the U-shaped sectional and I sit next to him, close enough for my thigh to press against his.

"What do you want to watch?" Sawyer asks, grabbing the remote from the big, stuffed ottoman.

"Whatever you want to watch." I'm not a big movie person, but Sawyer's always got a list of movies his friends have recommended to him.

He cues up an action movie, something with lots of car chases and explosions, and we settle into the couch. The food is delicious. Fragrant and savory. Made all that tastier because I know Sawyer made it for me.

When my plate is empty, Sawyer takes it and sets it down with his on the ottoman. Before he settles back again, he pulls the blanket from the back of the couch and spreads it over our laps. I sink into the cushions, my eyelids suddenly heavier than they were a moment ago. They drift shut, the sounds of the movie fade into the distance, and I relax into Sawyer.

He manhandles me, rearranges me so I'm lying on my side, covered in the blanket, curled into a ball with my head pillowed by his thick thigh. I sigh when his fingers find their way into my hair, when his arm is a solid weight draped over my body.

It's comfortable here. Peaceful. Calming. This is where I want to be. Always. Forever. And I slip into sleep.

SAWYER

I'm not surprised when Preston slumps against me, limbs loose and heavy. After a long day of work, with a full tummy, of course he falls asleep.

I guide him down so his head is on my lap and then cover him with the blanket. He stuffs his hands under my thigh like it's a pillow and soon his breathing slows.

His eyelashes are a dark fan across his cheeks. His thick black hair is silky between my fingers. His jaw is slack, lips parted. Any second now he'll start drooling. He's got a little beauty mark behind his ear and I can't resist stroking it lightly. He hums contentedly and snuggles deeper into me.

That moment in the kitchen earlier replays in my mind. Preston's hand on top of mine, both of us holding the wooden spoon. He shuffled forward to close the distance between us and gazed at me with a look in his eyes that I've never seen before, that I don't recognize.

My heart raced, thudding so hard and so loud I swear

he must have heard it. His lips were only an inch from mine and the way his head was angled, it felt like he might rise onto his toes and kiss me. Ridiculous, I know. But even as my brain rejected the idea as ludicrous, my body roared to life.

Blood rushed down to my dick and my balls drew up in anticipation. Heat pooled in my groin, in my joints, and ran like lava through my veins. My lips tingled, primed for a kiss. My head spun, dizzy with joy and need and want.

I'm usually a master at keeping my baser instincts under wraps around Preston. Commendable, I think, considering how physical we are with each other. But we were having such a good time, cooking together and being so domestic. Plus the relief that Preston might have gotten over whatever was plaguing him these past few weeks. All of it combined had me letting down my guard. And he slipped right in.

God, I wanted to kiss him so badly. My imagination played the scene out for me. Our lips would fit together perfectly. I'd bend him backward a bit to get just the right angle. He'd cling to me and whimper, and the sound would go directly to my cock. We'd end up on the floor of the kitchen, tearing at each other's clothes. And eventually, I'd sink into the tight heat of his body.

Fuck. I want that. I haven't let myself imagine sex with Preston in a really long time, and certainly never in quite so vivid detail. I figured out back in high school that fantasizing about my straight best friend to get off might not be the best idea if I wanted to keep him as my best friend.

To be honest, I'm not entirely sure when Preston went from a weird nerdy roommate to a best friend to something more. It happened so gradually, so naturally that now when I look back, it feels like I've always loved him.

His amazing brain. The ideas it's capable of generating go way over my head. He's devoted to his work, and he gets so passionate and excited when he talks about his research. The way he's adorably hopeless when it comes to any of life's practicalities. How touchy-feely he is; how he craves physical contact.

I love taking care of him. I love trying to decipher his complicated thought patterns and anticipate his needs before he's even aware of them. I love being his support system, handling the basics of life so he can focus that incredible intelligence on more important things. I love being his source of comfort, making him feel safe and secure and reassured.

I used to think I could get him to return my feelings. That it was just a matter of time before he realized how well we complement each other. When Madison broke up with him, I spent almost a year thinking that was my chance. Without Madison in the way, Preston would finally see how much I loved him, how much I could give him all the things that Madison couldn't.

But he never did. Things didn't change between us at all. Madison went from girlfriend to ex to childhood friend in a blink of an eye and Preston went on with his life as if it had always been that way. He never showed an iota of interest in me.

Thirteen years and counting now, I've been satisfying myself with being Preston's best friend. I still get to be at his side and share life together. So what if we don't have sex? We still cuddle. So what if we're not a couple? We still live together. Some days I think the life we have is enough for me, it's all I need. But then other days…

My phone buzzes in my pocket and I shift carefully to the side to pull it out.

FITZ

You wore me out today.

Attached is a photo of him shirtless, sprawled on a bed. He's smiling lazily into the camera, one hand teasing a nipple.

Guilt crashes into me, more forcefully than it usually does, and it's difficult to breathe.

I spent most of the day with Fitz, but I conveniently forgot him the second I got home. My world narrowed to Preston, feeding him, making sure he didn't hurt himself, forcing him to get some rest. Fitz hasn't existed in the past few hours—it's only been Preston, Preston, Preston.

That's not fair to Fitz. If I'm supposed to be dating him, how can I wipe him so entirely from my memory the moment I'm in the same room as Preston? That's not normal, right? That's not how relationships are supposed to work.

Does that mean I need to walk away from Preston to create space for Fitz? How am I supposed to do that? The past couple weeks, with Preston being all sulky and distant, have been awful. The thought of that becoming our new normal makes me sick to my stomach. The idea of pulling even further apart sets off a blare of alarm.

Preston stirs.

In my self-induced panic, I've inadvertently tightened my grip on his hair.

He stretches, shifting to lie on his back. "Sawyer?"

"Sorry." I comb my fingers through his locks, smoothing them out again. "Go back to sleep."

He takes a slow, deep breath and lets out a lazy, relaxed sigh. Then he notices the phone in my hand and stiffens.

"Fitz?" he asks, seeing the selfie on the screen.

Shit. I quickly shut the screen off and stuff my phone under a pillow. "Yeah," I croak, my throat tightening with guilt and shame.

Preston sits up and everything in me screams to pull him back, to rewind the last minute so we can return to the wonderfully idyllic evening we've been having.

Preston pushes the blanket off him, leaving it in a pile between us, a barrier that feels much more insurmountable than a mere piece of woolen fabric. He rubs the sleep out of his eyes. "You're seeing Fitz." His voice is tight, his tone slightly accusatory.

I feel like he's caught me cheating on him. I want to drop to my knees and beg him to forgive me. I want to promise that it'll never happen again. Except, I haven't been cheating. I haven't been disloyal. There's nothing to forgive.

Preston's sitting on the edge of the sofa, hands gripping the cushion, eyes downcast. Gone is his warm and sleepy expression, and in its place is tension and unease.

"Ye—" I stop to clear my throat. "Yeah, I am."

Preston nods once and curls in on himself. My heart breaks to see him like this. I don't like it. I have to fix it. I need Preston happy and relaxed and even a little silly like he was earlier this evening.

"You don't like Fitz," I say. I know he doesn't like Fitz, he hasn't from the very beginning. I thought he just needed time to adapt to a new person upsetting his daily routine. But it's been over a month now and Preston still get this visceral reaction whenever Fitz comes up. Could his distance these past couple weeks really be about Fitz?

But why? Why doesn't he like Fitz? "Is it something at the lab? Is he bad at research?"

Preston is so dedicated to his work he can't handle even the smallest hint of incompetence. But he gives a minute shake of his head. "No," he murmurs in a small voice that actually sounds kind of disappointed, like it's unfortunate that Fitz is a capable lab colleague. "He's good."

I try again. "Did he do something to upset you?"

Preston's bottom lip sticks out. "Not exactly."

But also not a complete denial. Maybe Fitz was right. Maybe Preston's moodiness does have something to do with him.

"What did he do?"

Preston curls in on himself even more then turns his head to peek at me over his shoulder. Vivid blue framed by black, the lost, longing look in his eyes hits me deep in my soul. The impact expels all the air from my lungs, and I grit my teeth against the pain.

Preston's hurting and I don't know how to make it go away. He's suffering and I don't know how to fix it.

I reach for him and for a split second, he resists. In that infinitesimal moment, fear floods every inch of me—am I the reason he's been hurting? Am I the problem? Am I going to lose him?

I can't lose him.

But then Preston relents and lets me haul him into my lap. He clutches at me, hands fisting in my shirt. I hold him just as tightly, trembling as the unexpected rush of adrenaline works its way through my system. It was only a second, barely a second, but even then, it was too much.

We sit there, clinging to each other. I feel ridiculous, reacting as if something happened when nothing did. He probably wasn't resisting anyway, just a little stiff from sleeping in an awkward position. It didn't mean anything. I'm overreacting.

And yet, in my heart of hearts, I know that's not true. Something did happen, something important and integral to my relationship with Preston. Something's changed. I'm just not sure what.

When my pounding heart slows to a reasonable rate, and Preston's in danger of falling asleep again, I urge him to his feet and send him down the hall to get ready for bed.

I shut off the TV and take our empty plates back to the kitchen. I load the dishwasher, wipe down the counters, and pour two glasses of water to bring back to my room. Preston's bathroom fan is still running when I start my own nightly routine.

I leave my door cracked open when I climb into bed, and it doesn't take long for Preston to slip in. He crawls in under the covers, but he doesn't scoot up against me— back-to-back—like he normally does.

I turn to see what's wrong and find Preston on his side —facing me. He's awake and watching me, so I flip over to face him too.

Wordlessly, I open my arms, and Preston burrows right in. His head is tucked under my chin, face pressed against my neck. His feet are all tangled up with mine. My nose is filled with his lavender scent and a shudder runs through me at how good—how right—it feels to hold him like this.

Despite all the cuddling we do, we've never fallen asleep like this before. Wrapped up in each other like we're desperate to occupy the same space, like I need to be inside him and he needs to be inside me. My cock fills at the idea and the more I try to make the erection go away, the larger it grows. But if Preston feels it pressing against his hip, he doesn't let on.

It doesn't take long for him to fall asleep, his breathing slowing into a steady rhythm. I press my lips to the top of his head and silently repeat the words I'll never be able to say out loud.

I love you. It might break my heart, but I love you.

PRESTON

I hate our weekly department meetings, but today's is especially awful. There's *discussion* and it keeps going on and on and on. Meanwhile, I forgot my tablet in the office so I can't sneak in some work during the endless chatter.

Instead, I'm ignoring the talking and obsessively glaring at Fitz. He doesn't seem to notice. He's contributing to the *discussion*, asking intelligent questions, and posing constructive ideas. He's smiling and laughing and whenever he talks, other people smile and laugh.

He's done every task I've given him in the lab, and he's done them exactly the way I told him to. He's got suggestions for every problem, good ones even I haven't thought of before. He's actually been helpful, and we've gotten more done on my research in the month he's been here than I did on my own all summer.

I hate him. He's so goddamn perfect, and I hate him. Why does he have to be so smart? So cooperative? Such a team player?

I've tried to like him. Okay, that's a lie. I've tried to tolerate him, tried to not hate him so much. He almost won me over a couple times. We'd be in the lab, he'd say something that sparks an idea, and we'd start brainstorming. The next thing I know I'm smiling and enjoying myself. Then I remember he's having sex with Sawyer and the hot bitterness roils inside me again.

I tried to stay away from Sawyer. I tried to give him room to have a relationship with Fitz, and I tried not to be upset about it. Sawyer deserves to be with someone he likes. He deserves to be happy, find love, and have a partner. But why does he have to have those things with Fitz?

Why can't he have those things with me?

Time slows to a standstill. The voices around me fade to silence. I'm paralyzed by the thought, lungs and limbs frozen. The only organ still functioning is my heart, which is racing like I've been injected with a giant syringe of adrenaline.

Why can't Sawyer have those things with me? Happiness. Partnership. Love. With me?

Do I even want those things? I don't know. I've never thought about it before.

I jolt as everyone around me pushes their chairs back and stands up. For a moment, I'm completely disoriented. Where am I? What's going on?

Oh. The meeting's ended and everyone is leaving.

I hurry to leave, dodging between my colleagues to rush out of the room. I need quiet. I need to be alone. I need to figure out what the hell is going on with my thoughts.

"Preston!"

I'm almost around the corner when I hear my name,

and I make the mistake of slowing down rather than speeding up. Fitz is on me in a flash.

"Hey! You ran out of there pretty quick."

"Yeah," I mutter as I scurry toward the stairs. What does he want? Hasn't he rubbed his perfection in my face enough today? I've got more important things to think about than him.

"So, um, I was hoping to talk to you—about Sawyer."

I nearly trip down the stairs and only just catch myself on the banister before I tumble head-first to my death.

"Whoa, you okay?" Fitz grabs my arm—a few seconds too late, ha, he's not that perfect—and waits till I find my footing before letting go.

"Yeah, I'm fine." I shrug him off and cling to the handrail. Fitz might want to talk about Sawyer, but I don't. Sawyer's the last thing I want to talk to him about.

I turn and continue down the stairs, keeping one hand on the banister this time. Fitz falls into step next to me.

"Do you want to grab coffee?" Fitz asks as if we're friends, as if grabbing coffee was a perfectly normal thing for the two of us to do.

"I'm busy." I mutter, trying to hurry without tripping over my own feet.

Fitz, to his credit, doesn't have any trouble keeping up. Asshole. "Yeah, sure, of course. Maybe tomorrow then?"

"I don't know. Probably not." Reaching the basement, I push my way out of the stairwell and turn right for the grad student office. Why is Fitz still following me? Why is he still trying to talk to me?

Just as we reach the office, Fitz steps in front of me and blocks the doorway.

"What are you doing?" I glare at him. "You're in the way. Move."

Fitz doesn't move. "Preston," he says. His usual boisterous enthusiasm is nowhere in sight. His expression is serious and he looks me straight in the eye.

"What?" I back up as an uneasy feeling slithers through me.

Fitz hesitates, opening and closing his mouth a couple times like he doesn't know if he should say what's on his mind.

"I wanted to tell you that I really like Sawyer."

I stagger backward as his words hit me like a sledgehammer. Not that it's news to me, but to hear him say it so matter-of-factly, directly into my face—it knocks the air out of my lungs and my diaphragm refuses to contract. My heart feels like it's in my throat, beating so rapidly I'm dizzy from the sudden rush of blood.

"I think Sawyer and I have something really special and I want to see where it goes."

My vision goes a little fuzzy around the edges and the hallway tilts on an axis.

"I know you guys are best friends, and I'm not trying to replace you or come between the two of you. So I was hoping we could talk? Come to an understanding?"

I bump into something behind me—the wall. The contact jolts my diaphragm into action again and I suck in a huge breath of air. But the disproportionate influx of oxygen only throws my senses into further disarray.

"Preston? Are you okay?" Fitz comes toward me, hands outstretched. "Do you need help?"

I knock his hands away and manage to get around him without falling on my ass. I burst into the office and grab the first coat I see. Then I spin around and race away as fast as my legs can take me.

"Preston! Stop!"

I know better than to stop this time. I need to get out of here. I need to find Sawyer.

I don't want him to have "something special" with Fitz. I don't want him to have a relationship with Fitz at all. Happiness. Partnership. Love. *I* can give him those things. He should be getting it all from *me*. Sawyer's mine. He's mine, and I'm not letting anyone take him away.

I must black out for a time because I'm not entirely sure how I make it home. Before my brain has caught up with my body, I'm suddenly standing in front of our building. Except I don't have my keys. Or my phone. The coat I'm wearing isn't mine. Damn it.

I desperately scroll through the intercom system and buzz our apartment, leaning on the button until Sawyer unlocks the door for me. It doesn't unlock. There's no tinny voice asking who I am. Sawyer's not home.

Shit. If Sawyer's not home, then where is he?

The gym. It's the afternoon. He's probably working.

I take off at a run, not certain where I'm going. I've been to Mars Fitness before, but I don't really pay attention to things like addresses. I know it's not far from our place and I know it's around the corner from a bar that Sawyer likes to go to.

I circle a couple blocks before I spot the lit-up sign, a crest with the name Mars Fitness in big block letters. I wrench the door open and stumble inside.

It's loud in there, music pumping through invisible speakers, a blender whirring at full speed, the crash and clang of metal against metal, a chorus of shouts and grunts. There are people everywhere, some in their coats, others in shorts and t-shirts or sweatpants and hoodies. I've stepped into an alternate universe and I don't know what to do.

"Preston!"

My head snaps toward the sound of my name, yelled in a familiar voice. Sawyer's voice. He's here. Somewhere. Where is he?

"Holy shit, Pres. What happened?" Sawyer materializes out of the chaos and I collapse into his arms.

Only then do I realize how fast my heart is beating, how much my legs are burning, and how difficult it is to breathe.

"Jesus Christ. Did you run here?" Sawyer half-guides and half-drags me past the people, past the front desk, and into a quiet, empty room. There are couches in it, a table with chairs, and a mini-kitchenette. He deposits me on a couch, then pops away to fetch me a bottle of water.

He twists off the lid and hands the bottle to me. "Here, drink this. I'll be back in a second."

I grab his wrist with a speed and strength that surprises even me. No, I just found him. I can't lose him again.

He covers my hand with his and leans in so our heads are bowed together. "Shh, it's okay. I just need to take care of a member. I'll be right back, promise."

I stare into his blue-green eyes. Eyes that have never lied to me. Eyes that have always given me exactly what I need. I force myself to loosen my grip and let Sawyer slip through my fingers.

It feels like hours, like days, like forever, but it's probably only a few minutes before Sawyer's back. He pulls a chair from the table and sets it in front of me to sit down.

Why is he sitting in the chair? Why isn't he on the couch with me? Hugging me? Holding me?

"I couldn't find you." The words spill out of their own accord. "You weren't at home."

Sawyer's elbows are braced on his knees, his feet planted wide, his hands clasped together. His brows are furrowed in concern. "It's Thursday afternoon. I'm usually working on Thursday afternoons."

"I forgot what day it is," I admit.

"Preston, what happened? Fitz messaged me and said you ran out wearing someone else's coat. You left your bag and your phone at school."

Fitz. Fucking Fitz. It's always fucking Fitz.

No, not anymore. I'm not letting Fitz steal Sawyer away. I can give Sawyer everything he wants, everything he deserves. He doesn't need to find happiness or partnership or love anywhere else because he can get all of it from me and more.

I'm moving before I've consciously decided to do so. The open bottle of water slips from my hands and drops to the floor, spilling water everywhere. I reach for Sawyer, grabbing him with my hands on either side of his face. His cheeks are prickly under my palms.

I drag him to me, pulling him out of his chair, and smash my mouth onto his.

SAWYER

What. The. Fuck. Is. Happening.

I'm paralyzed. Half out of my seat. Hands hovering in mid-air. Eyes opened wide.

And my lips are pressed flush against Preston's.

I can't move. I can't breathe. I don't dare.

Preston is kissing me. Preston. My straight best friend. My roommate since high school. The guy I've been hopelessly in love with for years. He's kissing me. On the lips. With his lips. On mine.

Granted, that's all he's doing. There's no movement. Absolutely no tongue. It's not so much a kiss, more like one part of his body resting on the same part of mine. Like maybe his lips were tired and he's using mine as a pillow? No, that's ridiculous. Even for Preston.

It's more like he's trying to kiss me, but he doesn't know how. He understands that kisses involve lips, but he's not sure what to do once the first step is completed.

So I show him.

Because I'm a fool, I'm a sucker for punishment, and I'm hardwired to help Preston at all times, even to my own detriment... I purse my lips, increase the pressure, part them slightly to catch him in a gentle nip.

Preston gasps and my tongue moves on auto-pilot, slipping out to lick at the opening he's given me. He whimpers and strains toward me, and that's when my brain truly breaks. Completely short-circuits. Flash. Fizzle. Wisps of smoke.

I grab him. Haul him into my lap. Preston spreads his legs so he's straddling me. My one hand goes under the coat his wearing and the other to the back of his head to guide him through the kiss. His arms snake around my neck like he's never intending to let me go.

I lick, swiping my tongue across his chapped lips. He tries chasing it with his own and I let him catch me. Our tongues touch and it sparks a fire that rips straight through me, landing in my groin where my cock has gone from zero to a hundred in a microsecond. My hips tilt up as I pull Preston down so I can grind my erection into his ass.

He hugs me tighter, threatening to strangle me, but I don't care. This is fucking Preston, in my arms, in my lap, kissing me. I could die and go to heaven right this second and have no regrets.

My tongue tingles as it slides over his, the nerve endings on high alert and sensitive. Preston squirms against me, wriggling his ass on my cock and pressing himself more fully against my body.

He tastes exactly the way I always imagined he would. Sweet and smoky, herbal and woodsy, a complex mix that is uniquely Preston. The taste winds its way through me, sinks its claws in deep, and turns me into its captive. I love this taste. I'm addicted to it. I'll never get enough.

"Sawyer? Oh! Uh…"

We both jump. Preston flies backward and lands on the couch with an *oomph*. My head snaps around to find Beau standing in the doorway, expression wavering between confused and amused.

"Sorry to interrupt?" Though he doesn't look very apologetic at all. He looks altogether too smug.

"No! You're not!" I shoot to my feet and the chair topples over behind me. I scramble to pick it up and slide it back under the table. Only then do I notice the water spilled all over the floor. "Shit."

I rush to grab paper towels and mop up the puddle. As I move, my limbs don't feel entirely under my control. They do what I want, go where I want, but I'm so removed from my body, it feels more like a puppet I'm directing.

"Whenever you're finished up here, there's something I could use your help with," Beau says from the doorway.

"Yep, yeah, sure thing. Be right there," I say, on my hands and knees pushing around the soaked paper towels.

Beau slips out and I let out a breath, head falling forward as my brain rushes to catch up with reality. Preston. My straight best friend, Preston. Kissed me. And I kissed him back. My lips are still tingling. My dick is still chubby. I want to kiss him again. Desperately.

I slump back onto my heels.

Preston's curled into a ball on the couch, knees pulled to his chest. His eyes are wide with fear, and the sight of him like that pierces me right through the chest.

"Sorry," he whispers and the single word twists the blade in my heart.

What in the fucking world is he sorry for? For kissing me? For whimpering into my mouth? For writhing in my arms? Because I'm not sorry about any of that. I've dreamed about this every fucking day for over a decade. This is a fantasy come to life for me.

"No," I shuffle on my knees over to him, not caring that my pants are getting wet. "Don't be sorry. Never be sorry."

It's awkward with his legs folded between us, but I get as close as I can. My chest is pressed to his shins and I brush his hair back from his face. I don't know why he bolted from school without his things. I don't know why he was so frantic to find me. I don't know why he kissed me.

But there is one thing I do know—I love Preston and I never want him to feel sorry or regret for anything.

If it means I pretend the last fifteen minutes never happened. If it means I get my heart trampled on and broken. If it means I satisfy myself with only ever being his friend. Then that's what I'll do.

"Everything's going to be okay," I say. No matter what the problem is. No matter what it takes, I'll make sure of it.

A throat clears behind me and fucking hell, I hate that I'm at work right now. I glare over my shoulder and feel only mildly contrite when Beau cocks an eyebrow at me.

Fuck.

I swallow down the curses poised at the tip of my tongue and give Beau a reluctant nod.

"Hey, I've got to go back out there for a bit," I murmur to Preston who grabs me like he's afraid I'll disappear if I'm out of his sight. My soul aches at the gesture. "I'll come back. I'm not leaving."

"Promise?" he asks in a small, fragile voice.

"Promise." I take his hand and place it over my heart. "I promise."

I pry myself out of Preston's grasp and it absolutely kills me to pull away from him. But I can't just walk out on Beau and Gavin in the middle of my shift.

I scoop up the sopping pile of paper towels, dump them into the trash bin, plaster a smile on my face, and march out to the front desk.

Music blares. Logan's blender whirs. People shout at each other. Equipment crashes and bangs as it's being thrown around. When did this place get so loud?

"Here he is!" Beau waves me over. "Sawyer's our front desk manager. He'll get you registered and all set up in the system. Remember that first free personal training session I mentioned? Sawyer can get that booked in for you too."

I've never disliked my job as much as I do at this moment. Meeting a new member, cracking jokes to make him feel comfortable, answering his questions—all the things I normally love about my job, today, I hate. Because it's taking me away from where I really want to be: with Preston.

But I grit my teeth and fake my way through it, even taking him back to the main floor to show him a specific piece of equipment. I go above and fucking beyond, all while the love of my life waits for me in the break room, freaking out.

By the time I get the dude out the front door, it's been twenty minutes.

"Hey, Sawyer!"

I ignore whoever is calling my name and race back to the break room, seized by the sudden fear that maybe I imagined everything. Maybe Preston didn't burst into the gym having just hightailed it from school. Maybe he didn't launch himself at me. Maybe we didn't share the hottest, most perfect kiss in my entire life. Maybe I'll round the corner and find the break room empty.

But it's not. Preston's still there, exactly where I left him, curled in a ball on the couch. The relief is so staggering I have to grab the doorframe to keep from collapsing. Fuck. I didn't imagine it. He did kiss me. And I kissed him back.

Fuuuccckkk. Preston kissed me. My straight best friend. And I kissed him back. The full weight of it hits me and it's a good thing I'm already holding the doorframe because otherwise I'd be on the floor.

Why— Wha— How—

My brain threatens to short-circuit for the second time today as the reality of what happened collides with what I know about me and Preston. He kissed me. I kissed him back. That's not supposed to happen. That's not even supposed to be possible.

"Sawyer?" Preston regards me from across the room, his blue eyes big and watery with unshed tears. He's so precious, so exquisite, and god, I love him so fucking much.

I stagger toward him, land on the couch, and immediately pull him to me. He curls into my side, head automatically tucking under my chin, face pressed against my neck.

I love him. And right now, that love is so big and it fills me so completely, I'm bursting. It's consuming me, burning me up and devastating me.

How did I ever think I could be with anyone else? How

did I ever believe there was anything left of me to give to another person? There isn't. I've already given everything I am to Preston.

But one kiss doesn't mean Preston loves me the way I love him. I'm not so foolish to assume it does. Preston's straight. He's asexual and aromantic. Something happened to make him kiss me. He didn't suddenly, after all these years, just feel like it.

And I think I know what—or rather who—that something is. Fitz.

Preston started acting strange the moment Fitz came into the picture. I thought he just needed time to get used to a new person, but he never did. If anything, he got worse, moodier, crankier. Now that I think about it, the closer I got to Fitz, the more distant and weirder he became. It all goes back to Fitz.

Was he afraid Fitz would steal me away? Did he think I would leave him for Fitz?

Oh, Preston. I hold him tighter and he nuzzles in deeper.

I would never. I could never. He doesn't need to kiss me to make me stay. He doesn't need to offer himself up as some sort of sexual tribute just to keep me. The absolute last thing I want is to pressure him into something like that —the thought of it makes me sick.

"It's okay," I murmur, as much to myself as to Preston. "We're going to be okay. Everything's going to be okay."

Beau appears in the doorway again and my stomach sinks. I *really* don't want to leave Preston to go back to work.

But Beau is the absolute best boss in the world. "Do you need to take off early today?"

"Can I?" Gratitude and relief pour through me.

He quirks his lips like he's being put upon, but his eyes are understanding. "Go on, get out of here. We'll manage without you for half a day."

"Thank you. So much. I'll make it up to you, promise."

"Yeah, yeah." He waves me off but flashes me a quick smile before turning away.

I give Preston a little shake. "How about we get out of here?"

He nods and sniffles, pulling away from me to wipe his damp cheeks with the back of his hand. His long black lashes are clumped together with moisture. The whites of his eyes are tinted red. His bottom lip is bruised and swollen like he's been chewing on it. He's the most gorgeous person I've ever laid eyes on.

"Come on." I stand and pull Preston to his feet. "Let's go home."

PRESTON

Sawyer takes me home. He keeps his arm around me the entire time and never lets go. Not until he settles me on the couch in our living room and tucks a blanket around me.

"Want something to drink?"

I shake my head, hugging my knees to my chest.

"I'll get you some water anyway." He leaves me and even though he only goes into the kitchen, I feel so much colder and more alone when he's not touching me.

Sawyer brings back a glass of water for me and a beer for himself. The second he sits down, I burrow under his arm and plaster myself to his side. He holds me to him, nose buried in my hair.

My eyes drift shut as I breathe him in, minty and fresh, like toothpaste. It's familiar and comforting and safe.

Sawyer takes a swig of his beer, then after a moment of silence, he asks in a quiet voice, "Pres?"

I hum and nestle in closer.

"Can you tell me what happened? Before you came to the gym?"

I don't answer. I don't know how. I was at school, going to my office, and Fitz was talking to me. He said he really liked Sawyer, that they had something special. But I don't want Sawyer to have something special with Fitz. I want Sawyer to have something special with me.

How do I say that? How do I explain that I want to keep Sawyer to myself? That I don't want to share him? It's selfish and unfair, but it's what I want.

"You were with Fitz?" Sawyer prompts.

I nod.

"Were you talking?" Sawyer combs his fingers through my hair. It's rhythmic and relaxing and I melt into him.

"Yeah."

"What were you talking about?"

"He wanted to tell me that—" The words catch in my throat. I don't want to say it out loud. It feels too real that way.

"What did he want to tell you?"

I'm already pressed as close as I can get to Sawyer's side, but it isn't close enough. I toss off the blanket and throw my knee over Sawyer's lap so I'm straddling him like I was back at the gym.

It's better this way, with my whole front flush against his, my arms wrapped around his body, my face tucked into the crook of his neck. It's better, but nowhere near enough. I want to be inside Sawyer, and I want him inside me. I want us so close I can't tell where I end and he begins.

Startled, Sawyer doesn't react right away. But then he

sighs and settles his arms around me. He rubs my back and brushes his fingers through my hair.

"You're mine," I murmur into Sawyer's neck. "He can't have you."

The only indication he hears me is the slight pause in the run of his hand over my back. It takes Sawyer a few long minutes to respond, but when he does, he clears his throat. "I'm all yours. No one's taking me away, promise."

Sawyer's promise sinks into me, reassuring and comforting, and yet, there's still a seed of doubt deep inside my amygdala. Am I enough for Sawyer? Can I actually give him everything he needs? I'm not cool like Fitz. I'm not charming and easy-going. Will Sawyer be satisfied with just me?

"Is that what the kiss was about?" Sawyer asks. "You're afraid I'll leave you?"

I nod and hug him tighter, like I can physically keep him with me by never letting go.

"Oh, Pres." Sawyer sighs and presses a kiss into my hair. "You don't need to kiss me to make me stay." His voice is rough and low, almost growly.

I tilt my head back and peer up at him. There's a furrow in his brow and his lips are pressed tightly together, turned down at the corners. He looks like he's upset but he doesn't want me to know. Like maybe *I've* upset him and he doesn't want me to blame myself.

But I do. Sawyer's been my rock for so long. He takes care of me and protects me. He's my safe place, my happy place. He gives so much of himself to me, and what have I given him in return?

I rack my hippocampus and come up with nothing. I make him worry. He feels responsible for me. But have I brought anything positive to our friendship? Or do I just take?

That's wrong. How did I not notice until now? How did I not see how uneven and lopsided our friendship is? I want to fix it. I need to fix it.

"What if I want to kiss you?" The question slips out, formed more by my subconscious than the Broca's area of my brain. The moment it's voiced, though, the desire to kiss him again overwhelms me.

Back at Mars, I wasn't thinking when I launched myself at him. It felt like the right thing to do at the time, like it was the only option in light of my tumultuous emotions.

The instant my lips touched Sawyer's, I froze, partially out of shock and partially because I wasn't sure what came next. The only other person I've ever kissed was Madison and she always took the lead.

Then Sawyer kissed me back, and it was absolutely nothing like the kisses I shared with Madison. Those were mechanical, merely physical movements that never held much appeal. I never understood why everyone is so obsessed with kissing. It's just smooshing lips together. What's the big deal?

Until Sawyer. Kissing Sawyer isn't just smooshing lips together. It's… transcendent, magical, otherworldly. I felt the kiss from the top of my head to the tips of my toes. My internal temperature skyrocketed and I burst into flames. When our tongues touched, it was like a lightning strike shot through me and left me burned and sizzling in its wake.

Kissing Sawyer brought me to life like nothing else ever has. And I want to do it again.

Sawyer makes a strangled sound. "You do?" he croaks.

I nod, then slowly slide my hands up his chest, up his neck, and cradle his face between my palms. "I do."

Sawyer's Adam's apple bobs as he swallows. "Bu—but, why?"

I tilt my head at his odd question. "Because it feels good."

Sawyer's eyebrows rise. "It does?"

"Yeah." I brush my thumb over his lips. They're so soft, a fascinating contrast to the scruff on his chin and cheeks.

"Bu—but, I'm a guy."

I drag my gaze from his lips back to his eyes. Blue and green swirl in a hypnotic dance. Of course he's a guy. What kind of statement is that? Did Sawyer hit his head? Does he have a concussion I'm unaware of?

"I know."

"You aren't supposed to like guys… right?"

I'm not? I've never thought about it before. I didn't realize it was something I was supposed to think about, that I needed an answer to. I've never *liked* anyone before, not in the way other people seem to *like* each other.

I liked Madison because she was there and our parents wanted us to be together and I didn't have a fundamental objection to it. But that fuzzy, warm, obsessive feeling people talk about? I never felt that for Madison and certainly never for anyone else.

Except maybe Sawyer? I do feel warm and fuzzy when I'm with him. I miss him when I don't see him all day. I'm obviously a little possessive when it appears someone might steal him from me. Is this what everyone's always going on about?

Do I like Sawyer? Like, *like* like him?

"I… don't know? Does it matter?" I ask.

Sawyer's jaw drops and he looks like he wants to say yes. "I guess it doesn't?"

The fact that Sawyer's a guy seems moot to me. My feelings toward him don't really have anything to do with his gender. He's my best friend. He takes care of me. He makes me feel safe. Would I still feel this way if he was a girl? Maybe? I don't know, and I don't think I care.

"I still want to kiss you," I say, refusing to be distracted from my goal. "Is that okay?"

Sawyer studies me, focusing so intently on my face I want to duck away and hide. I'm not much to look at and I don't know what he's searching for.

"Just kissing?" Sawyer's voice is hoarse again. "Or more?"

Hmm, that's a good question. I've done more than kissing with Madison, but again, that was because she wanted to. I was pretty indifferent. With Sawyer, though? If kissing Sawyer was so good, maybe doing more will feel even better?

"Maybe?"

Sawyer nods stiffly, then clears his throat, which turns into a small coughing fit. "Sorry." He thumps his chest with his fist. "Um, how about we stick to just kissing? For now?"

He adds the last part quickly when he sees my reaction. My disappointment must have shown on my face. It was never a concern before, but now that he's brought it up, I definitely want to try more than kissing. But I can settle for just kissing… for now.

"Okay," I agree. "Can we start now?"

Sawyer's Adam's apple bobs again. "Mmhmm," he hums squeakily.

I lean in, pausing before we make contact. Last time, I was so preoccupied, so stuck in my head I didn't fully appreciate the feel of Sawyer's lips on mine. This time, I want to feel every second of it, I want to catalog every sensation.

Sawyer lets out a breath, the hot air washing over my chin, smelling wheaty and hoppy from his beer. He tilts his chin like an invitation for me to drink from his lips. And suddenly, I'm parched.

I close the remaining distance, and the instant my lips touch his, heat unfurls in me. My lips tingle. A shiver runs down my spine. An ache settles in my groin, and the only way to alleviate it is to add pressure and friction. My hips push forward and a moan escapes my throat as Sawyer's hard, flat stomach provides a surface for me to grind against. The relief is so immense it feels like my bones are melting. But reprieve is only temporary.

Sawyer nips at my mouth, catching my bottom lip lightly between his. Pleasure shoots through me, increasing the tightness in my groin faster than I can relieve it.

Sawyer tightens his grip on my hips and pulls me firmly into his lap. A bulge digs into my ass and my entire bottom half clenches with a desire I've never felt before.

I'm overheating. Everything's sensitive. I'm full to bursting and yet so empty at the same time. I don't know how to fix it. I don't know how to satisfy the ache.

"Sawyer, please," I plead, clutching at him as I rub myself over his body.

He growls and then I'm flying through the air. But

Sawyer's hold on me is solid and sure, and he lowers me gently onto the couch. He presses me into the cushions, and his hips push my thighs wide. His weight is deliciously heavy, trapping me underneath him.

The bulge I felt in Sawyer's lap is now flush against the ache in my groin. It's my penis, I realize, it's erect because I'm aroused. Which means the bulge in Sawyer's joggers must be his penis, also erect because he's aroused.

By me. Because of me. I'm doing that to him. I'm the cause of his arousal. The knowledge curls through me like liquid fire, spiking my temperature until I'm feverish.

Sawyer's mouth is hot, too, where it slants over mine. His tongue snakes over and around mine and the appendage seems to reach so much farther than just my mouth. I swear I feel it all the way down my throat, down to my stomach, where it's stirring everything up, turning me inside out.

I grasp at Sawyer, whimpering and writhing with a need I don't know how to express. "Hot." That's the only coherent word I can produce.

"Hot. Hot. Hot," I mumble around Sawyer's tongue, then against his mouth.

He props himself onto his hands and I use the space he's created to tear at my shirt. My fingers are clammy and tingly, and there are so many damn buttons with such tiny holes. I can't stand another second of this heat, so I grab the two sides of my shirt and rip them apart. Buttons fly everywhere, landing silently on the couch and area rug.

Sawyer's eyebrows shoot up and his bruised, red lips form a perfect O before he breaks out in laughter. "Sure, that's one way to do it."

"I'm so hot," I whine, struggling to get the shirt off.

"Yeah, you really are." Sawyer's eyes twinkle. He must feel the heat radiating off me. He sits back onto his heels, still between my thighs, giving me more room to maneuver. "Here, let me help."

He's so practiced at undressing me he's probably better at it than I am. It's only mildly cooler with the skin of my upper body exposed directly to the air. Maybe our thermostat needs to be adjusted? My hands go to the buttons of my pants.

Sawyer's still wearing his zipped Mars Fitness hoodie.

"Aren't you hot?" I ask as I lever my hips up to push my pants down.

"Uh…" Sawyer lifts my legs so they point straight up and then helps me tug my pants off. He grabs my ankles and strips my socks off too. "I, uh, I guess I'm a little overdressed?"

My feet drop to either side of his hips and I don't bother waiting for him. I reach for the zipper of his hoodie and yank it all the way down.

"Yep. Okay. Guess that's going." Sawyer shrugs it off and throws it to the floor with my clothes. His Mars t-shirt stretches across his chest, his shoulders. It hugs his torso all the way down to his hips. I can see his nipples poking through the fabric.

And suddenly I'm gripped with the need to see them in the flesh. I need to see their dusky pink hue. I need to feel their pebbled stiffness under my fingertips. I need the broad expanse of Sawyer's bare chest dragging across my own.

I tug on the hem of his shirt, but it's too tight for me to make any headway.

"I got it." Sawyer crosses his arms, his hands grab the

hem at either hip, and in one fluid motion, he rolls the shirt all the way off. He hops quickly to his feet to push down his joggers, revealing blue boxers with purple and pink polka dots. They're bright and fun and such a contrast to the plain black briefs I've got on.

I settle my hands on his hips when he climbs back between my legs. My thumbs graze across his abdomen, right above the waistband of his boxers, and Sawyer sucks in a breath.

I glance at him. His one hand is curled into a fist at his side and his other is crushing the back cushions of the couch.

"Is this okay?" I ask and when he nods, I flatten my hand against his stomach. He's burning up too, his skin scorching hot under my touch. I can feel the rapid pace of his breathing and when I slide my hand up his chest, his heart beats in a frantic rhythm against my palm.

Sawyer covers my hand with his own and when I look up, our gazes collide. The impact drives the air from my lungs and there's only one remedy that will get me breathing again.

Sawyer. Only Sawyer.

SAWYER

Preston is murdering me. With every touch, every look, every goddamn word out of his mouth, I'm dying a little. When he started ripping at his clothes, I thought my head was going to explode. I've seen him naked a thousand times, but never like this, with him at a fever pitch.

When he asked whether it mattered if he liked guys, when he said he wanted to kiss me again, it took every ounce of self-control to not shove my tongue down his throat. Because, yeah, the part of me that's been in love with Preston for years is setting off fucking fireworks at this unexpected development. But the part of me that's best friends with Preston is waving red flags and sounding alarms.

Preston might want to get naked and make out tonight. But will he still feel that way tomorrow? Or the day after? What if this is merely an experiment and he decides he wants to go back to how things were before? What if this fundamentally changes our friendship and we find we can't go back anymore?

Is it worth risking what we have for whatever this might turn out to be? If I'm honest with myself, if I let myself think too deeply about it, I'm pretty sure I'll land on, "No." It's absolutely not worth it. What I currently have with Preston is all that is precious and good. It isn't everything I want it to be, but I'd rather this than nothing at all.

Except Preston is splayed out before me, wearing nothing but his tight briefs, his cock hard and leaking under the cotton. His legs are spread around my thighs and he keeps thrusting his hips forward like he's looking for something to grind up on.

I'm only a man. I have limits. When the guy I've been in love with since puberty starts tearing at our clothes, there's only so much I can resist.

His hand is on my chest, over my heart. Can he feel how fast it's beating? Does he know how long it's beat for him?

I watch him as he touches me. The wonder on his face, the light in his eyes. Jesus Christ. It should be illegal for anyone to look like that, so pure and innocent and unblemished.

I lift his hand from my chest and plant a kiss on his palm. He sucks in a shuddering breath. I lean down and cover his mouth with my lips as he exhales. Breathing in the air that was just in his lungs, I hold it inside me for as long as I can, letting my body absorb as many of the microscopic, invisible molecules as possible. It's a tiny bit of Preston that's now a part of me, something of him that I'll carry with me forever.

Preston slides his arms over my shoulders, pulling me down on top of him. The skin-on-skin contact overloads my brain's circuits and the sparks pop as the evolved portion of my mind shuts down and primal instincts take over.

I crush Preston into the couch. His knees come up on either side of my hips and he locks his ankles behind me. His cock is a hard length against my stomach and I line us up for a couple good thrusts.

Preston mewls and arches into me. His heels dig into my ass and his fingers scrabble against my back. His body couldn't have shouted "more" any clearer.

I plunder his mouth, licking into it and searching out every dark recess. I pet his tongue with mine, suck on it, push it around in a dance that mimics the one our bodies are dancing.

The pleasure is indescribable. It's better than anything I've ever experienced. It's so good, so perfect. The sounds Preston makes—god, they're so obscene and yet so sweet. The way he fits against me, all his sharp angles perfectly cushioned by the curves of my muscles. I know Preston doesn't have much experience with sex, but Jesus fucking Christ does he know how to turn on the sexy when he wants to.

The air is heated and thick, filled with the musky aroma of our mutual arousal and the sour scent of our sweat. I kiss Preston's jaw, press my lips on the beauty mark behind his ear, and lap at the saltiness on his neck. Preston's fingers find their way into my hair and he holds me to him, like he can't get enough. Pleasure shoots through me, racing down my spine and straight to my balls. They're pulled up, high and tight, primed to turn themselves inside out.

But I can't come before Preston does. In no world, in no universe is that okay. Preston absolutely, without a doubt has to come first.

I take his mouth again and he whimpers into it. I swallow it down as my hands wander, eating up all those acres of skin I've never let myself touch. His sides, his hips, his thighs. His spine, the small of his back, his ass. I palm one perfectly round globe and it fits in my hand like it was made to measure.

I squeeze and pull him tighter to me. His movements grow more frantic, more desperate as he bucks against me. I sink my weight into him, a hard, solid surface for him to chase his orgasm on. His sex sounds grower higher and higher, louder and louder, and his whole body is shaking like he's right on the edge.

"Come for me, Preston," I murmur against his lips, and like magic, he does.

He throws his head back, screaming, and liquid warmth gushes between our bodies.

He's so fucking beautiful. The sounds he makes are music to my ears. His cum has soaked through not only his own underwear but mine too. His cum is on my skin, on my cock. I did this to him. I made him come. I love him so fucking much.

My own orgasm explodes, harder and stronger than any I've ever had. It tears through me, ripping me open from the inside out. I roar as I keep frotting against Preston, like I can somehow work our combined cum into our bodies so we don't lose a single drop.

I come so hard, I think I black out for a second. Aftershocks are still rumbling through me as I cover Preston's body, my face buried in the crook of his neck. His arms and legs are still wrapped around me. He's still trembling too.

I want to stay here forever. I never want to move. I don't want to deal with whatever comes next, whatever consequences are waiting for us on the other side of this moment.

Here. Right now. This is paradise.

"That was good," Preston says. His voice is quiet and lazy, but there's a distinct note of surprise in it.

"Yeah?"

"Better than I anticipated."

I push myself onto my elbows and gaze down at Preston.

"We're going to have to do this again," he says with a soft, sleepy smile. His eyes are heavy-lidded, but the blue of his irises is clear and sharp. He might still be riding high off his orgasm, but he almost looks like he's thinking about his research. "Make sure we get a good sample size."

He's lost me. "Sample size?"

"To ensure this wasn't a fluke."

Fuck me.

This was supposed to be just kissing. Some simple making out to test the waters and see if Preston's comfortable with guy-on-guy action. We weren't supposed to get naked and sweaty and introduce our dicks to each other—albeit between two layers of cotton. We weren't supposed to have mutual orgasms. We weren't supposed to have sex. And now he wants to do it a bunch more times to confirm that yes, he might actually be gay?

Fear and want battle inside me—I want more too. I

want everything with Preston. It would be so easy to take anything and everything he's willing to give, consequences be damned.

Would we survive all that? Our friendship is the most important thing in my life. If I lost it or it changed for the worse, I don't know what I would do. I don't know if I could go on.

But when Preston gazes adoringly at me, what real choice do I have? I smile back and slowly lift myself off him. Preston doesn't let me get far, following me up and tucking himself into my side like he can't bear to lose the skin-on-skin contact.

Without a word, we head to my bathroom. "How about you take a shower?" I say, trying to untangle myself from Preston.

He just clings to me harder. "With you?" He peers at me with those beautiful blue eyes, rimmed with long, dark lashes.

How can I say no to him? I love him. I'll never say no. Even if it means testing the very limits of my sanity. Hot shower, soapy, naked. Despite having just come, my dick twitches in interest.

All I can do is nod.

He releases me then, and I turn on the water, waiting for it to heat up before pushing my boxers off. I don't look behind me to see what Preston's doing. I don't dare. Instead, I step in under the spray and brace my hands on the wall, letting the water pour over my head.

My only reaction when Preston sets his hands on my hips is a hitch in my breath. Then he slides his hands to my stomach as he presses himself flush against my back.

His lips land on the nape of my neck. His soft dick is nestled in my ass.

My stomach clenches with the urge to spin around and haul him into my arms, to rub myself on him until he smells like me, until he wears burns from my stubble and bruises from my hands. I want to sink into him, fill him up, flood him with my cum, so he's covered in me inside and out.

The desire is staggering. It knocks me over and makes it difficult to breathe.

Preston's hands roam over my front, his fingers seeking out all the bumps and dips of my muscles. He moves up to my pecs, palming them and squeezing them until my nipples are so hard they ache. Then he flicks his thumbs over them and I let out a deep, guttural groan.

"Does that feel good?" Preston asks.

I nod jerkily.

He does it again and I let go of the wall to grab his hands. It's too much. It's not enough. He's killing me and it's the sweetest death.

"Sawyer?" Preston's lips move on the back of my neck and he squeezes my pecs again. He stretches, rubbing his body across my back, his cock starting to grow against my ass.

I can't stand it anymore. I turn to find Preston gloriously wet. His black hair is slicked away from his face. Water droplets hang from his clumped lashes, from the tip of his nose. His normally pale cheeks have taken on a rosy hue and his lips are swollen and bruised from my kisses.

I growl and grab him. I can't help it. This is my every dream come true, my wildest fantasies. How can I walk away from this? How can I set boundaries when Preston presents himself so unassumingly?

Preston makes a soft, moaning sound when I capture his lips. My arms wind around him, bending him backward to mold him to me. He hugs me tight around the neck and hikes one leg up my hip. We're both hard again, this time without the barrier of underwear between us.

His cock is caught between our stomachs and he keeps rutting against me like he can't stop himself. There's something incredibly erotic about Preston using me to get off. Like I'm nothing more than a convenient surface, a toy he happens to have on hand. He's seeking his own pleasure, laser-focused on it, determined to chase the climax and I'm just a tool he uses to get there.

My hands move to his ass and I've never been so thankful for all the weight lifting I've done over the years. I widen my stance on the slippery tile floor, bend my knees for stability, and hoist Preston off his feet.

He squeals at being airborne, but his legs automatically go around my waist and he clings to me like a koala to a tree. I shuffle to the side and pin him to the wall with my weight.

Shower kisses with Preston might be better than normal, non-shower kisses with Preston. It's slippery and messy and wet and somehow, we both end up smiling and giggling as we nip and lick at each other. I follow the rivulets of water as they sluice down his neck, lap at the hollow of his collarbone, and take his pulse with my lips.

He has a smattering of dark hair in the middle of his chest and it narrows to a thin trail like an arrow pointing the way to his cock. His beautiful, flawless specimen of a cock. He's not super long or super thick, but when I curl my fingers around it, it's a perfect fit.

I hold it for a moment, savoring the feeling. The weight of it, the heat of it, the veins running along its length. The bulbous mushroom head is swollen and smooth, just begging for me to wrap my lips around it.

I give it an experimental stroke and Preston drops his head back against the wall with a strangled cry. His lashes flutter and his mouth hangs open.

I pump my hand again, squeezing a little tighter this time. He cries louder and digs his fingers into my shoulders.

I swipe my thumb over the head, circling around and around the slit.

"Sawyer!"

Fuck, I love the sound of my name when he says it like that. Pleading. Desperate. Wild and untamed.

I jerk and tug on his cock, watching the expressions flitting across Preston's face to find just the right pressure, rhythm, angle. My own cock throbs where it pokes Preston's ass, so close to his hole, so close to being inside him.

Preston's voice is frighteningly high, and his body grows taut as he nears his climax. I don't stop, don't let up, pushing him hard and fast toward the finish line. When he comes, his cum spills from his cock and covers my hand.

I bring my hand up to my mouth, licking up the salty, bitter goodness before the shower can wash it down the drain. Preston watches me with half-lidded eyes, and when my hand is clean, he pulls me to him.

I don't realize what he's doing until he thrusts his tongue between my lips, licking and searching. Fuck. He's

trying to eat his own cum from my mouth. It's so unexpected, so unlike Preston, so fucking hot, that it tips me
over my own finish line.

I reach under Preston's ass as I hit the peak and I jerk
myself the rest of the way. I spray the wall while Preston
sucks up every last, lingering drop of his cum.

I love this man. I love him so fucking much. I'm so
fucked.

PRESTON

Madison does a double take when I walk down the center aisle of the chartered plane that will take us to Boston for Thanksgiving weekend. Sawyer's right behind me and Madison narrows her eyes, her gaze flitting from me to him and back to me again.

"Ho. Ly. Shit." Madison drops her phone in her lap. "You two had sex!"

She's sitting by the window in a large recliner-sized seat upholstered in soft, cream-colored leather. It's in a group of four—two seats facing forward, two facing backward, separated by a wide table bolted to the floor. A group of two is across the aisle and a couch sits in the rear of the cabin. I take the other window seat, opposite Madison, leaving Sawyer with the seat next to mine.

"Jesus, Mads!" Sawyer shoots a pointed look toward the back of the plane where the flight attendant is working in the galley.

Madison claps her hands excitedly. "I'm right, aren't I? You guys finally had sex!"

"Keep your voice down!"

"Why? The crew won't care," Madison says at full volume. "This is something to celebrate! Actually—" She turns to yell at the flight attendant. "Excuse me! Do we have any bubbly on board?"

The flight attendant takes a few steps in our direction. "Yes, we do. Shall I bring three glasses?"

"Yes, please! Thanks!" Madison sits down with a smirk.

"Seriously?" Sawyer's slumps into his seat, sliding down low so he can hide his face behind his hand while his elbow is planted on the armrest.

"Yes! Come on!" Madison kicks at Sawyer's leg. "Preston's lost his v-card for the second time. This is momentous."

"I've lost my what?" I'm pretty absentminded, but I don't think I've lost anything recently, especially not a v-card since I have no idea what that is.

"Oh god." Sawyer's voice is muffled as he slaps his hand over his face. "How do you even know?"

"Please," Madison scoffs. "I smelled the sex on you the second you stepped on board."

She could? I lift the collar of my sweater and sniff. We both took showers this morning. We shouldn't smell like sex at all.

"Not literally, silly!" Madison exclaims. "I mean, you're practically glowing! You both have that smug, satisfied look that only comes from good sex. It was good, wasn't it?"

"Don't answer that," Sawyer interjects before I can say that, yes, it was indeed good.

The flight attendant brings three glasses of champagne on a tray and as he hands each to Madison, she passes them to me and Sawyer.

"Fine. I don't want the details anyway. Here. Take this."

"We'll be pushing away in a moment, so please have your seatbelts fastened for takeoff." The flight attendant directs us before disappearing toward the back of the plane again.

"Cheers!" Madison holds up her glass. "To really great sex!"

I clink mine against hers and take a sip, the carbonated wine tickling my nose as I swallow.

"Kill me now," Sawyer says, but he clinks his glass and takes a sip too.

"What's with the attitude, dude?" Madison asks with a laugh. "Haven't you wanted to bang Preston for forever?"

"Mads!" Sawyer hisses at her.

Wait, what? He's wanted to have sex with me for a long time? That can't be right. Wouldn't he have told me?

"What do you mean?" I ask, glancing from Madison to Sawyer.

He looks like he wants to drop through the floor of the plane, even though we've started barreling down the runway. Madison's eyes widen, her lips press together like she's accidentally let slip something she was supposed to keep secret.

"What do you mean?" I ask again, more forcefully this time.

Madison and Sawyer have both known me for a long time and they're my bestest friends. They each have their own way of looking out for me, of taking care of me. And

I'm really grateful to them for everything they do. But sometimes… sometimes I wish they weren't quite so protective. I'm not made of glass. I won't break with the slightest contact.

"Nothing," Sawyer finally says. "It's nothing."

It's not nothing. I can tell from the way Sawyer shifts uncomfortably in his seat and how Madison's gaze darts back and forth between us. There's something, and it has to do with me and Sawyer having sex, but they won't tell me because they don't want to hurt me.

It's only been a couple days since I went to Mars to find him, and then he took me home and we had sex. Maybe Sawyer didn't actually want to have sex with me? Maybe he did it only to appease me? He seemed so enthusiastic, though. Is it possible to fake something like that?

I thought Sawyer wanted sex—he had sex with Fitz after all—but perhaps I'm wrong? A sickening feeling grows in my stomach at the thought that I forced myself onto Sawyer, and I gulp down my champagne.

Madison lets out a laugh that sounds a little strained. "It's nothing. Ignore me. I'm always running my mouth. You know me. I don't know what I'm talking about."

When I glance at Sawyer, he's staring daggers at Madison who diligently pretends not to notice.

I hate it when this happens. Neither of them says a word but somehow manages to communicate with pointed looks and subtle body movements. It's like they know a secret language I've never learned. Maybe I'm paranoid or sensitive, but I'm certain it's about me. They've got good intentions, they're trying to protect me, but then I end up being left out.

I turn toward the window and sulk while watching the

clouds float past. This isn't a great way to start the weekend, but I suppose I should set my expectations appropriately before we touch down in Boston. Time with my parents is always strained, and these weekends usually feel more like obstacle courses than vacations.

Silence descends upon the plane as I stew and neither Madison nor Sawyer try to fill it. Sawyer pulls out his laptop to do some schoolwork and Madison types madly on her phone. I dig through my bag for my tablet, opening up the analysis I've been working on this week. I stare at the screen, but the letters and numbers blur together as my mind wanders.

I'm not the son my parents wanted. I'm too antisocial and nerdy, too wrapped up in my research and uninterested in the things that are important to them. They want a bright, charming, savvy son who will one day take over the company business. It doesn't matter that that's not who I am.

The flight attendant comes by with snacks and drinks a couple times, and then we're landing in Boston. Sawyer's the first out of his seat and off the plane. Madison catches my arm before I can follow him.

"Hey, Pres," she says, voice lowered. "You know I was just teasing earlier, right? I'm sorry if I made you uncomfortable."

"That's okay," I say, and I mean it. Madison would never intentionally hurt me, and I wasn't exactly uncomfortable either. Ironic that I didn't understand enough of the subtext to be bothered by it.

After we climb into the big SUV that will take us to my parents' house, Madison clears her throat. "So, um, how do you guys want to play this?"

Sawyer stares at Madison. "Play what?"

"This." Madison waves a finger between us. "Are you together now?"

Sawyer stiffens next to me, but I don't understand why. Sawyer and I have always been together. We're best friends. We've lived together since we were in high school.

"I hate to break it to you, but you're literally glowing. People are going to have questions," Madison continues.

"What do you mean? What kinds of questions?" I ask.

Madison's voice is gentle as she speaks. "You guys have always been way too touchy-feely and co-dependent for a normal set of best friends. But this?" She looks pointedly to where my thigh is pressed flushed against Sawyer's, where my hand is snugly ensconced in his. "That's a lot, even for you. People are going to notice that something's changed. And they'll want to know what happened."

The question brings me up short. Why should anyone care about me and Sawyer? Why is it any of their business?

Sawyer fidgets. "I don't know. We—I haven't thought that far ahead. This is… a pretty recent development."

Madison winces like she's about to give us bad news. "Then you might want to…" She waves at our clasped hands again. "Not do stuff like that."

I take in the way my hand fits inside Sawyer's, the roughness of his palms, the callouses at the base of his fingers, the slight color variation between his skin and mine. I like holding Sawyer's hand. I like being pressed up next to him. I like cuddling and being held by him.

Sawyer clears his throat. "You're right. Maybe we should tone it down for the weekend." He squeezes my fingers quickly before letting go, then shifts so there's an inch of space between us.

If Sawyer thinks it's the best thing to do, then I trust him. Except now my side is cold and I don't know where I'm supposed to put my hand. I tuck it under my thigh to keep myself from reaching for him again.

Madison regards me for a moment before asking, "Are you okay with that, Pres?"

I nod, even though I'm not sure I am. I have no reason not to be okay, but I don't like the unsettled, unmoored feeling I get when I'm not physically touching Sawyer.

"It's just a few days," Sawyer says, though he sounds unconvinced. "It'll be fine."

Mom greets us at the front door when we arrive at the house. It's already fully decked out for Thanksgiving with red, orange, and yellow leafed wreaths and garlands decorating every surface. On the table in the middle of the foyer sits a giant cornucopia surrounded by pumpkins, apples, grapes, and corn. Sunflower arrangements as tall as Sawyer line the walls. The scent of pumpkin spice fills the air.

"Madison!" She holds out both arms to give Madison an elbow-clasping hug and air kisses on both cheeks.

"Hey, Mrs. Boyer. How are you?"

"Oh, you know, busy, busy. There's so much to do for Thanksgiving."

"Let me know if you need help."

"You're a darling, Madison." Then Mom turns to me and does the elbow-clasping and air kissing thing, but only on one side. "Preston, how is the research going?"

"Uh, fine." I don't bother to explain how it's *really* going. Not only would she not understand, but I don't think she actually cares. Asking after my research is just the polite thing to do.

"That's wonderful. And Sawyer!" Mom gives him a slow once-over. "My, my, I swear you get more muscular every time I see you!" She squeezes his arm like she's testing the firmness of his bicep.

Sawyer chuckles good-naturedly. "Thanks, Mrs. Boyer."

"Come in, come in!" Mom spins around and leads the way through the foyer and into one of the sitting rooms. "You'll have to excuse Mr. Boyer and I. We're accustomed to a set dinner hour, so we've already eaten. But I've had Chef make up a few things for you to nibble on."

She twirls around with a flourish, gesturing to a sideboard that holds enough food for an entire party of guests. There are more varieties of meat and cheese, crackers and fruit than I can count. Mini pumpkins and gourds sit among decorative branches and more colored leaves.

"I'll pour drinks for everyone. We have a new pumpkin brandy that's absolutely yummy. You all have to try some."

Sawyer hands me a plate and I dutifully hold it while he piles food on it. When it's full, he guides me over to a couch by the fireplace.

"Ahem." Madison purposefully clears her throat when she joins us. Before I can figure out what she's trying to communicate, Sawyer shifts away from me.

I'm about to close the gap between us when I realize what's happening. I sat down too close to him, and we're supposed to be inconspicuous. I bite my lip as I fight the urge to touch him. It's a physical itch, like an irritant that can only be soothed with physical contact.

I know I agreed to—what did Sawyer call it?—tone things down, but this can't be what he meant, can it? We always sit like this, close enough to touch, even before we started having sex.

Mom brings over glasses of dark amber liquor, handing them out before settling herself into an armchair. She doesn't immediately launch into conversation like she usually does. Instead, she watches us—me and Sawyer—for a long, silent moment before taking a drink.

There's something in her eyes that makes me squirm. Mom is always so perfectly put together, with a practiced smile on her lips and a measured laugh at the ready. It's not often she lets the veneer drop, but when she does, there's something unmistakably sharp and discerning in her demeanor.

I hate it when she looks at me like that. Like she's trying to cut open my skull and rummage around inside my brain. Like she's trying to figure out what's wrong with my neural pathways.

I don't know why I'm the way I am. I don't know why I can't be the person she and Dad want me to be. I slump into myself, as if I can escape her scrutiny if I make myself smaller.

Sawyer's knee bumps into mine—then stays there. He's shifted forward on the couch, legs spread wide as he rests his elbows on his knees. It looks like a casual position, convenient for munching on his plate of food. But the light and consistent pressure tells me it's not. It's deliberate. My lungs relax enough to draw in a full breath. Sawyer's got me. Even when it appears he doesn't, he still does.

"Mrs. Boyer," he says, breaking the silence. "The decorations this year are really cool. You've gone all out."

There's a slight lag in Mom's reaction, but when she turns her attention to Sawyer, her signature smile is firmly in place again.

"Yes, Mrs. Boyer." Madison chimes in. "I love the wreaths on the doors! Where did you get those?"

Mom laughs politely in response. "There's this wonderful little flower shop…"

As the small talk flows effortlessly around me, I scoot a little closer to Sawyer.

SAWYER

I'm getting ready for bed in one of the Boyers' guest rooms when the door slowly creaks open. A smile pulls at my cheeks even as a weird sour feeling churns in my stomach. It isn't the decadent charcuterie we had for dinner. Or the awful pumpkin brandy Mrs. Boyer foisted upon us.

The blue room is my "usual room" when I stay with the Boyers. It's decorated with a mix of antique furniture and simple, clean lines. A large four-poster bed sits in the middle of the room, and by the window is a seating area with a loveseat and armchair.

"Sawyer?" comes Preston's whisper, then the snick of the door latching shut behind him.

I turn from my duffle bag on a luggage rack—yes, the Boyers keep hotel-style luggage racks in their guest rooms —to find Preston dressed in plaid pajama pants and an old varsity t-shirt of mine from high school.

It's much too big on him and he swims in it, but the sight makes my heart clench so hard it hurts. God, he looks so good wearing my clothes. It's so cliché, and yet I can't help the possessive satisfaction it gives me. Preston's mine. I've put my mark on him.

Fuck. This whole situation is so fucked up.

I love him. I want to shout it from the rooftops. I want everyone to know. But I can't.

In the few days since Preston came charging into Mars, all freaked out, we've had quite a bit more sex, but we're still very much in the honeymoon phase. Any minute now, Preston could tell me this has been a huge mistake. It's why I suggested we tone things down for the weekend. There's no point in raising suspicions when there will be nothing to suspect in a couple weeks.

I've managed to avoid Fitz too. The timing happened to work out in my favor—Fitz left the city early for Thanksgiving, and we've only had a couple text messages back and forth.

I won't be able to avoid him forever, though. I'll have to break up with him after Thanksgiving. No matter what happens between me and Preston, even if he wants nothing to do with me tomorrow, I can't in good conscience keep dating Fitz. It wouldn't be fair to him—or to me. Fitz is a nice guy, sweet, smart, attractive. But he doesn't hold a candle to Preston. I was fooling myself to think he could.

Preston takes a few steps forward, then hesitates. "Is this... is this okay?"

I hate the uncertainty in his eyes, the waver in his voice, as if he's not sure where he stands with me. That should never be in question. I will always be here for him —nothing will tear me away.

"Of course it is. Come here." I wave him over and he

rushes forward, arms snapping around my waist like a vise, face burrowing into the crook of my neck.

I hold him, nose in his hair, breathing in his lavender scent. It takes a few seconds for the tension in Preston's body to melt away and he relaxes into me, letting me bear some of his weight.

Thanksgiving and Christmas are always fraught for Preston, and this weekend hasn't gotten off to a great start. First the grilling from Madison. I know she didn't mean him any harm, but what the fuck, Madison. Then Mrs. Boyer keeping us company by the fire downstairs.

Despite being a socialite, Mrs. Boyer has an eagle eye and she doesn't miss anything. She rarely lets on how perceptive she is, but I have no doubt she keeps dossiers on every person she meets, and she's not afraid of using the intelligence to her advantage.

Madison was right to warn us about limiting our PDA. It wouldn't take much to trigger Mrs. Boyer's suspicions. And once she's got a scent in her nose, there's no stopping her from tracking down the whole story.

There was a moment after we sat down with our food and drinks. Mrs. Boyer got this look in her eyes as she regarded Preston. It was calculating and shrewd and scary as fuck.

Then she turned it on me and for a second, I could've sworn she saw right through the inch of air I'd put between me and Preston. I fully expected the first words out of her mouth to be along the lines of, "How dare you touch my son. Get the hell out of my house."

We managed to evade an interrogation tonight, but we're by no means out of the danger zone. The fact that Mrs. Boyer didn't say anything now, might just mean she's saving it for a more advantageous opportunity later on.

Which is why, when we called it a night, I pushed Preston toward the house's family wing while I retreated meekly to the guest wing. Not that I expected him to stay there; he knows where I usually am.

"Don't want to stay in your old room?" I ask, already knowing the answer.

He shakes his head. "It's cold in there."

It's not—every room has independent temperature controls. Preston just thinks it was because he was alone.

"Warmer now?" I rub my hands briskly up and down his back.

"Mmhmm."

"Good." I don't bother asking whether he wants to stay with me tonight. It's a given. I won't turn him away when he's come to me.

Preston shifts and suddenly I feel soft lips against the base of my neck. They travel up to the point of my jaw, then down toward my chin before sliding over my mouth.

He makes a soft moaning sound that goes straight to my dick. There's a hint of minty fresh toothpaste on his lips and they part when I nibble on them.

Kissing Preston is such a head rush. I never imagined I'd be allowed to, that I'd ever know what it feels like, what he tastes like. It's so much better than anything my imagination can conjure up.

But before we get too carried away, I break off the kiss, soothing Preston's whine with a quiet hush. With my forehead resting against his, I whisper, "Are you sure about this? In your parents' house?"

He stands stock-still for a moment before pulling away

to look up at me. There's confusion in his eyes and I could fucking kick myself.

"You don't want to?" The hurt in his voice is clear.

"Of course I want to." I brush my thumb across his gorgeous, gorgeous cheekbone. Then across his damp, rosy bottom lip.

"You're not doing it just for me?" His limbs stiffen as some tension returns to his body. He tries to step back, despite his hands fisting the hem of my shirt.

"What are you talking about?" I sway us slowly from side to side.

"You don't have to have sex with me if you don't want to. I won't be hurt. I'll understand," he says, eyes trained on my collarbone. He's such a bad liar.

I lift his head with a finger under his chin. "I very much want to have sex with you." I tug him closer so my hard-on is pressed against his stomach. "Feel that?" I say, lowering my head to growl in his ear.

Preston nods breathlessly.

"That's because of you. You make me so fucking hard, Pres."

A shudder runs through him and an answering bulge grows against my hip.

I snag his earlobe between my teeth and bite down gently. The bulge at my hip grows bigger and Preston lets out a helpless, fragile sound that fuels my own erection.

He squirms, scrabbling at me and arching into me, like he wants something but he doesn't know how to ask for it, and he's getting more frantic with each passing second.

I walk us toward the bed. "What do you need, Preston? Tell me what you need."

I have to hear him say it out loud so there's zero doubt

where he wants this to go. So I don't end up second-guessing myself later when I wonder if I pushed him too far.

"Please, I want... I need..." Preston says, barely audible.

"Tell me." I work my way up his jaw to that beauty mark behind his ear. The one I've been fascinated with for as long as I've known it was there.

His fingers drag over my scalp as I suck on that spot. "I... I... need to orgasm."

I hum and murmur against his skin. "I can make that happen. How do you want me to do it? With my hand? My mouth?"

I'm already salivating at the thought of getting Preston's cock between my lips.

A tremble races through Preston at my suggestion. "Your... your mouth?"

I hum again. "Yes, good choice."

I strip my t-shirt off Preston, then push the pajama pants off his hips. He's not wearing anything under them—minx. Then I carefully ease him down to the bed.

His cock lays on his stomach, hard with thick veins running along its length. His foreskin is pulled back, revealing that bulbous head, swollen and wet with pre-cum. I push his legs apart so I can kneel between them, pausing for a moment to give him a chance to object to being spread wide. But Preston only spreads himself wider. Fuck.

I run my hands up his legs, thumbs grazing his inner thighs. At the crease between his hips and legs, my thumbs slip under his balls to his taint. Preston lets out a cry, with his eyes wide open, staring unseeingly at the ceiling while he pants through his mouth.

"This okay?" I ask, checking in.

He lets out a strangled sound.

"Preston? Is this okay?"

He nods frantically. "Uh huh."

I scoot down, open my mouth, and take his balls into my mouth.

"Oh fuck! Sawyer!"

I hum at my name on his lips, incontrovertible proof that he knows who he's in bed with. Me—Sawyer—I'm the one sucking his balls. But we're not alone in the house and the last thing we want is someone knocking on the door to save Preston from me.

"Shh," I say. "They'll hear."

That's all Preston needs to slap one hand over his mouth. But his other hand lands in my hair, pulling me close, pushing me deeper into his groin. I lave at his ball with my tongue, increasing the pressure before letting it plop out to subject the other one to the same treatment.

Preston smells divine down here. Musk, with that lingering hint of lavender. I breathe him in, filling my senses with him until I'm lost in him.

Preston. My Preston. My best friend. The man I've been in love with for years. He's such an integral part of me I don't know who I am without him.

I pause for a moment, resting my face in his groin, overcome with the emotions roiling inside me. Gratitude, joy, love. Disbelief that this is finally happening. Fear that it will be torn away.

Preston's fingers card through my hair and after a few minutes, he sits up, planting kisses along the back of my head and shoulders. I lift my head and catch his mouth with mine. I groan while Preston whimpers.

I might have only tasted his lips a handful of times, but I'm already addicted to it, to the way they feel, how he tentatively sneaks his tongue out, the way he shudders when I swipe my tongue against it. I could spend all day kissing those lips, nibbling and devouring them.

But I promised Preston a blowjob, so I push him back down, and take his cock in my hand. I savor the weight of it in my palm before licking a long strip from the base to the tip. He hisses and his hips come off the bed as I wrap my lips around the swollen, tender head.

"Ah! Sawyer!" It slips out before Preston remembers to be quiet. He rolls his lips between his teeth and whines.

Letting the head of his cock run along the top of my mouth, I sink all the way down. Like Preston himself, his cock is long and slender, and it fits snugly in my throat as I swallow. I push forward until my nose is flush against his pelvic bone, his cock blocking off my airway. My stomach clenches at the satisfaction of being stuffed full of Preston, of having such a delicate and vulnerable part of him suffocating me.

Holding him in my throat, I rub circles on his perineum and roll his balls in my palm. Underneath me, Preston thrashes, body undulating and thighs clenching around my shoulders. He's covered his mouth with an elbow, but that doesn't completely muffle the sound of my name as he babbles incoherently.

My lungs protest and my head feels a little faint. I reluctantly pull off him to drag in a breath of air, but I take the opportunity to probe my tongue into his slip. I'm rewarded with a burst of pre-cum and it's the most delicious thing I've ever tasted in my life—light, clean, only a hint of musk.

Preston's muffled cries turn a little frantic, a little alarmed—he must be close. I up my efforts, increasing my suction. I tug lightly at his balls and press my thumb more firmly into his taint. With all the spit I'm drooling, my thumb slips down and runs over Preston's hole. It wasn't my intention to go there, but it does the trick. Preston screams into his elbow and he tenses with his orgasm. Sweet, sweet cum spills into my mouth.

I rub my thumb over his hole as his muscles contract and relax like he's trying to suck me inside. God, I really want to be in there. I want to taste his ass, then sink myself deep inside his body. I want to wrap myself around him and thrust into him. I want to see the expression on his face as I stretch him wide and touch him where no one has ever touched him before. I want to flood him with my cum, fill him up with it.

Without thinking, I press my thumb into his hole. He's not loose enough for me to get in, but more cum shoots into my mouth. I swallow it down, every single precious drop.

Preston's trembling with aftershocks when I kiss my way up his delectable body. When I get within range, he attacks my mouth, his tongue searching out every nook and cranny like he's trying to taste himself on me. There isn't much left, I've swallowed as much of it as I can.

Then suddenly, with his hands on either side of my face, he pushes me away to look me in the eye.

"I want you to ejaculate on my face."

My brain short circuits. "What?"

"I want you to ejaculate on my face," he says again,

slower this time, enunciating clearly so there's no way for me to mistake his words.

"Uh…"

My hesitation makes Preston second-guess himself. "Is that okay?

I hurry to nod. "Yep. Mmhmm. That's definitely okay. I can definitely do that." I roll off him, strip naked, and I'm back on the bed in less than half a second.

"Like this." Preston tugs me into position.

My brain is legit exploding as I kneel on the bed with his head between my knees. Preston's eyes are glued to my dick, hard and leaking, pointed directly at his face.

He opens his mouth and angles up to take my cock between his lips like he's a seasoned cocksucker. He swirls his tongue around the head, wiggles his tongue into my slit, and grazes his teeth ever so lightly over the sensitive flesh.

"Oh, fuck." I grab the headboard to keep from shoving myself all the way down his throat.

Preston furrows his brow. "Shh."

Oh god. It's so incredibly hot when he shushes me. I turn my head and bite my arm.

Then he turns his attention back to my cock with a look of intense concentration, the same one he gets when he's deep into his work. "Can you stroke yourself? I want to see how you do it."

How can I possibly say no? I spit in my palm then take myself in hand. My spit combines with Preston's and it's way more erotic than it has any right to be. I start slow, with long, even strokes. Preston's mouth hangs open as he watches, eyes following every move.

Gradually, I pick up speed, adding a twist at the end.

Preston makes a surprised little sound like he's stumbled upon the most interesting scientific discovery.

His lips are red and bruised. His cheeks are flushed and rosy. His hair is in disarray on the pillow. He's the most beautiful thing I've ever laid eyes on.

He opens his jaw wide and sticks his tongue out like an invitation. I can't resist. I gently rest my cock on it, sliding an inch into his mouth. He hums and tugs on my hips, encouraging me forward.

"Are you sure?" I ask in a strangled voice.

He nods. "Mmhmm." And he tugs on my hips harder.

I'm careful as I ease in farther. His eyes roll backward and his eyelids flutter as he moans. The vibrations travel up my dick, hitting me deep, and it takes all my self-control not to come right then.

I don't give him more than an inch or so, pulling out well before I trigger his gag reflex. Slow and gentle, it's more like I'm stroking his tongue with the head of my dick than any kind of face fucking. But god, it's so good. My balls draw up, my stomach clenches, and when Preston lets out another satisfied groan, it's too much for me to hold back.

I don't pull out fast enough and the first spurt lands on his tongue. His eyes fly open and his jaw drops as more cum shoots from my cock. It lands on his chin, his cheeks, his nose, ropes and ropes of cum until my balls are turned inside out.

Without thinking, I rub my cock over his face, spreading my cum around. Preston lets out a satisfied moan as he turns his head side to side to make sure I don't miss any spots.

Jesus Christ. I've given Preston a facial. I've painted his

face with my cum. Seeing him so innocent and yet so debauched only makes me love him more.

I scoot down and clean him up with long, thorough licks. Then I feed my cum to Preston who hums like it's the most mind-blowing thing he's ever tasted. And fucking hell, if I wasn't so drained, I'd come all over again.

When he's finally clean, I cuddle up behind him—my big spoon to his little one. That's how we fall asleep. I've never slept so well in my life.

PRESTON

It's a family tradition to play football on Thanksgiving before the big meal. It's Dad's show these days, but Grandpa is the one who started it. Guests are divided into two teams. It's supposed to be a fun game, but nothing is ever just for fun when Dad's involved. He always stacks his team—which means he gets Sawyer—and if the other side knows what's good for them, they'll let him win. No one wants to spend the rest of the day around grumpy, passive-aggressive Dad.

The big field behind the house is marked out with flags and a massive tent is erected with chairs and refreshments for the spectators. Only the old and infirm are excused from playing. Every able-bodied person is required to spend at least a few minutes on the field.

Despite having been forced to partake in this tradition every year, I have no idea how football works. There's a ball. It gets thrown. People run. And then some people cheer and other people groan. I just try to stay out of everyone's way.

Sawyer's wearing a form-fitting long-sleeve shirt and black leggings under his shorts. His cheeks are flushed and he's grinning from ear to ear. When he's playing, he's so laser-focused, eyes trained on his target. His legs are a blur as he races down the field, and the air around him ripples with fog from the heat his body projects.

When he scores—and he scores a lot—he breaks out into complicated dance routines. During every lull in the game, he runs around giving people high fives. His voice rings out over everyone else's as he shouts encouragements to his teammates and friendly shit talk to the opposing team.

It's not the first time I've seen him play like this, of course. I've watched him hundreds of times before. Every year at Thanksgiving, sure, but also at his rugby games during high school. He's always been mesmerizing on the field. So athletic. So determined. The energy that exudes from him is infectious and intoxicating. He makes everyone run a little faster and throw a little harder. He brings everyone together.

He's a vision. Captivating to watch. Impossible to turn away from.

"Hi, Preston." I jump, but it's only Sawyer's mom. She's been coming to these Thanksgiving parties just as long as Sawyer has.

"Hi, Mrs. Paige," I say, trying not to shrink away from her. Sawyer's mom is really nice, but I've never quite gotten over the impression she made the first time we met. She was so intimidating back then, and even though I've known her for years, she hasn't lost that effect on me.

"How's your research going?" Mrs. Paige asks, and unlike my own mom, there's a sincerity in her voice that makes me believe she actually wants to know.

Some of my nervousness eases. "It's going really well. I ran into some problems with my coding earlier in the semester, but once I figured that out, there's been significant progress in the past couple months."

"I'm so glad to hear that! Does that mean you'll graduate next spring? Sawyer mentioned you might push back your defense."

I bite back a groan. Professor Graves still won't entertain the idea of delaying my defense, and since Fitz came on board, things have only sped up, not slowed down. I still don't want to graduate in the spring, because I still haven't figured out how to avoid being recruited into Dad's company. At this rate, though, I might not have a choice.

"I don't know yet," I say, hedging my answer.

"I bet your parents are eager for you to be done with school."

"Yeah," I mutter under my breath.

Mrs. Paige pulls in a deep breath, then lets it out in a sigh, as if she can feel how despondent I am. "Your parents are good people." Her voice is softer now, as if she's trying to comfort me.

I chew on my inner lip, not sure where she's going with this.

"They're smart, accomplished, ambitious people." She bumps me with her shoulder in a move that reminds me so much of Sawyer. "You've inherited a lot of great qualities from them."

I nod in agreement. As much as I don't get along with

my parents, I know I'm lucky. Despite their objections to my life choices, they've never tried to block me from pursuing academia.

"I know they have... expectations of you. And, I'll be honest here, all parents have expectations of their kids. But, at the end of the day, I think they just want you to be happy."

I glance at Mrs. Paige and she's wearing a kind smile that looks so much like Sawyer's. I want to believe she's right, that my parents will suddenly change their minds about my future. They must know how unfit I am for business and how disastrous it would be if they put me in charge of anything. I want them to approve of my academic career. But I can't see that happening. My parents are stubborn. They don't give up on what they want so easily.

"Preston!"

I hear my name, but it takes me a second to react. I glance up, trying to figure out which direction the shout came from, and—

Crunch. Pain explodes across my face and I crumple to the ground.

"Oh my god, Preston!" Mrs. Paige's small but tough hands tug on my shoulder, but it hurts and I curl into myself. "Sawyer!"

"Out of my way! Coming through!" Someone falls to their knees next to me, then another set of hands settles gently on me. These ones are bigger, stronger, but no less careful as they slowly turn me onto my back.

My vision is blurry and it hurts to breathe. Something wet runs down my face and into my mouth. A coppery tang coats my tongue.

I'm bleeding. I've been hit in the face, and I'm bleeding.

"Jesus, that came out of nowhere. I didn't even have time to react."

"Preston? Preston, can you hear me?" Sawyer asks.

I recognize his voice despite the ringing in my ears. But the only response I can manage is a gross gurgling sound.

Someone—Madison, I think—hisses. "Oh shit. That doesn't look good."

"I think his nose is broken." Mrs. Paige.

"Goddamn it, Preston. You can't even duck an incoming ball?" Dad.

"Stop it." *Whack.* "You didn't have to throw the ball so hard." Mom.

"It's football. That's how you throw the ball." Dad.

"Do we need to call an ambulance?" Madison.

"It'll be faster if we drive him to the hospital." Mrs. Paige.

"No, no ambulance, no hospital. I'll call our private clinic." Mom.

"Hey Pres, you okay?" Multiples of Sawyer's face appear in front of me, fading in and out of focus. "I mean, other than…" He winces as he waves his hand in my general direction. "Does anything else hurt?"

I shake my head, then gasp and whimper as pain shoots through my skull.

"Try to avoid any sudden movements. Can you sit?" He threads his arm behind my neck and shoulders and helps prop me up.

The slight change in altitude makes my nose throb and a new gush of blood pours down my face and into my mouth. I try to spit it out, but it spills into my lap.

"Here, hold this." Sawyer presses a balled-up piece of fabric against my face. It's the shirt he was wearing, and even through the pain and the overwhelming scent of blood, I register Sawyer's unique smell. "Alright, I'm going to pick you up now. Grab onto me."

He loops my arm over his shoulder, then tucks one of his under my knees. Bracing me against his bare chest, he stands to his feet, lifting me as if I weigh nothing more than a feather. I cling to him, curling myself around him as much as I'm able. Every step he takes is jolting, the impact of his feet on the ground sending fresh bursts of pain across my face. More blood gushes from my nose and Sawyer's shirt is already soaked through.

"No! Not through there! You'll get blood all over the house. Go through the staff entrance into the kitchen."

Sawyer growls deep in his chest, but he changes directions at Dad's protest. The house shouldn't be far, but it feels like ages before Sawyer's lowering me into a hard plastic lawn chair.

"Okay, I called the twenty-four-hour clinic. The doctor's on his way."

There's a lot of commotion around me, voices speaking over one another and bodies jostling my chair. I hunch forward, letting the blood and snot and tears drip onto the tiled floor.

Sawyer tries to move away, but I latch onto his wrist and don't let go. I need him. With me. Next to me. Touching me.

"Shh, I've got you." He lays his arm across my back, heavy and warm, solid and secure. "Hang in there. You'll be okay."

SAWYER

It's taking every ounce of self-control I've ever possessed to keep myself from marching over to Preston's dad and knocking his teeth out. What the actual fuck. Preston wasn't playing. He wasn't even on the fucking field.

I don't want to believe Mr. Boyer deliberately tried to hit Preston with the ball—not even he is sadistic enough for that. But we didn't have any players in the vicinity. There was no reason for him to throw the ball in that direction. It's not like Mr. Boyer doesn't know how to aim.

And the fact that he hasn't even fucking apologized. Fucking fucker. As if I needed another reason not to like him.

"The doctor's almost here," I say, trying to comfort Preston, even though I have no idea how far the doctor is.

Preston whimpers and leans into me. He's got a death grip on my hand, like he's afraid I'll let go. I squeeze back just as hard—I'm not going anywhere.

Mom's right. Preston's nose is definitely broken. He

probably needs stitches too, seeing as he almost bit through his lip. He'll be sporting double black eyes for a few weeks at least. Tears leak out of his swelling eyes and mix with the blood and snot running down his face. He really doesn't look good. And yet, he's still the most beautiful person I've ever laid eyes on.

I love him. God, I love him so fucking much.

Terror and panic paralyzed me when it became apparent the ball would make contact with Preston's face. Jesus fucking Christ. Time slowed to a crawl while the ball inched its way closer. I tried to shout his name, to tell him to duck, but the message from my brain to my vocal cords got stuck somewhere along the way. By the time I managed to get them to work, it was too late. My heart dropped through my stomach, then shot up to my throat, and it's been lodged there ever since.

Preston starts shivering. Fuck. He's going into shock.

"Mom!" I don't know where she is, but when I call for her, she's right there—with blankets in hand. Thank fucking god. She always comes through when I need her.

"Here." She helps me wrap one around Preston's shoulders.

"Thanks." I rub my hand briskly up and down Preston's back, trying to warm him up.

One of the Boyers' staff hands Mom a basin filled with warm water and a towel. She sets them on the floor at Preston's feet.

"Preston, can I take a look?" She slips her fingers around Preston's wrist and guides his hand away from his face.

The bleeding hasn't stopped completely but it's not

gushing anymore. Thank god. Preston whines and shrinks into me.

"It's okay, Pres. Mom's just trying to assess the damage."

He whines again and Mom shoots me a stern look. Okay, so maybe "damage" wasn't the right word to use. I mouth a silent "sorry" to her.

"I'm going to clean you up a bit, okay?" She dips the towel in the water, then wrings it out before bringing it to Preston's face. With one hand on his chin to hold him still, she drags the cloth carefully over his skin.

It comes away bloody and soon the water is tinged bright red. Inch by inch, she wipes the mess away, revealing more of his injuries. He looks like he got hit in the face by a truck, not merely a football.

By the time Mom's done, Madison is leading the doctor in. "He's right over here."

The doctor sets his bag on a nearby table and crouches down next to me. "Hey, Preston. I'm Dr. Myers. Let's take a look at what's going on here."

Preston is folded in half, face hanging over his knees. The doctor bends to the side trying to get a look at his face, but the closer he gets, the more Preston turns away from him.

"Sorry, doc. Hold on a sec." I pull Preston to his feet long enough for me to take his spot, then I drag him down again so he's sitting on my lap, back against my chest. It's still a little awkward, but at least the doctor doesn't have to crawl around on the floor.

"Football to the face, huh?" Dr. Myers says as he puts on a pair of disposable gloves. "This is going to hurt a bit, okay?"

Preston stiffens and I squeeze him tighter. He flinches when Dr. Myers touches his cheeks and his nose, but he doesn't pull away. Pride surges through me at Preston being so brave, and before I realize what I'm doing, I've planted a kiss on the back of his neck.

Mom and Madison are standing behind the doctor. Mom's eyes narrow in suspicion and I stifle a groan. I'll be getting a talking-to once Preston's sorted.

Madison's gaze snaps to a spot over my shoulder. The alarm in her eyes tells me Mrs. Boyer is somewhere back there. Fuck. I really hope she didn't notice the kiss.

"It's most likely broken, though I can't be sure without an x-ray. It doesn't feel crooked, though, so that's good."

"He won't end up with a bump on his nose, will he?" The question comes from Mrs. Boyer. She comes around to peer at Preston's face.

Preston ducks his head and my simmering rage bubbles to life. Jesus, what is wrong with his parents? Is that really what she's concerned with right now?

"We'll get a better sense of alignment when the swelling goes down. If anything looks unusual, we can try to push it back into place. Any clear discharge from the nose?" Dr. Myers asks, looking at me.

"It's hard to tell with all the blood," I say, answering for Preston. "But I don't think so?"

"You didn't hit your head on the ground when you fell?"

"No," Preston mumbles, sounding nasally.

"Good. Let's take a look at your lip. Can you open your mouth?"

Preston makes a distressed sound, but he cooperates when Dr. Myers peels his lip back to examine the cut.

"I'll have to put a stitch or two there."

Preston shrinks back against me at the doctor's pronouncement.

"Is it going to scar?" Mrs. Boyer asks.

Mom catches my gaze and gives me a tiny headshake to warn me. I grit my teeth together before I spit out something impolite.

"It might. But even if it does, you shouldn't be able to see it. It'll be on the inside." Dr. Myers turns to his bag and starts pulling out supplies.

"Hey, it's okay," I whisper to him. "Scars are sexy."

He gives me such a baleful look I almost kiss him again.

"In that case, I'll leave him in your capable hands," Mrs. Boyer says before skirting around me and exiting the room.

It wasn't clear whether she was referring to me or the doctor, but it doesn't matter. I'll make sure Preston's taken care of.

"Alright, I'm going to numb the area before putting the stitches in," Dr. Myers explains as he turns back to me and Preston. "That means you won't be able to feel anything for a couple hours. You can still eat and drink, it'll just be a bit tricky, so be careful. I've got some painkillers for your nose. Make sure you keep icing a few times a day for the next several days. And you'll need to sleep with your head upright for a while too. Just stuff a bunch of pillows behind your head."

I nod, making mental notes of the doctor's instructions. "I'll make sure he does all that."

"Great." The doctor smiles at Preston. "You're lucky to have such a caring partner. You'll be better in no time."

Preston doesn't seem to react to Dr. Myers's words, but they hit me right in the gut. Partners. Me and Preston. That's what I want us to be. That's the dream.

I hold Preston as the doctor works, but it doesn't take long for him to put the stitches in. He gives me instructions for the medication and Mom brings over a glass of water for Preston's first dose. Then we guide him upstairs to my room.

"Need anything?" Mom asks.

"Not at the moment. I'm going to get him into bed."

Mom glances down at Preston's clothes and grimaces. "Maybe a shower first?"

He's still covered in blood and dirt. "Yeah, good idea."

"Get him settled," Mom tells me with a pointed look. "Then we need to talk."

Crap.

Mom leaves us to head back downstairs, and I bring Preston into the bathroom. After cranking the water all the way up, I help him wrangle his shirt over his head. All those nights of undressing Preston while he's half asleep have been practice for this very moment.

When steam starts curling up toward the ceiling, I lead Preston into the walk-in shower. He's filthy. His hands, chest, legs. He's even got blood and dirt in his hair. With a washcloth, I gently wash the grime away, being extra careful around his stitches and anywhere that looks too tender.

Through it all, Preston is in a daze. He stands where I put him, moves when I direct him. The drugs might have something to do with it, but I think it's more than that. Coming home is never fun for Preston, but this weekend might take the prize.

I wish I could turn back the clock and stop Mr. Boyer before he threw that ball. Or push Preston out of the way. Or take his spot and catch the ball with my face instead. It wouldn't be the first time I've been hit. Preston doesn't deserve this. He deserves so much more than parents who are preoccupied with a party, with his appearance rather than his injuries.

Once the water runs clear, I bundle us both into bathrobes and hustle him toward the bed. His head is lolling now and he can barely keep his eyes open. The drugs are definitely doing their job. I tuck him in under the covers, making sure there are plenty of pillows to keep his head upright. He's out before I'm done.

I sit next to him, holding his hand and giving myself a moment to breathe. The emotional rollercoaster of the past couple hours is catching up with me—anger, fear, guilt, worry. It's just a broken nose and a split lip—people get those all the time. In the grand scheme of things, they're minor injuries and he'll recover quickly.

But when I saw Preston's head snap back at the impact of the ball. When I watched him crumple to the ground and I was too far away to catch him. God, it felt like the world was ending. All the worst-case scenarios flashed through my mind. Concussion. Traumatic brain injury. Broken neck. Paralysis. The possibility of losing Preston became frighteningly real.

The mere thought of it sends pain slicing through me and I rub my chest where there's a lingering ache. I never want to experience anything like that ever again. If that pain is even a fraction of what it's like to lose the person I love, I'll never survive the real thing. I won't want to.

When I manage to pull myself together, I slip quietly

out of the room and head downstairs in search of dinner. Mom's in the kitchen when I get there, sitting off to the side and chatting to Nina, the Boyers' chef, as she directs the rest of the kitchen staff.

"How come you're not having dinner in there?" I point to the formal dining room where the rest of the party has gathered.

Mom rolls her eyes. "Please, as if I want to sit through a stuffy meal with them." Then her expression softens. "How is he?"

I take a slow breath, still a little shaky from the adrenaline. "He's okay. Sleeping."

"Good." Mom waves me over to a small table in the corner that's already set for two. "I asked Nina to make up these for us. I figured you wouldn't be in the mood for Thanksgiving dinner with a roomful of strangers."

We take our seats and Mom cuts right to the chase. "Alright, talk to me."

I set my fork down again without taking a single bite, not sure where to start. This whole thing happened so suddenly I haven't really had time to process it myself. "I… Preston and I…"

Mom doesn't speak, waiting me out with her practiced silence.

"We…" *had sex.* Yeah, I'm not saying that to my mother. Fuck. How am I supposed to talk about this without mentioning sex to my mother? "There's been a development."

"A development."

"In our relationship."

Mom scoops up a forkful of stuffing and lifts it toward

her mouth. "You finally admitted your feelings to each other?"

Her question is so unexpected it completely throws off my train of thought. I've never told my mom about my feelings for Preston. "Uh… what?"

Mom sighs like she's explaining the most obvious thing in the world. "Your feelings, that you and Preston have for each other."

"How do you—wait, no. It's not— Preston doesn't— It's just my—"

Mom cuts me off with a simple raised hand. "You're in love with Preston. You have been since high school."

Not that it's news to me, but hearing it come out of her mouth so matter-of-factly shocks me into a stupor. "How did you know about that?"

"Sawyer, please. I have eyes. I've been in love before. It's not like you're very subtle. Preston's in love with you too. Maybe not since high school, but for long enough."

"No, he isn't. He isn't into guys." My gut twists as the words leave my mouth. He seemed plenty into it while I was sliding my cock in and out of his mouth last night. The problem is, how long will that last? When will he lose interest? When will he decide that, actually, he's not that fond of dick after all?

Mom looks unconvinced. "Are you sure?"

"Okay, okay, he might be into guys—for now. But he's not in love with me."

"But *you* are in love with *him*," she says pointedly.

"Well, yeah," I respond in a mutter. I grab the fork and push food around my plate to keep my hands occupied. I'm suddenly not hungry anymore.

I suppose I shouldn't be surprised Mom knows how I feel about Preston, that she's apparently known for years. She and I are close, even though I haven't shared this particular part of my life with her. And she's always had that creepy mom thing where it feels like she can read my mind.

"And you told him?"

"No."

"I thought you said—" Her eyebrows shoot up as understanding dawns. "Oh, I see, the developments are more physical in nature?"

I groan and drop my head into my hand.

"Hence the 'into guys' thing." Mom nods pensively. "Why do you think it's only for now?"

"Because," I say with a note of incredulity. "Preston's never shown any interest in guys before. He's probably just experimenting. He is a scientist after all."

Mom cocks her head thoughtfully. "Has Preston ever shown any interest in anyone?"

The unexpected question takes me aback. "Uh, no, not really. Why?"

"There's a term for that, isn't there?" She grabs her phone and starts scrolling through it. "I listened to a podcast about it recently. What did they call it?"

I blink at the sudden shift in the conversation. "Do you mean asexual?"

"Yes!" She points at me. "Asexual. And there are a bunch of variations, aren't there?"

I sit back in my chair, dumbfounded. "Yeah."

I'd always assumed Preston was some sort of asexual or aromantic. But what if he's actually demisexual? "If he's demisexual, then he'd only feel attraction to people he already has an emotional connection with. That could explain why he's never been interested in anyone before."

"So maybe he hasn't been 'into guys' before now because you're the only guy he spends any significant amount of time with?"

My heart thuds at the possibility. "Maybe?"

Mom plants her elbows on the table and clasps her hands together, leaning forward to stare me straight in the eyes. "Sweetheart, listen. I saw the way he looked at you earlier. That boy is just as in love with you as you are with him. The difference is, he probably doesn't realize it yet."

I stare back at her, letting her words sink in. God, I really want her to be right, but I don't know if I'm brave enough to believe her.

Mom breaks the stare first, going back to her dinner. "How did this whole physical development come about anyway?" She waves her fork at me when she says "Physical development", and I have to suppress a shudder.

"Um, Preston showed up at Mars a few days ago and kissed me?"

Mom's eyebrows skyrocket. "Just like that? Out of the blue?"

It certainly felt out of the blue when Preston launched himself at me in the break room. But as much as I want to deny it, there have been signs since September. I just didn't know what they meant.

Mom narrows her eyes thoughtfully before I can answer her. "Haven't you been seeing a new guy recently?"

I groan as the reminder hits me with a fresh burst of guilt. "Yeah, Fitz. It was going really well too."

"Oh, honey." She smiles like the answer is already written on the wall.

I grimace, not wanting to acknowledge the suspicion that's been teasing at the back of my mind.

"You know what I'm going to say, don't you?"

I push away my plate so I can bang my forehead on the table.

Mom doesn't spare me. "Let me recap. You start seeing someone else, spending time with that someone else, maybe spending less time with Preston? Could it be that he got jealous?"

"But I've dated other people before," I object. "He's never reacted this way with any of them."

"True. But you said things were going well with Fitz. Better than with other people?"

"Yeah, but..."

"But what?"

I hesitate. Preston's always been this forbidden fruit. I can get close, I can even touch, but I can't take. And now that I've taken, I'm waiting for the curse to strike. Because it can't possibly be this easy. It's too good to be true.

"You're scared," Mom says. A statement, not a question.

My heart thuds against my ribs and my throat is tight with emotion. "What if he doesn't love me back?" I whisper, afraid that speaking the words too loudly will make them come true.

Mom waits several beats before answering me in the same hushed tone. "That's a risk you'll have to take."

I shake my head. "It's too risky. I can't do it."

"Yes, you can." There's such confidence in her voice, a level of conviction I certainly don't feel. "Every relationship is risky. But that doesn't mean we don't try. You can't let fear keep you from living your life. You have to go after the things you want, even if you might not get them. That's especially true when it comes to love."

The prospect is terrifying, and it would be so much easier to stay where it's comfortable and safe. But I'm not sure that's an option anymore, not after the events of this week. I really, really hope Mom is right. The alternative is unacceptable.

PRESTON

The room is dark when I blink my eyes open. At first, I can't figure out where I am. Then it all comes back to me.

Thanksgiving at my parents' house. The football. My face.

I'm in Sawyer's room, and my head is propped up at an awkward angle with a pile of pillows. Sawyer's next to me, fast asleep.

I lift my hand gingerly to my face. I'm all swollen and disfigured, and my sinuses feel inflamed. The painkillers must be wearing off.

Moving slowly, I slip out of bed and make my way to the bathroom, making sure the door is closed before flipping on the light. It's bright and I wince, then hiss as the muscles in my face protest.

Bracing myself on the bathroom counter, I peer at my reflection in the mirror. My face is double the size of what it's supposed to be. Black splotches cover my cheeks and eyes. The stitches in my lip pull uncomfortably. I look hideous.

Tears sting the backs of my eyes as I lower myself onto the covered toilet seat. I'm not even sure what I'm crying about. I don't usually pay attention to my appearance, never mind actually care about how I look. But maybe I'm vainer than I originally thought because I'm ugly now.

Sawyer's so perfect. Handsome and athletic. Charming and smart. Everyone loves him.

Meanwhile, I can't even duck an incoming football. I'm not athletic or charming, and now I'm not even handsome. I don't know how to socialize, and people think I'm weird.

I'm no match for Sawyer. I'm not strong or confident like he is. He knows who he is and what he wants and he's not afraid of what other people think. He's so sure of himself.

I'm not sure of anything. I don't understand emotions, forget about expressing them out loud. I don't know what I want and have even less clue about how to get them. I'm afraid of standing up to people, so much so that I'd rather sabotage my academic career than tell my parents that I don't want to join the family company.

I'm not good enough for Sawyer. He deserves so much better than me.

"Preston?" A quiet knock sounds at the door before it's cracked open. Sawyer slips into the bathroom, sleep-rumpled with his hair sticking up in all directions. "Why are you sitting in here?"

"Sorry for waking you," I say. I sound nasally and my voice is slightly slurred.

"Don't worry about that. What's wrong? Did something happen?"

I shake my head and the tears stream down my cheeks at his kindness, his attentiveness. Sawyer is so good. So wonderful. What is he doing wasting his time with me?

"Babe, hey, it's okay." He grabs the toilet paper and winds a wad of it around his fingers. Gently, he dabs at my face, careful not to press too hard. He lets me cry and doesn't try to stop me or force me to talk. He just waits until the tears dry up on their own.

"I know this sucks," he says when I'm reduced to hiccups. "We'll get through it, though. And I'm sure Madison will love to teach you how to use makeup to cover up the bruises."

I shake my head again, and Sawyer sits down on the floor in front of me.

"What is it?" he asks, holding both my hands in his.

His fingers wrap around mine, firm and sure. He's got tiny golden-blond hairs on his knuckles and his nails are cut short. His hands always make me feel safe. I love his hands.

My heart beats faster, drumming against my ribs so hard I can feel it in my face. I keep my gaze glued to our clasped hands as I whisper, "Why are you friends with me?"

Sawyer stills, his fingers tightening a fraction. "What?"

"Why are you—" My voice breaks, but I suck in a breath and force myself to keep going. "You're so cool. You've got so many friends. Any one of them would want to be your best friend. I'm nothing compared to them. Why do you even bother with me?"

"Are you serious? What kind of question is that?" There's a hardness to Sawyer's voice that I'm not used to hearing. "Pres, look at me. Please."

Slowly, I work up the courage to meet his gaze. What I see there takes my breath away. The blue-greens of his eyes are vibrant under the bathroom's fluorescent lights. There's such intensity in them, so much determination and fierceness it takes my breath away.

"Preston." Sawyer's voice is thick with emotion, and even though I don't understand why, my eyes start tearing up again.

"I could never not be friends with you," he says. "You're so fucking smart. When you nerd out, I have no idea what you're talking about, but your eyes light up and you become so animated—it's captivating."

Every word he utters hits me like raindrops falling from the sky. They hurt a little when they land, stinging and sharp. But then they seep through my skin, penetrate my bloodstream, and speed through my body, warming me from the inside out. I can't help but squirm a little under the onslaught.

"You're wonderfully honest. It's a little brutal sometimes, but also super refreshing. There's no guessing with you. You don't try to be someone you're not. You're gorgeous. Beautiful."

"No, I'm not," I say, turning my head away.

"Yes, you are." Sawyer takes my chin and nudges me to look at him again. "Even like this, you're stunning. But more than that, you're beautiful in here." He flattens his hand against my chest. "Your heart is so pure, simple, and good."

I sniffle. "Simple doesn't sound good."

"It is." He laughs. "Simple, uncomplicated, unpretentious. Innocent. Wholesome. Good."

Then he pauses with his lips parted, like he wants to

say something, but he doesn't know if it's a good idea. "Preston—" He swallows and his Adam's apple bobs. "Preston, I... I love you."

I cock my head at his admission. From the expression on Sawyer's face, I think it's supposed to be significant, but I'm not sure how. He's my best friend. Of course he loves me. "I know. I love you too."

"No, that's not—" Sawyer closes his eyes and shakes his head. "I mean, I'm in love with you. Like romantically." The last word comes out a little strangled and it takes me a moment to decipher it.

Sawyer's in love with me—romantically. That's different from friendship. It's more than friendship. It's— Madison's question from the car comes back to me. *Are you together now?* She meant whether Sawyer and I are a couple, dating, like I was with Madison in high school.

"Oh."

Sawyer hangs his head and a dry laugh escapes him. "Yeah, oh."

Am I supposed to say it back to him now? I love him as a friend, as a best friend. That's never been in doubt and I just told him that. But do I love him more than that? Am I in love with him? I don't know—what does that feel like? How do I tell?

Sawyer tilts his head and gives me a wry smile like he can hear the flurry of thoughts in my mind. "It's okay, You don't have to say it back if you don't feel the same way."

"No, I just... I'm not sure. I've never really thought about it." I grip his hands tighter, hating that I don't understand my feelings as well as Sawyer does, hating that I don't know how to express them as eloquently as he can.

He loves me. I know it's significant. I know it's important. I just don't fully understand what it means.

Sawyer bows his head, burying his face in my lap. Careful of my injuries, I place a small kiss on the back of his head. Silence stretches between us and with every second that ticks by, I feel worse and worse. Sawyer's right about me being simple. But he's wrong about it being a good thing.

"I'm sorry."

Sawyer shakes his head and slowly tilts it up to meet my gaze. "No, don't be sorry. I don't want you to say things you don't mean. And if you need time to figure out how you feel, then we'll make sure you have time."

He rises to his knees, cups either side of my face with his hands, and presses a kiss to my relatively undamaged forehead.

"I love you, Preston Boyer. I love you enough to wait. For as long as you need. For eternity."

We end up going back to bed, me topped up on painkillers and pillows buttressing me on all sides. Sawyer falls asleep while holding my hand and I follow as soon as the drugs kick in.

The next time I wake up, the sun is shining through the window and the spot next to me is empty. The bedroom door opens as I push the covers away and Sawyer comes in carrying a tray with two silver domes.

"Morning!" He smiles, wide and bright, and my breath catches at the sight. "Brought you breakfast. You must be starving. You didn't have dinner last night."

My stomach grumbles in agreement. I follow Sawyer to the little sitting area by the window and sit on the loveseat when he nods at it.

"How are you feeling?" he asks.

"Okay, I think." The painkillers I took in the middle of the night are wearing off again and the space behind my eyes is starting to ache.

"Take this." Sawyer hands me a glass of freshly squeezed orange juice, then shakes out my medication onto his palm.

Once I've swallowed down the pills, he lifts the silver domes with a flourish. Each plate is artfully arranged with a fancy rolled omelet, cubed hash browns, and a mix of fruit.

Sawyer takes the glass of juice from me and replaces it with a plate and fork. He's just settling in beside me with his own plate when there's a knock at the door.

"Hello? You guys decent?" Madison's voice calls out.

"Yes, you can come in," Sawyer calls back to her.

Madison strolls in, already dressed for the day, hair and makeup perfectly done. She drops into the armchair opposite us.

"How's your face?" she asks me.

"I'm okay," I mumble, nibbling on a piece of omelet.

Madison sighs. "I mean this in the nicest way possible, but your dad is an ass."

My gaze darts from the plate to Madison, eyes growing wide at the annoyed expression she's wearing.

"Hear hear," Sawyer mutters before shoving potatoes into his mouth.

"Why do you say that?"

Madison waves her hand in the air like the answer should be obvious. "Because he is. And I don't just mean the whole football situation. That's just a symptom of the underlying problem." She leans over the low table between us and snatches a strawberry from my plate.

I've only had a few bites of food, but my appetite vanishes. "What underlying problem?"

Sawyer shifts and clears his throat. When I glance at him, he's glaring at Madison.

"He can't keep living like this," she says to him, doing that thing again where they're talking about me like I'm not here.

Sawyer doesn't respond, just scowls as he takes a giant bite of omelet.

"What is it?" I ask again, a familiar frustration bubbling up inside me. Maybe it's the side effect of the medication, but instead of pushing it down like I normally do, this time, I let it out. "You can tell me!"

My outburst stuns them both into silence.

"You don't have to talk about me like I'm not here," I say in a more subdued tone. "I'm not a child. I can handle it."

Madison's expression grows contrite and Sawyer moves to set his plate on the table.

"You're right, Preston," Sawyer says. "You're not a child, and we shouldn't talk about you like that."

"Sorry," Madison offers.

"I'm sorry too." Sawyer lifts his arm and lays it across the back of my shoulders. Even though I just said I wasn't a kid, I still lean into him, taking comfort in his touch. Sawyer kisses the top of my head. "Madison and I kind of disagree on something."

"What thing?"

"Standing up to your dad." Madison gives a little

shrug. "Or both your parents. I think you need to but Sawyer..."

"I don't want you to do anything you don't want to do," Sawyer says, cheek pressed to my hair.

Madison rolls her eyes. "But that's life! We all have to do things we don't want to do!"

"Mr. Boyer isn't that easy to stand up to," Sawyer argues back. "He doesn't listen to anyone."

"I didn't say it'd be easy!" Madison throws her hands in the air. "He's a prick. Of course, it's not going to be easy."

I don't need to see Sawyer's face to know he's glowering at her.

"Pres, what are you going to do? Stay in school forever so you never have to join your dad's company? Or, god forbid, actually take a job there and be fucking miserable for the rest of your life? Don't take this the wrong way, but you'd suck at any job they give you."

"Mads!"

"I'm just laying it out there." Madison gestures to my face. "This football bullshit? Do you really think it would've happened if Preston had just told his dad to piss off?"

Sawyer doesn't respond, which means he thinks the answer is no.

"Pres, you just said so yourself. You're not a kid. You can handle it."

Sawyer's arm tightens around me, and I start chewing my lip, remembering too late that it's injured. I did say I could handle it, but I meant with Madison and Sawyer.

Standing up to Dad is something else entirely, something I've never been able to do. I wouldn't even know where to start. He's always been so forceful and imposing, and he always gets his way.

Your parents just want you to be happy. Mrs. Paige's words come back to me.

What if I tell them outright I want to stay in academia rather than delaying the inevitable by applying for one program after the next? What if I refuse to join Boyer Pharmaceuticals and stop pretending to go along with their plans?

Will they be happy about that? I want to believe they would be, but a lifetime of experience tells me they won't.

SAWYER

We end up heading back to New York early. I make up a fake emergency at Mars and Madison says she's got a last-minute date with some guy she's seeing. Preston comes with us, of course, since we're all taking the same chartered flight home.

Preston sleeps the rest of the weekend, waking up to eat and go to the bathroom before I shuffle him off to bed again. By the time Monday rolls around, he's feeling a lot better, even if his face is still a mess. I convince him to spend an extra day at home before returning to school, which he agreed to only because he can access all his research from his tablet.

Which leaves me with the dreaded task of breaking up with Fitz. Fuck.

We've had a few text message exchanges over Thanksgiving weekend, so I haven't exactly ghosted him. But I haven't been as enthusiastic as I usually am. I don't know if he's been able to tell over text, and I'm not sure whether it would be better or worse if he has.

We agreed to meet at a bar around the corner from Mars about an hour before my shift starts. Maybe that's cowardly of me, but can you really blame me for wanting an excuse to leave if things turn ugly or awkward.

I'm early and waiting at a high top at the back of the bar, nearly crawling out of my skin I'm so nervous. I've never had to break up with someone before. I don't usually get that serious with the people I date, and the few times it has, we've always ended up drifting apart. I don't want to hurt Fitz, but I have a feeling it's inevitable.

I feel terrible about how things have gone down. He deserves to be treated better than how I've treated him. It's not that I've led him on, per se, but I haven't been honest with him, or myself, or well, any of us. Because even if Preston and I go back to being just friends—I'm still expecting him to call things off any day now—he would always take priority over anyone I date. I can't in good faith pursue anything with Fitz. Preston's it for me. It'll always be Preston or bust.

"Hey, Sawyer."

I jump, head snapping up. I was so caught up in my own thoughts I didn't notice Fitz entering the bar.

"Hey!" I exclaim with way too much fake enthusiasm.

Fitz blinks once in surprise then leans in for a kiss— shit. I dodge it at the last second, turning my head so his lips land on my cheek and I lean in the rest of the way to give him a brief hug.

When he pulls back, confusion is written plainly across his face.

"Um, do you want a drink?" I raise my hand and flag down a waiter.

"Sure," Fitz says, sounding not at all sure. After the waiter leaves with our order, he continues. "Uh, how was Thanksgiving? You went to Preston's house, right?"

"Yes! It was good!" I cringe. "Well, not really. Preston got hit in the face with a football."

"Oh shit. Is he okay?" Fitz sounds genuinely concerned, and that only makes me feel worse.

"He is. Or he will be. Anyway, how was your Thanksgiving?" My voice is a little too high, sounding almost hysterical.

Fitz gives me a funny look—he's definitely noticed. "It was good. We don't do anything fancy. Just hanging out with the family, you know?"

"Mmhmm, yup, yep, hanging out. Awesome."

The waiter comes back with our drinks, and I take my beer, downing almost half the glass in one go.

"Um, are you okay, Sawyer? Is something wrong?"

"Hmm? Oh, no, nothing's wrong." I cringe again. "Uh, well, that's not true. Uh… fuck."

I cover my face with my hand. Why didn't I think about what to say before I got here? I should've written it down. Hell, I should've rehearsed it.

Fitz shifts back in his chair, straightening his posture and folding his arms across his chest. He's a smart guy. He's probably guessed what's going on. But he doesn't make it easy for me. He sits and waits, letting me make a fool of myself as I fumble for words.

"So, um, I wanted to talk to you because, um, well, Preston and I…" *are a couple now?* No, that's not entirely correct. *We're sleeping together?* Yes, but that sounds crude. It's more than just sex. I love him and even though he's not sure where he stands, I know Preston cares for me.

I don't need to finish my sentence because Fitz squeezes his eyes shut, his lips flatten into a straight line and his jaw starts ticcing.

"You and Preston." He huffs, a short, annoyed, angry sound. "Are you fucking kidding me?"

I'm pretty sure that is a rhetorical question so I don't try to answer.

Fitz pins me with a glare that's so intense and fierce that it shines through his black-rimmed glasses and hits me square in the face. I've seen that look before—or at least, it reminds me of one. Thirteen years ago. When I was moving into Westbourne, and Preston walked into the room.

I sit back in my chair, jaw hanging open in shock. How did I not notice it until now? Black hair, blue eyes. Short, slim frame. Smart, nerdy. Even the glasses are similar to the ones Preston wore before his parents made him get laser eye surgery.

Holy fucking shit. I blink a few times, hoping that the similarities will disappear, that they're a figment of my imagination, maybe a trick of the light. But, nope. The more I stare at Fitz, the more I see the resemblance. He looks *so much* like Preston, it's hard to believe.

"What?" Fitz spits out when he notices me studying him.

I shake my head, dumbfounded. "Nothing, I just..." *realized I liked you because you reminded me of Preston* is probably not the right thing to say at the moment. I clear my throat. "Sorry. I'm sorry."

Fitz huffs again. "You're un-fucking-believable. I asked you if anything was going on between you and Preston."

"I know," I say quietly, bracing myself for the daggers I fully deserve.

"You swore up and down that there was nothing there. That you and Preston were only friends. That I wasn't walking into the middle of some fucked-up, twisted, co-dependent bullshit."

I grimace as the daggers hit their target, but I don't try to stop him. "I know."

"Hell, I even asked Preston!"

"You did?" I didn't know he'd done that.

"Yeah, I did. Told him that he only needed to say the word and I'd back off. Much fucking good that did." Fitz grabs his beer and takes a few gulps before slamming it down on the table. "That's why he's such a jerk to me, isn't it? Why he ignores me all the time, only talks to me when absolutely necessary. I've been doing everything I can fucking think of to ingratiate myself to him. And for what? Nothing. Because he's punishing me for dating you when I fucking asked both of you if it was okay!"

Fitz's voice is loud enough to draw attention from the bartender and a few other nearby tables. I force myself not to shrink back, to take the full brunt of his anger and let everyone see just what an asshole I've been. It's the least I deserve after what I put Fitz through.

"I'm sorry."

"You better fucking be sorry. This is my career you guys have been fucking with." Fitz leans forward, jabbing his finger on the table's surface. "Preston's my fucking mentor in the department, he could screw me over with one fucking word in the right ear."

"He wouldn't do that," I say. Coming to Preston's defense is second nature to me.

"Sure, he wouldn't." Sarcasm drips from Fitz's voice.

"He wouldn't. And I'm not just saying that. He takes his research very seriously. He wouldn't undermine his work for a personal vendetta."

"Small mercies."

I can taste the bitterness rolling off Fitz and even though I don't fault him for it, I won't stand around and let him besmirch Preston. Fitz can say and do whatever he wants to me, but Preston is off-limits. "You want someone to blame. You should blame me. I'm the one who should've known better."

"Oh, I do blame you. I never said I didn't." His glare makes it clear just how much he does.

"Good. I mean, yeah." God, this sucks. I'm never breaking up with anyone again.

At least, Fitz seems to be losing steam. He takes off his glasses and rubs his eyes for a moment before putting them back on. "Listen, I'm pissed, obviously."

"And you have every right to be," I add quickly.

His eyes flash, not appreciating my attempt to reassure him.

"But I should've seen this coming," Fitz continues. "It's not like the signs weren't there, in bright fucking neon. I should've listened to my gut."

Instead of to me. "Sorry." I almost want to suggest he punch me in the face—it might make both of us feel better.

Fitz picks up his beer and chugs what remains. When he sets it down again, he holds the back of his hand to his mouth and takes a few deep breaths. "How long?"

"Huh?"

"When did you and Preston—" Fitz gestures vaguely with his hand. "Was it when you and I were still—" He waves back and forth between me and him.

"Oh! No!" I'm quick to confirm. "No, Preston and I only started… you know, that day when he freaked out at school and ran out on you."

Fitz nods. "I figured. But I needed to be sure."

"Yeah, of course. I wouldn't—I mean, uh, yeah."

Fitz glares at me for a few more seconds before speaking again. "Anyway, like I said, I'm pissed, but don't think I'm heartbroken or anything. I liked you, but I didn't love you. I'll get over this, so you can stop with the whole kicked puppy routine."

I sit up a little straighter and clear my throat. I'm not sure a kicked puppy is the right metaphor since I was the asshole, but I get his point. "Sorry."

"Yeah, well, I'm going to go." Fitz stands but doesn't walk away immediately. He taps his fingers on the table a few times. "I guess I'll see you around."

"Yeah, I'll see you around."

I watch him walk out of the bar, then hang my head with a sigh. That went as well as could be expected, I suppose.

The waiter comes back with the bill and as he slides the paper toward me, he says, "At least you didn't end up with a face full of beer."

"Thanks."

I pay the bill and head over to Mars where Logan, Everest, Beau, and Donnie are all gathered around the front desk. The moment I approach, they fall silent.

Donnie pretends to study the paperwork in front of him. Beau and Everest look everywhere but at me. Only

Logan is staring at me wide-eyed, like I caught him with his hand in the cookie jar.

"What is it?" I demand.

"Nothing!" Logan exclaims, his voice squeaking a little.

"It's obviously not nothing. Just out with it."

Donnie—the only mature one in the group—sighs and takes off his reading glasses. "Logan saw Fitz through the window and he looked really pissed."

I sigh and slump against the counter. "Yeah, he is."

"See! It does have something to do with Sawyer!" Logan elbows Everest in the side.

"Ow! I never said it didn't!"

"Remember you told me you're meeting with Fitz before work today? And then I saw him storming past the windows. He looked like he wanted to burn the place to the ground. So… what happened?"

"Jesus, Logan, give the guy a break," Beau says. "At least let him take his coat off and stash his stuff."

Logan rolls his eyes. "Fine, go. I'll interrogate you later."

And he does, except not later. No, Logan follows me into the staff locker room and hovers next to me as I change into the Mars staff uniform, peppering me with questions.

"I told you Preston would get jealous of you and Fitz," he says when we head back out to the lobby.

I have a vague memory of him saying something to that effect, but I don't want to give him the satisfaction of being right. "Did you? I don't remember."

"I did." Logan pokes me in the arm to emphasize his point. "So, he's the one, huh?"

I roll my eyes, but a grin tugs at my lips. "Not this again."

"Oh, come on." He bumps me with his shoulder. "He is, isn't he? Preston's the one. Just admit it. I'm right. I always am."

I don't bother pointing out all the times he's been wrong about his own love life, because this time, he is right.

"Yes, fine." I give Logan a playful shove and he dances away. "You're right. Preston's the one."

PRESTON

After Sawyer leaves for work this morning, I pull out my tablet and try to work on my AI algorithm. I stare at it blankly as the letters and numbers blur together on the screen and I give up after an hour.

My face still hurts. Not as much as it did a couple days ago, but if I move too suddenly, or hold my head in the wrong position, the space behind my eyes and nose throbs painfully. I try to sleep, but sleep doesn't come. I turn on the TV, but the light hurts my eyes. I wander the apartment, counting my steps as I go from room to room to room.

I keep replaying Thanksgiving. The conversation with Mrs. Paige where she claimed my parents just want me to be happy. Getting hit in the face with the football. Sawyer telling me he loves me while we're huddled around the toilet. Breakfast the next morning when Madison said I need to stand up to my dad.

I don't know what I'm supposed to do with all that. It's all people stuff, emotional stuff, stuff I've never been good at. It's stuff I've always ignored or went along with, or let other people take care of. But I don't think I can anymore.

I told Madison and Sawyer I'm not a child, that I can handle the difficult things they've always tried to shield me from. Except the truth is, I don't know if I can handle it. It's all so much and so big. It's so nebulous and ephemeral. There's no way to quantify it or measure it. It doesn't follow a prescribed set of rules.

It scares me. People stuff. Emotional stuff. It scares me.

All I want is to crawl back into the safe little space Sawyer's created for me, where I know he will protect me from everything. He would do it too, in a heartbeat, and without question. He would go on taking care of me the way he's always done... because he loves me.

Sawyer loves me.

And I don't deserve it.

Despite all the wonderful things he said about me while sitting on the bathroom floor, the truth is, I don't bring anything to this relationship.

Sawyer makes sure our apartment is cleaned, the bills are paid, and there's food in the fridge. He arranges for the laundromat to pick up my dirty clothes and drop them off again when they're clean. He reminds me to eat, sleep, shower. He even shows up at the lab when I stay too late and drags me home to rest.

What do I do for him? Nothing. Hell, I barely remember where his gym is.

That needs to change. *I* need to change. I need to be worthy of Sawyer's attention, worthy of his care and his love. I can't keep leeching off him, only taking and never giving anything back.

I need to fight my own battles rather than wait for him to fight them for me. I need to face up to difficult situations rather than hide behind him and bury my head in the sand. I need to take care of him as much as he's taken care of me—or try to, at least.

Which means I need to graduate on time. I can't keep putting it off because I'm afraid of what comes after. I need to tell Mom and Dad that I won't be working for the family company, that I'm staying in academia.

They won't like it. Dad will end up shouting at me. Mom will side with him. It'll be pretty ugly. But it's something I have to do, because it's what Sawyer would do if he were in my position, it's what he would want me to do if I wasn't such a coward.

And I need to start doing stuff around the apartment. Stuff like, I don't know, vacuuming. That's a thing, right? I glance at the floor, which looks pretty clean to me. How do you know when the floor needs vacuuming? And where is the vacuum cleaner anyway? I'm sure we have one… somewhere.

Okay, I'll leave the cleaning for now. What else can I do? Food. Dinner. I glance at the clock. It'll be a couple hours before Sawyer gets home from work. Maybe I can cook something? I go to the kitchen and open the fridge door. There's food in there, but I don't know what to do with any of it. And to be honest, I'm more likely to burn the building down than end up with something edible.

No cooking then. I'll order delivery instead.

I grab my phone and pull up the food delivery app.

There's this Italian place Sawyer orders from a lot—what is it called? I scroll and check menus until I find the one with the spaghetti and meatballs he's always raving about, and I place the order. There. Done.

The sense of accomplishment I feel is ridiculous. I placed an order on a food delivery app, for god's sake. It's not difficult or complicated. I've done it before. So why do I have the urge to call Sawyer so I can brag about it?

Forty minutes later, the food arrives and I even remember to tip the delivery guy. Except it's still another hour before Sawyer will be home and the food will get cold by then. Shit. I didn't think the timing through. I knew I was forgetting something.

PRESTON

I ordered dinner for Sawyer.

MADISON

Okay... congratulations?

He's not home yet and the food will be cold. What do I do?

Oh my god. Seriously?

Yes.

eye roll emoji Put it in the oven.

No, wait. Hold on.

The phone buzzes in my hand and I swipe to answer Madison's call.

"Don't just put the whole thing in the oven," she warns before I even say hello.

"Then what should I do?"

"Alright. Step one. Is there anything in the oven?"

I pull open the oven door. "No, just the racks."

"Okay, good. Do you know how to turn the oven on?"

"Um…" I stare at the display panel with buttons and dials and—

"Never mind. Let's switch to video and you can point the camera at the controls."

It takes me a moment to get the camera on and pointed in the right direction. Then Madison walks me through turning the oven on to the lowest heat setting.

"Okay, now take the food out of the bags. What kind of containers are they in? What material are they made out of?"

I untie the plastic bag, then unroll the paper one. There are three containers inside. "Aluminum and the tops are paper."

"Thank god. In that case, you can pop the whole thing inside, close the oven door, and you're good to go."

"That's it?" I ask, glancing from the container of food in my hand to the racks inside the oven.

"That's it!"

"Oh. That's not very hard."

Madison sighs and gives me a wry smile. "No, it's not. It's sweet that you got dinner for Sawyer, though. I'm sure he'll appreciate it."

I slide the three containers into the oven and close the door. Then I hit the lightbulb button and peer through the glass window. "I guess. It's just… how come I don't know how to do any of these things?"

"Because you've never had to before." Madison laughs. "You went from living at home with all that staff, to living with Sawyer who does everything for you. Why would you learn it if you didn't need to?"

I hum, staring at the food containers in the oven.

"It's cool that you're doing it now, though. I'm proud of you, Pres."

I hang up with Madison, then go to sit by the window. The sun's already set, but the sky is still bright from all the city lights. I fall asleep curled up in the armchair, my mind finally quieting enough for me to slip into unconsciousness.

The next thing I know, a strong hand is gently shaking my shoulder. I blurrily blink my eyes open to find Sawyer crouching in front of me. He's wearing such a kind smile and his eyes are filled with such tenderness. My chest expands with a ticklish, bubbling feeling at the sight of him.

"Tired?" he asks.

I shake my head. "No, just waiting for you to get back."

"Aw… miss me?" There's a teasing note to his voice, but it's true, I did.

I smile sheepishly. "Yeah."

Sawyer's eyes darken, and then he's pulling me to my feet and hauling me in for a hug. "I missed you too."

It's been less than half a day since we last saw each other, but relief washes over me as I mold myself to Sawyer. My eyes drift shut and I savor the feeling of being held safe and secure in his arms.

"Did you eat?" Sawyer eventually asks.

I stiffen because I haven't. I might've accidentally skipped lunch because I was so preoccupied. "I was waiting for you," I say instead. "I ordered food. It's in the oven."

Sawyer's eyebrows shoot up. "The oven?"

I'm not offended that he's surprised, but I pout anyway. "I called Madison to make sure I didn't burn anything down."

He chuckles and drops a kiss on my forehead. "What did you order?" He tucks me under his arm and guides me toward the kitchen.

"The Italian place you like?" At least, I hope I picked the right one.

"Mmm, I do like that place. You got the meatballs?"

I nod, glad that I remembered what he liked. "Yeah."

"Awesome."

Sawyer deposits me on a stool by the kitchen island, then pulls the food containers out of the oven. He dishes up two plates of spaghetti and meatballs and slices of garlic bread.

When we sit down to eat, I make an attempt at small talk. That's what people do right? Have conversations over meals?

"How's, um, how was your day?"

Sawyer pauses with his fork halfway in his mouth. He glances at me in surprise, then finishes the bite before speaking. "Uh, good," he says with a smile, like he knows what I'm trying to do. "I broke up with Fitz."

My eyes widen and that ticklish bubbly feeling comes back in full force. "You did?"

"Yup." Sawyer reaches for my hand. "I love you, Preston. I can't see other people when I'm in love with you."

My face heats and I drop my chin to my chest. He loves me. The reminder makes me feel all warm inside and I wish I could say it back to him, but I don't know how.

"How was your day?" Sawyer asks, deftly changing the subject like he knows I'm at a loss for words.

I take a deep breath and squeeze his hand, imagining I can borrow some of his strength through the contact. Which is silly since this is Sawyer and he loves me and I have nothing to be afraid of. But it's still difficult to voice my thoughts out loud. "I'm going to defend my dissertation in the spring."

Sawyer sits up straighter and leans toward me. "Yeah? That's great!"

I nod and charge onward. "I'm going to defend my dissertation, and then I'm going to graduate, but I'm not joining Boyer Pharmaceuticals."

I lift my chin, almost daring Sawyer to argue with me. But he doesn't. Of course he doesn't. He smiles with pride shining in his eyes.

"That's awesome."

"I am," I repeat, my voice rising as I gather steam. My pulse races as words spill unbidden from my lips. "I'm going to say no to Dad. I'm going to make him listen. I'm going to stand up to him."

Sawyer nods. "That's amazing."

"I can. And I will. I'll do it."

"I believe you."

"I'm going to talk to Professor Graves and tell him to schedule the defense."

Sawyer blinks and it looks like there's moisture in his eyes. "He'll be thrilled."

"And then I'll tell Dad. At Christmas." I blurt out the last bit on a whim. I haven't actually given that part much thought—when and how I'm going to have that conversation—but I'm determined to figure it out.

"I… I don't know how exactly. But I will."

Sawyer gives me one more firm, decisive nod. "I'm sure you will. And I'll be there to help if you need me."

I will need his help. And I know he'll be there. Because he loves me. I make a promise to myself that he'll never regret it.

Later, after we've finished cleaning up and are getting ready for bed, I sneak up behind Sawyer and slip my hands under his shirt. He turns and smiles at me with so much love in his eyes even I can't mistake it.

Carefully, I rise onto my toes and kiss him, melting into him when our lips connect. I lick at the seam between Sawyer's lips and he opens for me. I swipe my tongue across his and he moans, his arms tightening around me and hauling me against him. Heat races through me, creeping up my neck and making my head spin. I figured out there's nothing wrong with the thermostat in our apartment. All my overheating is Sawyer's fault. He makes me so hot. He makes me burn.

The thin t-shirts we wear are in the way and I'm desperate to feel his skin on mine. So I sacrifice the feast of his lips for a moment to tear at our clothes. When we're both naked from the waist up, I kiss him again.

One of my favorite things in the world now is how Sawyer's chest feels against mine. His skin is always so warm, so smooth, soft, and yet firm at the same time. I love rubbing myself on him, dragging my sensitive nipples over the mounds of his pectoral muscles.

"Fuck, Preston," Sawyer murmurs as he takes over the kiss. His hand on the back of my head angles me just right for him to ravage me with his tongue, his teeth, his lips.

I arch against him, searching for the friction that will

ease the ache in my dick—Sawyer said I'm not allowed to call it a penis anymore.

He kisses his way down my neck, stopping to suck on my collarbone until I shiver at the delicious sensation, then down farther to my nipple. He rakes his teeth across the sensitive flesh, then soothes it with the flat of his tongue. He flicks it, then sucks it into his mouth and the negative pressure feels like it'll turn me inside out.

My hands are in his hair, holding him to me, tugging at the strands. "Sawyer!" His name feels like a prayer, like a plea.

He growls and wraps his arms around me to pick me up like I weigh nothing. I curl my legs around him, locking my ankles behind his back. I love that he can carry me around. I love that he's strong enough to manhandle me however he likes. It makes me feel small and protected and safe. It makes me feel like Sawyer's got everything under control and everything's going to be okay.

He covers the short distance to the bed and we tumble onto it, me pinned under him, exactly where I'm supposed to be. Sawyer resumes his assault on my nipples, switching to the neglected one this time. I writhe and squirm, knowing that his weight will keep me anchored to the bed. He's solid, steady, strong.

Sawyer's hand goes to my pants, tugging the drawstring loose so he can reach inside. He cups my dick, massages it, and kneads it gently with his fingers. It's exactly what I need and yet not nearly enough.

"Sawyer!"

He rears up, grabbing the waistband of my pajama pants and briefs at the same time to strip them off my legs. Then he jumps off the bed to rid himself of the rest of his clothing too. But before he can take up his spot between my legs again, I stop him.

"Wait."

Sawyer freezes, one knee on the bed, the other foot still on the floor. The lust in his eyes is abruptly erased by concern. "What's wrong?"

"I want you to fuck me."

SAWYER

Multiple things happen in my body at once. My dick goes from pleasantly plump to rock fucking hard in an instant. My heart rate shoots through the roof and my lungs seize up. My brain flashes error messages as it tries to process the words coming out of Preston's mouth.

He wants me to fuck him.

Yes. Yes. Absolutely, yes.

Fucking Preston, being inside him, it's everything I've ever wanted in life. I've been avoiding it, satisfying myself with frotting and handjobs and blowjobs. And they've been plenty satisfying, don't get me wrong. It's all still sex and wonderful sex at that. But there's something next-level about cock in ass. Once we've graduated to fucking, there's no going back.

"Are you sure?" My voice is strangled as I force myself to ask the question.

"Yes, please." Preston's hand goes to his nipple, already red and swollen from my attention. He tweaks it and gasps. He drags his other hand down his torso and takes hold of himself. He's hard and leaking, and when he gives himself a stroke, a small gush of pre-cum spills out of his slit.

"Fuck," I mutter, eyes glued to Preston and how he's pleasuring himself. My balls ache in anticipation of flooding Preston with my cum, of painting his insides and leaving a part of me behind.

At my inaction, Preston tilts his head contemplatively. "Unless you don't want to?"

The laugh that escapes my throat borders on hysterical. "Oh, I want to. I definitely want to. It's just that… are you sure you're sure?"

"Yes," Preston says again with a little furrow in his brow. "I want you to fuck me. I wouldn't have said so if I didn't want it."

I squeeze my eyes shut and try to focus on drawing in deep, steady breaths. "But do you know what it means? What's involved?"

"Of course, I do." Preston sounds indignant now. "You put your penis in my rectum."

"Jesus Christ."

"I know there are different positions we can try, that we need to use lube because the rectum doesn't produce its own lubrication, and that we'll need to slowly stretch my sphincter so—"

"Okay, yep, yeah. Got it. You got the mechanics down pat, but…" I hesitate, studying Preston's curious and confused expression.

There is nothing I want more in the world than to fuck Preston, to show him how good it can feel, to be that inti-mate and close to him. But faced with it now, knowing what a big step it is... I've never had performance anxiety before, but...

"Sawyer?" Preston touches himself, pinching his nipple and stroking his cock. "Please?"

I gulp. How can I resist him when he's looking at me with so much heat in his eyes? I'll make this good for him. And if for whatever reason, I don't succeed, well, I don't give up that easily.

I slot myself between his thighs. "You have to tell me if you want to stop, okay?"

Preston nods. Eyes wide and bright with eagerness, bottom lip caught between his teeth.

"If it hurts or if you don't like it—anything—you have to tell me and we'll stop and we never have to do it again."

He nods again, more fervently this time. "Okay." The word comes out in a hushed, but excited whisper.

"Promise me you'll stop me."

When he hesitates, I push into the mattress with my hands and shake the bed. "Promise me."

"Okay, I promise, I promise."

Even with that, I don't start right away. I want to savor this moment, record it to my memory so I'll never forget. My first time fucking Preston. His boldness and determination, so coy and sensual. My love for him threatens to choke me, it's so thick.

"Can we start now?" Preston asks, his hands coming to my sides and sliding around to my back. He tugs me down and I drop to my elbows. His breath is hot as it blows across my chin.

This is perfect. Preston's perfect. I'll never get enough.

"Yeah, we can start now." I slant my mouth over

Preston's, careful of his bruises, and he whimpers into the kiss.

It's slow at first, our lips caressing each other, our tongues saying hello. But it heats quickly when Preston plants his feet on the bed and arches up into me. Using my weight, I press him back down, dicks grinding together, skin sliding across smooth skin.

Preston digs his fingers into my back, clawing at me like he can't get enough. He rips his mouth from mine. "Sawyer, please!"

I growl at the desperation in his voice, at the way he's writhing around, I grind myself against him. "Is this what you want?"

He arches against me. "Yes!"

"You want to take my cock?"

"Yes!"

"You want me to stretch you open and fill you up?"

"Yes! Please, Sawyer, please!"

His cries are a drug, sending me soaring and leaving me dazed. I pull back, pushing his knees up to reveal the entrance to his body. "Hold here," I instruct him and Preston immediately complies, hands coming to grip the backs of his knees.

"Yes!"

The single word rings in my ears as I dive in. Preston's hole is pink and wrinkled and—I never thought I'd ever say this—so goddamn cute. It flutters and winks at me, and when I swipe my tongue over it, it's fucking sweet. Assholes aren't supposed to be sweet, but I swear to god, Preston's is. It tastes like pure sugar and it's just as addicting.

I lick and lap and suck, fueled by the sounds Preston

doesn't try to contain. I stiffen the tip of my tongue and drive it into the center of his hole. More sweetness explodes in my mouth and Preston's voice goes up an octave. I fuck him with my tongue, scrape the stubble on my chin over his glistening pink hole, sink my teeth into the fleshy parts of his glutes.

Preston's cries gradually turn to sobs. On his stomach, his dick is leaking an impressive puddle. He wiggles his hips back and forth. "More. Please, Sawyer. More."

I scramble for the bottle of lube in my nightstand and slick up my fingers. With the opposite hand wrapped around his cock, I gently push a finger into his body. Watching it disappear, watching his hole stretch to let me in... Jesus fucking Christ, it's the most erotic thing I've ever seen. Better than any porn in any corner of the internet.

"Yes! Oh god, Sawyer! Yes!"

Preston's cock throbs in my palm, his hole clenches like it wants to suck my entire hand inside.

"More! More!"

I push a second finger in with the first. His hole relaxes into the invasion like he's a seasoned bottom rather than the anal virgin I know he is. It's so fucking hot to think of Preston as having a natural talent for bottoming, like he was made for this, made to be opened up and filled with cock. My dick spurts out a huge gush of pre-cum.

With two fingers inside him, I search for that little button that will drive him absolutely fucking wild. I'm not disappointed when I press on it. Preston screams, throwing his head back and rocking his ass on my hand.

"Sawyer, please! Please! I need you!" Preston reaches scrabbling fingers for me.

I need him too, but there's something we should clear up first. I lean over him, hands braced on either side of his head. "Preston, look at me. This is important."

I wait for Preston to blink and for the lust to clear from his eyes. "I'm on PrEP, I've always been careful with sexual partners, and I stopped by a rapid test clinic yesterday—everything came back negative. Can I—would you be okay if I—I mean—" Fuck, why can't I get the words out? How do I explain how much I want to be inside Preston without any kind of barrier between us?

He seems to read my mind, though. "Yes, yes, no condom, yes. Please. Fuck me, please, Sawyer."

Well, when he asks so politely…

I press a long, lingering kiss to his lips before sitting back to slick my dick with plenty of lube. Then I scoot forward, cock poised at Preston's hole. "Ready?"

"Yes, yes, please. Give it to me. Fuck me, Sawyer. Fuck me."

"I'm going to fuck you. I'm going to fuck you so hard."

"Yes, yes, I want it."

Despite the dirty talk, I'm careful as I gradually increase the pressure and guide myself into Preston's hole.

When the head of my cock pops in, he sucks in a huge gasp and goes still. His eyes are wide and unseeing, lips parted in a silent scream. I run my hand along his side, then give his cock a few encouraging tugs.

"That's it. Relax. Let me in. You're doing so good. So good."

I rock into him by degrees, pushing deeper as I feel his body loosen and grow lax around me. He whimpers and mewls, writhing and arching toward me when he thinks I'm going too slow.

By the time I'm fully seated inside him, we're both drenched with sweat. The air is thick with the scent of our sex. The sheets are damp underneath us.

Preston curls himself around me, arms around my neck, legs around my waist. My groin is flush against his ass and my nose is buried in the crook of his neck. I breathe him in, sweet lavender that winds through me, wrapping me up so I'm caught in its hold. I am his. All of me.

I don't fuck Preston. I can't. Not when I'm so full of love for him. I make love to him instead, pouring every ounce of affection and tenderness I've ever felt for him into my movements, into the kisses I plant on his neck, his shoulders, his jaw, his chin, his mouth.

I pull out until only the head of my cock is inside him, then I sink all the way back in. Again and again. Long and slow. He's so hot and tight around my cock, and it doesn't take him long to figure out how to relax as I'm going in and clench when I'm drawing out.

His lashes flutter and he opens his eyes. The bright blue of his irises is a thin ring around his pupils. His pale skin is flushed rosy pink, and his lips are curled into an ever-so-slight smile. He looks like he's in heaven, like having my cock inside him is the best thing that's ever happened to him. I don't think I've ever loved him more than in this moment.

"Preston." His name comes out in a sob, layered with all the emotions I've never been able to voice out loud.

"Sawyer."

I shudder at the little hiccup at the end. Preston is so good, so right, so perfect for me.

My hips start moving in earnest and Preston lets out a long, whining, "Yeeesss."

"Fuck, Preston."

"Yes, Sawyer, yes! Fuck me!"

I do. As fast and hard as I can, driving myself into him like I want to wedge myself in there permanently.

"You like this? Huh? You like it when I fuck you?"

"Yes! Yes! More!"

My hips slap against his ass, the sound mixing with the squelch of my cock as it pumps in and out of his hole. The bed squeaks. The whole thing is loud and obscene and it's fucking music to my ears.

My orgasm hovers at the edge of my consciousness, primed and ready to crash through me. But I hold it off. I can't come yet. Preston needs to come first. I need to make sure I take care of him before I can enjoy my own pleasure.

I squeeze my hand between us and wrap my fingers around his cock. He's rock hard and scalding hot to the touch. I swirl my thumb across the tip of his dick, just the way I know he likes it.

"Are you gonna come, Pres? Are you going to come for me?"

"Yes! Yes! Sawyer! Please!"

"Then come for me, Pres. Come for me."

He screams, body going taut as he clamps down around my cock. Cum spews out from his dick, all over my hand, over both our stomachs.

I slam myself into him, as deep as I can possibly go, and bellow out my orgasm. Blinding pleasure explodes, starting deep in my groin and radiating out, touching every cell in my body. Wave after wave buffets me, pulverizing me, with no end in sight.

When I finally have the strength to lift my head, I gaze down at Preston, amazed that I get to have this wonderful man in my bed, in my arms. I grow soft and slip out of him, and he blinks his eyes open with a whine.

"Was that okay?" I ask, suddenly worried I might've been too aggressive.

But the smile that spreads across Preston's face is pure sin. "Yeah, I want to do it again."

I laugh and roll to the side, bringing Preston with me. "We can do that as many times as you want."

PRESTON

"I don't think I can go in there with you, babe," Sawyer says, squeezing my hand. We're on campus, standing outside Professor Graves's office. I'm going to tell him that I want to graduate on time—this spring, to be exact. Sawyer's come with me for moral support.

I'm not afraid of talking to Professor Graves. I'm afraid of what comes after, of having to tell my dad that despite graduating on schedule, I won't be joining the family company. I'm dreading that conversation, so much so that I've projected my dread onto the meeting with Professor Graves.

"I know, I just…" I cling to Sawyer's arm.

"You don't have to talk to your dad yet. That's a problem for future Preston. Just focus on what's right in front of you now." Sawyer always knows what I'm thinking, always knows exactly what to say. "I'll wait right here for you."

I nod, take a deep breath, and steel myself. Then I march toward Professor Graves's door and knock.

"Come in!"

I shoot Sawyer one last glance and he gives me an encouraging smile, then I go in.

"Preston, how are you?" Professor Graves looks up from the papers he's reading and gives me a friendly smile.

I take my usual chair, perch on the edge of the seat, and fold my hands in my lap. "Hi, Professor Graves. I'm doing well. How are you?"

A little furrow appears in his brow and when he speaks, there's a bit of laughter in his voice. "I am also doing well. Thanks for asking. What did you want to talk about today?"

I clear my throat. "My defense."

"Oh good." He leans forward, folding his arms across the top of his desk. "Have you decided what you want to do? I still think you should go ahead with this spring, especially with how quickly your research is coming along. But ultimately, the decision is yours."

"Yes, I understand." My heart feels like it's untethered and bouncing around in my chest, trying to escape. "I, uh, I've decided to, uh, stay on schedule."

Professor Graves breaks out into a wide smile. "That's wonderful. I'm glad to hear it. In fact, I was just chatting with the dissertation committee chair about which doctoral candidates we need to fit into the defense sched-ule. I included your name in hopes you'd come around."

My heart is still racing, but now that the words are out and Professor Graves appears happy with my decision, I breathe a little easier.

"Yes, thank you."

Professor Graves studies me for a moment, then continues more softly. "It's going to be fine, Preston. Your research is solid. You know your material inside out. You'll blow them out of the water."

I nod as tension slowly eases from me and I slide deeper into the chair, slumping inward. "Yes, I know."

A look of confusion passes over Professor Graves's face. "So why do you look so worried?"

"It's not the defense," I say, too quietly for him to hear.

"What's that?"

I swallow thickly and speak up louder. "It's not the defense. It's after I graduate. My parents want me to go work for them, but I don't want to."

"Oh." Now he looks surprised as well as confused. "Do you have alternative options?"

I shrug. "I guess I can apply for post-doc positions." That's what most people on my career trajectory would do. But with the whole Sawyer-Fitz thing and the football incident, I haven't looked into any.

"In that case, you might just be in luck." Professor Graves turns to his computer and clicks on a few things. "We don't currently have any post-docs in our department."

"Yes, I know." It would've been the most obvious option for me.

"But we've been in discussion with the administration about carving out a budget for one."

I sit up at Professor Graves's announcement. "Really?"

He nods. "Really. The work you're doing is cutting-edge stuff, Preston, you know that. It would be a shame for us to lose that when you graduate."

I think I know what he's implying, but I don't want to jump to conclusions and get my hopes up. My heart starts racing again, but this time in excitement rather than fear.

"Now, there's no guarantee the budget will be approved, but we've made a strong case and I think the administration is willing to come on board."

I shift to the edge of my seat again. "Really?"

"And again, no guarantee, but if the budget is approved, you would most likely be our top candidate."

"I would?" This could be it. This could be the answer to everything. I'd have a job after graduation. A good job that I'd love. I wouldn't have to go to another school or move to a different city. Sawyer and I could stay exactly where we are, where we're happy.

"Yes, Preston, you would."

"I… I… I don't know what to say."

Professor Graves laughs softly. "You don't have to say anything right now. Nothing is set in stone. I just wanted you to know that we're pulling for you."

I nod. "Okay. Thank you."

"Don't thank me yet. We can celebrate when the contract comes through. Now, for your dissertation, how about we schedule a time next week to see what holes we need to patch up before your defense?"

We settle on a time, then I float out of his office in a daze.

Sawyer's exactly where I left him, waiting outside Professor Graves's office. "How'd it go?"

I slot myself into his side, winding my arm around his waist. "Good, I think. He said they might have a post-doc position for me."

"Oh?" Sawyer says as he directs me down the hall.

"Yeah, they'd be creating a new position."

"Just for you? That's amazing!" He gives me a gentle shake.

I don't try to fight the grin bunching up my cheeks. "It's not finalized yet, but it sounds promising."

"Still. We should celebrate." We step out into the cold early December air. "What do you want to do? Go get dinner? Drinks? Watch a movie?"

"Hmm." I smile up at him, doing my best to look seductive. "I want to go home. To bed."

Sawyer chokes on nothing at all, then nods frantically. "Mmhmm, yep, we can do that. For sure."

We grab a rideshare back home and the second we step into our apartment, I'm on him.

We leave a trail of clothes from the front door to Sawyer's—really, our—bedroom, and by the time we hit the bed, we're both naked.

"Sawyer, please." I press myself against him. I want Sawyer to take me, to fuck me, to pound into me and tear me apart.

But he doesn't, he slows down. He holds my face between his palms and peppers featherlight kisses all over my forehead, my eyes, my cheeks, my jaw, the corners of my mouth. The bruising on my face has mostly faded, with only a few lingering yellow spots near my eyes. Still, he's gentle with me and I feel like the most precious treasure under his attention.

"You're beautiful," he murmurs. "Gorgeous. Stunning."

It's not the first time Sawyer's said these things to me. In fact, he seems to say them more and more these days. The words make me whimper and tremble. My instinct is to deny them, to hide from them, but I force myself to stay in Sawyer's embrace and endure his praise.

He kisses down my neck to suck on that spot where my pulse is strongest. I drop my head back to give him access and my hips go forward, looking for something to grind my hard dick against. Sawyer slips his knee between my legs and I rub my aching dick along his thigh.

"Please, Sawyer, please."

With a growl, Sawyer grabs me around the waist and hoists me into the air. It's a few steps to the bed, then he drops me onto the mattress and I squeal in delight as I bounce. I scramble backward as he comes after me.

Sawyer catches one ankle, then the other, holding me open so he can wedge his shoulders between my thighs. Before I can prepare myself, my dick is in his mouth.

"Sawyer!" I cry out, hips coming off the bed as Sawyer takes me deep into his throat. It's so hot, so searing, that sweat immediately breaks out across my skin. "Oh god!"

Sawyer doesn't let me go. He holds me in his throat, swallowing around the head of my dick like he wants to consume me whole. I want him to have every single part of me. I want him to take me apart and make me his.

He's panting and breathing hard when he finally pulls off. My dick glistens with his saliva, the foreskin retracted and the head so engorged it's red.

"So pretty," he murmurs before tracing his tongue up and down my length.

I squirm and thrash when he turns his attention to my balls, pulling each one into his mouth, sucking on them, tonguing them. The sounds Sawyer wrings out of me don't sound human anymore. They're low and guttural, like they're coming out of the deepest, darkest parts of me. They're high and squeaky when Sawyer works his way down to my perineum, bathing it with long, slow licks, nipping with his teeth. The sounds skyrocket when he pushes my legs up to expose my hole.

"Sawyer!" I scream as he bends down to eat me out. His tongue is so dexterous and strong, probing at my hole and pushing inside. He scrapes his teeth across my sensitive skin and rubs his stubble all around too. Everything is on fire, burning through me, ravaging me.

"Please, Sawyer, please! I need you."

Sawyer, ever the athlete, moves quickly, reaching across the bed to fish the lube from the nightstand. Then he turns back to me and carefully eases me onto my side.

"Yesss," I hiss. This is my favorite way to get fucked. From behind, with his body molded to mine, his wide chest against my back. Sure, it's harder to kiss this way, which is a shame, but we make up for it with lots of kissing before and after. "Hurry, please, hurry."

"I'm here, babe, I'm right here. I'm gonna give you what you need, everything you need."

Sawyer slots himself behind me and his erection seeks out my hole like it's a precision-guided missile. I push myself back, moaning as he slides into my body.

The stretch is divine. The fullness is so satisfying. I would live every moment of every day like this if I could, with Sawyer seated entirely inside me.

Our size difference means I fit perfectly into the curve of Sawyer's body, his dick aligned with my hole, his chin hooking over my shoulder to kiss my ear and nuzzle my neck. I was designed for this, for Sawyer to use me like this. I was made to take his cock.

"Fuck, Preston, you feel so goddamn good," he murmurs, hauling me against him.

I whimper and snuggle back some more.

Sawyer's got one arm trapped under me, bent so he can reach my chest and nipples. His other arm roams freely, gripping my hip, flattening across my stomach, reaching down to cup my balls and stroke my dick. He does it all, torturing my sensitive zones, lighting up my nerve endings, while he pumps himself steadily into me. Everything is hot, everything tingles. Every touch and stroke sends pleasure bursting through me.

"Sawyer." My voice is softer now, wistful and intimate. I whisper into the small space between us, this little bubble we've created where nothing exists except our bodies, connected so deeply I don't know where I end and he begins.

"I love you, Preston," Sawyer murmurs, the words winding through me and lighting me up from the inside out. "It shouldn't be possible to love someone so much, but I do. You're the air I breathe, the sustenance that fuels me. You're a drug and I'm so addicted to you I'll die without you."

"Yes, yes, yes," I agree because he is all those things to me too. My eyes prickle with tears and my dick grows harder in Sawyer's palm. I tremble and quake as my orgasm draws near.

"You're the reason I wake up every morning. The reason I eat and sleep and live. You're my reason for being, my purpose in life."

The tears spill over, hot on my cheeks and soaking into the pillow. I dig my fingers into his muscled forearm and clench tightly around Sawyer's cock in my body. I want to keep him inside me. I'm empty without him. I'm nothing without him.

"I love you, Preston. I love you with every fiber of my body, every neuron in my brain, every molecule of every cell."

I'm close, so close, and Sawyer's going to make me come with his words. His thrusts are steady and unwavering, hitting me deep inside my body, in my soul.

"I love you, Preston. I love you. I love you. I love you."

I explode with Sawyer's endearments echoing in my ear. The orgasm rips through me, turning me inside out, pleasure so profound it makes me sob.

Then Sawyer is orgasming too. Fully sheathed inside me, pouring his cum into my body. There's no barrier between us, nothing separating us. In this moment, we're one entity, one heartbeat, one life.

SAWYER

Across the Mars lobby, Logan holds a banana to his lips and mouths the words "One… last… time…" as he lip-syncs to Ariana Grande's song. I'm not quite so dedicated, but I sing along too, dancing behind the front counter as I swipe in a group of members and hand out towels.

"Have a good workout! Leg day today? Ouch! Good luck!" Everyone gets a high five as they pass through. "Yeah, you got thiiis! Do iiit! Look at that pump!"

Things have been busy today and Gavin has stepped out of his office to help me keep things flowing.

"So, I hear you've gotten together with your best friend?" he asks during a small lull in activity.

My cheeks suddenly feel hot, even though I'm not usually one to blush. "Uh, yeah, Preston."

Gavin gives me a sly look. "Nice. Welcome to the straight best friend club."

I laugh at the reminder of how he and Beau ended up

together. Everyone knows their story. Beau was the straight best friend and Gavin was hopelessly in love with him for years. Then Beau got divorced from his wife and Gavin helped patch him up—in all the ways. Theirs is a romantic happily ever after that I would *love* to have with Preston.

"Thanks, but, uh, we're not quite there yet."

I take every opportunity to tell Preston I love him, but he has yet to say it back. I'm not worried, per se. The more I think about my conversation with Mom over Thanksgiving, the more I'm coming around to the idea that she's right: Preston loves me, he just hasn't figured it out yet. It takes time for him to sort through his feelings, to understand and accept them. But that doesn't mean the feelings don't exist. It doesn't mean that he feels them any less potently.

I just have to be patient.

Another wave of members come through and while I'm passing towels out, Gavin gives me a nudge with his elbow.

"Hey, isn't that him?"

"Who?" I follow Gavin's gaze toward the front door where the last person I expect to see is standing just inside.

Preston.

Cheeks rosy from the cold. Eyes wide as he takes in the unfamiliar surroundings. Hands clutching nervously at the strap of his bag.

What the hell is Preston doing at Mars? Memories of the last time he showed up out of the blue flash through my mind, and I drop the towels I'm holding to run out from behind the front counter.

"Preston!"

He turns at the sound of his name and his face breaks out into a wide smile. My heart lurches at the sight, but it doesn't appease my worry.

"Are you okay? Did something happen? Are you hurt?" I grab him by the arms and scan him up and down. He doesn't look injured, and he's wearing his own coat this time.

"I'm fine. Everything's okay. I wanted to, um…" He glances around us and shuffles closer to me. "I thought I could hang out here? If that's okay?"

"Oh." I'm dumbfounded. People hang out here all the time. It's why we have the tables and chairs in the lobby. But Preston's never shown any interest in doing that before. Hell, he's never shown any interest in Mars at all.

"Um, I can leave, if I'm not allowed." He tries to take a step back, but I haul him forward.

"No! I mean, of course you can stay and hang out." I loop an arm around his shoulders and bring him farther inside. "Did you want to grab one of these tables? Or you can use the break room if you want something quieter."

Preston nibbles on his lip as he considers his options, then he turns to me. "Where will you be?"

It takes a second for me to answer as my heart ping-pongs around in my chest. "Out here, mostly. We're pretty busy today." I wince. "So I might not be able to spend much time with you."

Preston brightens. "That's okay. I brought my work and noise-canceling headphones. I just… wanted to be close to you."

God-fucking-damn. Love and pride well up in me, so much that I'm bursting. "I want to be close to you too."

I bend to give him a quick, chaste kiss on the lips, but

Preston melts into me and makes a needy little whimper. What can I do but linger and savor the taste of him a little longer? Until we're interrupted by catcalls—assholes.

Preston's already rosy cheeks redden even more, and I turn around to give Logan and Everest—when did he show up?—the middle finger.

"You remember Logan and Everest?" I ask Preston as I guide him to an empty table. "I think you met them at my birthday party last year."

"I think so?" Preston says, meaning he absolutely does not remember them. But he still gives them a hesitant little wave and I feel another rush of pride.

Ever since we got back from Thanksgiving, it's like he's become a different person. Or rather, he's trying to become a different person—a better person. I'm one hundred percent happy with who he is, but I can tell that this is what he wants. He wants to grow, to challenge himself, to step outside his comfort zone. And I couldn't be prouder of him for it.

I get Preston settled at his table with his tablet and portable keyboard, noise-canceling headphones on. Then I plant a kiss on the top of his head and head back to the front counter.

"Sorry about that," I say to Gavin, who has watched the whole thing unfold.

"No worries." He considers Preston for a moment before speaking again. "He's pretty special, isn't he?"

I struggle to breathe around all the emotions swirling in my chest. "Yeah, he is."

I keep an eye on Preston while I work. Most of the time, when I glance over, he's bent over his tablet, brow furrowed in deep concentration. Every once in a while, I catch him watching me, just sitting there gazing at me with his elbow on the table, chin in hand.

Donnie stops by to do some paperwork. Beau checks in a few times too. Neither of them mentions Preston directly, but the encouraging smiles they give me say they've both seen him sitting there.

At the end of my shift, Logan comes bounding up to me. "Hey! Are you coming to drinks after work? Connor can't make it, but Everest and I are still game. Preston's invited, of course."

I glance at Preston just in time to catch him in the middle of a yawn. "I don't know. I should probably get him home."

Logan tilts his head and gives me a pointed look. "Why don't you ask him instead of making the decision for him?"

Goddamn. I glare at Logan and his uncharacteristically wise piece of advice. "Fine."

I jog out from behind the front counter and plop into the empty chair at Preston's table.

He lights up when he sees me and pulls his headphones down around his neck.

"How's it going?" I ask, pointing at his tablet.

Preston nods enthusiastically. "Good. The last set of results is really promising. I think I just need a few more tweaks to really nail it."

"That's awesome," I say, and Preston beams. "Logan asked if we want to get drinks after work."

"Oh, uh…" Preston peeks over at Logan who's still leaning on the front counter. Logan gives him a wave and Preston ducks his head shyly.

"We don't have to. We can go home if you want," I say,

not wanting Preston to feel pressured by Logan's exuberance.

"But you would normally go with them, right?"

"Yeah," I admit. "Normally, I would."

Preston lifts his chin and looks me directly in the eyes. "Then let's go."

"Are you sure?" I don't want Preston to push this "new and improved" scheme too far and end up crashing and burning. Baby steps are key to things like this.

"Yes, I'm sure. Let's go." His tone is final and I fall a little more in love with him right then.

After work, Everest, Logan, Preston, and I go to the bar down the street.

"Are you coming to the New Year's Eve party?" Logan asks, as we take our seats. But before any of us can answer, he charges on. "Jay's coming. My boyfriend. We've been seeing each other for six months now. Well, almost six—five and a half."

"And we'll finally get to meet this mysterious boyfriend at New Year's?" I ask. Despite listening to Logan talk nonstop about the guy he's dating, none of us have actually met the guy before.

"Yes, you will," Logan says with determination. "There's nothing mysterious about him. He's normal. Perfectly normal. He's perfect."

"I'm still not convinced he's real," Everest says.

"He is real!" Logan exclaims.

"Uh huh, sure. I'll believe it when I see it."

Old Preston would have tuned out by now. Hell, old Preston probably wouldn't have agreed to come to begin with. But new Preston is valiantly trying to follow our conversation, gaze flitting back and forth between us as we speak.

Under the table, I take his hand and intertwine our fingers. He scoots his chair over so it's flush with mine and leans his head on my shoulder.

The waiter comes by with our drinks. Beers for me and Everest. A margarita for Logan. And a glass of wine for Preston.

"I still can't believe you know nothing about the guy," Everest says, picking up where he left off.

Logan scoffs. "I know tons about Jay!"

"No, you don't," Everest says with a laugh. "What does he do for work? What company does he work for? Where is he from? Does he have any siblings? What about his parents? You haven't even been to his place before or met any of his friends."

"I know he likes red wine, he listens to true crime podcasts, he likes the theatre." Logan ticks each item off on his fingers.

"You've just described ninety percent of the city's population," I point out, taking a sip of my beer.

"Whatever," Logan says haughtily. "What's important is that he's a good person and he's kind to me and I love him."

Which isn't nearly as shocking a statement when it comes from Logan, but next to me, Preston shifts.

"You good?" I whisper the question to Preston as Everest and Logan continue arguing.

"Mmhmm." He shifts again. "Your friends are funny."

I laugh out loud, but Everest and Logan are too wrapped up in their argument to notice. "Yeah, they are. You tired?" I ask, noticing Preston's eyes drooping a bit.

"A little. But this is nice. We don't have to go yet."

I blink a few times to let Preston's comment sink in. He never would've said something like that before Thanksgiving. He's trying so hard and he's doing so well. I always knew he could do anything he set his mind to, and I was right.

PRESTON

I think I've cracked it. I think I've found the fix in the code that will generate the most accurate output Stable Diffusion has ever achieved. Now, if only the computer will hurry the fuck up and process the data with the updated AI algorithm.

Tap, tap, tap. Tap, tap, tap.

The sound of a pen bouncing on a hard surface invades my thoughts and my head snaps up to find the source. It's Fitz, sitting at the workstation across from me. He's studying me intently, and I suddenly wonder how long he's been there.

"What?" I ask, annoyed and self-conscious at the same time. The swelling on my face has receded, but the bruising is still pretty dark. Madison showed me how to cover it up with makeup, but I'm not good enough at the application to hide it completely.

Fitz chuckles softly, but he doesn't sound like he's laughing. "I spoke with Sawyer."

The words bring me up short. I thought Sawyer broke up with Fitz. What does he mean he spoke with Sawyer?

Fitz rolls his eyes and tosses the pen onto the table with a clatter. "Relax, Jesus, he broke up with me. He's all yours."

"Oh."

"Yeah, oh." Fitz shoves his fingers through his hair, then leans forward, arms folded across the table. "So can you stop being a jerk to me now?"

I jolt like Fitz's comment physically slapped me in the face. "Can I—what?"

"Can you stop treating me like I'm the gum stuck to the bottom of your shoe?"

It takes me a second to understand he doesn't mean actual gum on my shoes.

"I'm good at my job. I've been helpful in the lab. I've done everything you've asked me to without complaint. And now, I'm not even trying to steal your boyfriend anymore. So maybe you can conjure up a little common courtesy?"

I stare at Fitz, the Wernicke's area of my brain scrambling to process all the words he's tossed in my direction. When I finally land on something I know how to respond to, I say, "Sawyer's not my boyfriend."

Fitz regards me for a moment, like he can't believe what he's heard. Then he bursts out in laughter that sounds almost like sobs. "Sawyer's not your boyfriend. Right. Fool me once, shame on you. Fool me twice..."

He shakes his head and walks around his workstation toward me. Leaning a hip against my desk, he crosses his arms over his chest. I don't like how close he is, how he looks down at me from that angle, so I push my chair away and roll backward a few feet.

Except when I glance at Fitz again, he's wearing a pensive expression.

"You really don't think Sawyer's your boyfriend, do you?"

I don't know how to answer that question. Sawyer's mine. He's my best friend and my roommate. I guess he's my lover now too, since we're having sex. Does that mean he's my boyfriend? That I'm his? He hasn't asked me to be his boyfriend, though. Isn't that supposed to happen first?

"I… I don't know," I answer honestly.

Fitz shakes his head. "I think, for all intents and purposes, you and Sawyer have been boyfriends for a long time. Maybe you don't call each other that, but you certainly behave like a couple."

I think back to the relationship I had with Madison in high school. It's not a great comparison, I know, but it's the only reference I have. Madison and I spent a lot of time together—when I wasn't busy studying. But Sawyer and I spent a lot of time together too. Madison helped me with life stuff and I helped her with homework. It was the same with Sawyer. Madison and I had sex occasionally. I didn't do that with Sawyer back then, but I do now… which means…

I blink at Fitz as my brain arrives at the most reasonable conclusion. "Oh."

Fitz chuckles, but this time it sounds more resigned than bitter. "Yeah, oh."

And Sawyer loves me—romantically, the way people do when they're a couple. I could tell when we were in the bathroom at my parents' house that he wanted me to say I love him too.

I do love him. But what's the difference between loving a best friend and loving someone romantically? Is it the same thing, just at a larger magnitude? Or is it completely different? And different how?

"How do you know if you're in love?"

Fitz's eyebrows shoot up to his hairline. "Uh, I'm not sure I'm the right person to ask."

"But you are." I roll my chair closer. "You understand science and logic and reason."

"Yes, but what does that have to do with—"

I push to my feet, chair flying across the room, and pace as my thoughts finally start transforming themselves into words. "What are the parameters to love? Are there units of measurement that can be quantified and tested? If I can posit a hypothesis, then I can build an experiment to prove it. Then I'd have a definite answer. I'd know if I'm in love with Sawyer."

Fitz raises a hand to stop my pacing. "First of all, I don't think love works that way. There are no 'units of measurement'—unfortunately. And second of all, you don't know if you're in love with Sawyer? Are you kidding me?"

"No, why would I be kidding? This isn't something to joke about."

"Oh my god." He straightens and comes to stand in front of me. We're about the same height, so I don't have to crane my neck up at him.

Taking my arms in his hands, he stares into my eyes as he speaks, "Preston, of course you're in love with Sawyer. How is that even a question? You nearly derailed my career because you're so in love with him that you couldn't stand to see him with me."

"I… I didn't derail your career."

Fitz throws his hands in the air and spins around. "Jesus Christ, haven't you been listening to anything I said?" When he's facing me again, he holds up one finger. "You've been in love with Sawyer for god knows how long.

He holds up a second finger. "Sawyer and I start dating." Third finger. "You get super fucking jealous." Fourth finger. "You take out your jealousy on me by treating me like shit at school." Fifth finger. "I tell you I want to get serious with Sawyer and you freak the fuck out and go throw yourself at him. Have I missed anything?"

When he lays it all out like that, I can finally see how the dots connect. "No, I don't think so."

"And the argument only works because of the first premise—you're in love with Sawyer."

I run through Fitz's argument again, testing his logic for any holes. I don't find any. Which means… which means the first premise must be correct.

"I'm in love with Sawyer." The realization is staggering and I drop into my abandoned chair. Then I jump to my feet again—I know how to answer Sawyer now. "I'm in love with Sawyer."

"No, shit. I should start charging you guys by the hour."

"I have to go. I have to tell him." I scramble to toss my things into my bag and I'm halfway to the door before I stop in my tracks.

I'm in love with Sawyer—and I treated Fitz like shit because I only managed to figure it out now. Oops.

I spin around to find Fitz leaning against the desk, hands braced on either side of his hips. "I'm sorry."

Fitz cocks an eyebrow. "What for?"

"For what you said, being mean to you." I take a step toward him, hoping he'll believe me even though he has no reason to. "I never would've jeopardized your career, though. I know I haven't treated you very well, but I've always thought you were good at your job. And I've said so to Professor Graves. You're a—" How did Professor Graves put it? "—a valuable addition to the team."

He heaves a sigh and rolls his eyes. "Yeah, okay, fine, apology accepted. As long as you start treating me with a little respect."

I nod my head earnestly. "I will. I promise."

Fitz makes a shooing motion with his hand. "Alright, get lost. Go tell Sawyer you love him. Christ, I need a drin—"

I'm out the door before Fitz can finish his sentence and it takes me no time at all to race home. When I burst into the apartment, Sawyer's on the couch, laptop propped on a pillow.

"Hey," he says, looking up from the screen.

I drop everything on the floor and rush forward. He sees me coming just in time to set his laptop aside and catch me as I launch myself at him.

"I love you," I try to say while kissing him at the same time. It comes out more like *I-ub-bu* and I hiss as I bump my bruised face against Sawyer's hard cheekbone. "Ow…"

"Oh my god, are you okay?" Sawyer maneuvers us so I'm sitting securely on his lap.

"Yeah, I forgot."

He swipes his fingers gently across my mottled skin. "You've got to be careful, Pres."

His voice is tender and his eyes are so filled with love. It's so obvious, now that I know what I'm looking for. I can't believe it's taken me this long to recognize it.

"I love you."

Sawyer blinks, stunned, then a smile blossoms on his face—bright and shining and the most beautiful thing I've ever seen.

"Yeah?"

I nod enthusiastically. "Yeah. I love you. I do. Fitz helped me figure it out."

"Fitz?" Sawyer's smile goes a little strained around the edges. "I don't think he likes us very much right now."

I shrug. "I apologized."

"I did too." Sawyer relaxes. "We'll have to make it up to him sometime. But right now... you love me?"

I nod again. "I love you. I wasn't sure how to identify it at first. I didn't know what the markers were. But Fitz broke it down for me and now I can see it. I love you. I love you a lot. I love you more than anything in the world."

With each word that leaves my mouth, Sawyer's smile grows wider. "I love you too, Pres."

SAWYER

My life is pretty fucking perfect right now. I spent the last couple days decorating Mars with Logan and Everest until it looked like an elf vomited all over it. I wrote the final exams for the two courses I'm taking this semester and did really well. Most importantly, I'm in love with my best friend and he's in love with me.

Now we're heading to Boston for Christmas. Since Preston and I moved to New York, flying on private planes has become pretty common for me. But no matter how many times I've been on one, it still kind of blows my mind that we can hop on a plane like it's a taxi cab.

Preston's in the window seat and I'm on the aisle. Madison's across the aisle from me, engrossed in her phone. I brought the new thriller novel Preston surprised me with as an end-of-semester present, but I gave up on reading when Preston couldn't sit still. The closer we get to Boston, the twitchier he's gotten.

He's decided the conversation with his parents will

happen sometime during this trip. I told him Christmas is already pretty high-stress, so it's okay to postpone it until the new year. But this new Preston is determined to push through, no matter what.

I have to say, new Preston is fucking hot. Like, H. O. T. Don't get me wrong, I've always been attracted to Preston, to his nerdiness and his awkward honesty. But the resolve that shines in his eyes these days, the way he's applied his single-mindedness to his life outside of academia... goddamn, it's impossible to resist. Especially when he brings that sense of purpose into the bedroom.

We've been having a lot of sex. Like, a lot. My dick is a little raw with how often we're fucking and my balls are perpetually dry. I'm a young guy, an athlete with lots of stamina, but Preston is putting me to shame. He's insatiable.

He's on me the second we're alone. He's developed a taste for good morning orgasms. I don't know where or how he learned to eye-fuck, but Jesus Christ, he is so good at it. More than once, I've almost come just from having him regard me with lust in his eyes.

"Excuse me." The flight attendant comes up from the galley at the back of the plane. "We'll be landing soon. Can I gather your empty glasses and plates?"

Preston's hands shake as he picks up his untouched plate of crackers and cheese. I take it from him and pass it to the flight attendant.

"Hey, you alright?" I ask, drawing him in as close as the fixed armrests will allow.

He nods and turns his head up for a sweet, lingering kiss.

"Ugh, get a room." Madison groans. When I glance toward her, she looks so pleased with herself.

"Shut up," I reply, though there's no heat behind my words.

"You're sure you want to talk to your dad on this trip?" Madison asks.

"Yes, I do," Preston says, his voice a little shaky.

"I'll be there—right outside the room, at least."

"I won't be," Madison says with an apologetic grimace. "Sorry. I would, except my mom needs help getting stuff ready for the Christmas party."

Preston nods, then reaches for my hand, intertwining our fingers. "That's okay. I'll be fine."

Madison and I exchange a look at Preston's tone. He doesn't sound like he believes himself, but we've decided not to baby him anymore. He wants to face the challenges on his own, and we'll be there to lend a hand when he needs one.

The plane lands and when we disembark, two cars are waiting for us: one for Madison and the other for me and Preston.

We hug Madison goodbye, with promises to let her know how Preston's conversation goes. Then we climb into our respective cars and Preston cuddles up to me in the back seat.

"Do you want to talk to them tonight?"

It's the twenty-third. Preston and I are supposed to go to my mom's apartment for Christmas Eve tomorrow, then the big Christmas bash at Madison's the day after.

"I guess?" His voice is smaller than it was on the plane. That doesn't bode well.

"Or you can wait until tomorrow morning. That way

you have an excuse to leave in case they want to drag things out." Apparently, this has become my strategy for giving people bad news.

"Maybe." He turns his face into my shoulder. "I don't want to put it off though. Won't that make it worse?"

I sigh. Dread rolls off him in waves so palpable, I can feel the weight of it. I want to protect him, to fight off anything that scares him and banish it forever. But that's what I would do with old Preston, and this is new Preston. "How about we play it by ear? See how you feel when we get to the house?"

"Okay."

Except, when we get to the house, the decision is made for us. The Boyers aren't home. One of the house staff greets us at the door and informs us that Mr. and Mrs. Boyer are out at a Christmas party and aren't expected home until late. Chef Nina left us some food in the oven for dinner, though, if we're happy to help ourselves.

I reassure her that we're definitely happy to fend for ourselves and she can go home to her family. She gives me a grateful smile, then disappears into the bowels of the house.

Decorations from Thanksgiving have been replaced with Christmas ones. The theme this year is white—white trees, garlands, snowflakes. The table normally in the middle of the foyer is gone and in its place is the world's largest poinsettia. It sits on the floor but the white flowers stand as high as my chest. Fake snow drifts line the walls and fill the corners. The big Christmas party might be at someone else's house, but details like that have never stopped Mrs. Boyer from making sure her house is seasonally appropriate.

I turn to Preston to find his shoulders slumped and a slightly despondent look on his face.

"Hey, hey, it's okay." I pull him into a hug. "So they're not home tonight. That just means you talk to them tomorrow morning. Then we escape to my mom's right after. It'll be great. You'll see."

Preston tries to give me a rallying smile, but I can still feel the tension in his body.

"Come on. First, let's put our bags away, then get something to eat, then find a way to distract ourselves. How does that sound?"

"That sounds good."

So we do just that. I carry our things to the blue room—my usual guest room—then we eat dinner—or at least, we try. Preston's so wound up he's practically coming out of his skin. By the time I'm putting the dishes in the dishwasher, I've made up my mind. Tonight calls for some hardcore distraction techniques.

I close the dishwasher, wipe my hands clean, and pull Preston into my arms, back to chest, just the way he likes it. I curl myself around him, cocooning him, and he wriggles backward into me.

"I want to fuck you so bad, Pres," I murmur into his ear, and a full-body shiver races through him. Oh yes, this is definitely what he needs.

"I love being inside you, being a part of you. I love the way you feel, so hot and tight, clenching around me like you never want me to leave. I love coming inside you, painting your insides, and leaving a part of me behind."

With every word I speak, Preston's knees give out a little more, until he's clinging to me. If I let go now, he'll melt into a puddle on the floor. But I'm not letting him go. I would never.

"Do you want that, Pres? Hmm? Do you want me inside you? Leaving my cum inside you?"

He nods, the movement both languid and frantic at the same time.

"Let me hear you say it, Pres."

"Yes, yes, please, Sawyer. Please, come inside me."

"So polite." I plant a kiss on his cheek. "How can I refuse?"

I spin him around, then bend my knees to get a good grip around his waist. As I hoist him up, he wraps himself around me like an octopus, and I carry him to the bedroom like that. When we get there, I toss him on the mattress, and Preston bounces with a delighted little shriek.

"Shh," I say, crawling up the bed after him. "We have to be quiet. We don't know how many staff are still around. Wouldn't want them running in, wondering why you're screaming."

The likelihood of that happening is basically zero—I'm pretty sure we're the only ones in the house by now. But Preston clamps down on his bottom lip, eyes wide and sparkling in excitement. He's so fucking adorable my heart pulses in my chest like one of those cartoon hearts, threatening to escape my body.

He scrambles up the bed, but I'm faster and I pin him down before he reaches the pillows.

"Where do you think you're going?" I tease.

Preston shakes his head. "Nowhere," he answers in a whisper.

"That's right." I rest my weight on him, trapping him. "I've got you right where I want you."

Preston gasps when I wedge a thigh between his, putting pressure on his cock and balls. I drink down the sound and it tastes just as sweet as it sounds. Like every other sound he makes when we're having sex. I love that he's so vocal, that he feels absolutely no inhibition about expressing everything he feels. For someone normally so quiet and shy, Preston is incredibly and delightfully unrestrained in bed.

We grind against each other, making out like teenagers. His hands are on my hips, gripping my ass, holding me to him as he arches against me.

"Hot," he murmurs into my mouth. "Hot."

That's the signal for clothes to start coming off. I slip my hands under Preston's shirt and push the fabric up to reveal his skinny torso. I trace each one of his ribs with my tongue, working my way from left to right, right to left, from his sternum up to his nipples.

I torture them both—tongue and teeth and lips on one while I twist the other with my fingers. When Preston starts squirming under me, I switch my mouth and fingers to torture him some more.

Preston's hands are in my hair, blunt fingernails scraping over my scalp. Shivers of pleasure travel from my head down to every corner of my body.

An endless stream of "Yes, Sawyer, yes, more, hot, so hot, more…" tumbles from his lips and it makes me suck his skin harder and pinch his nipple tighter.

"Sawyer! Sawyer!" Preston's voice is getting loud. His fingers dig into my shoulders, clawing and pushing at the same time. "It's hot. So hot. Too hot."

I prop myself on my elbows and gaze down at him. His chest is bright red from stubble burn. His nipples are swollen and bruised and almost grotesque. His chest rises and falls so fast, he could've just run a sprint.

I help Preston pull the shirt off all the way, then undo his pants and get rid of them, along with his briefs. His cock pops out, hard and leaking, standing straight in the air. It's beautiful like this, but it doesn't quite match his nipples. I'll have to do something about that.

Preston likes it when I focus on the tip of his cock, licking around the engorged mushroom head, playing with his slit. He likes it so much that he starts shouting as I work his cock with my mouth. I reach up, intending to put my hand over his mouth. But instead, my fingers land between his lips and he closes around them.

Fuck. Jesus Christ. A gush of pre-cum bursts from my cock, still trapped in my underwear. Preston bathes my fingers, winding his tongue in between and around them. He moans, then sucks on them like he's sucking my dick.

I won't last long like this. I need to get inside him.

Reluctantly, I let Preston's cock fall from my mouth and extract my fingers from his. My clothes fly in all directions —I don't care where they land. Then I scramble for the lube in my bag and race back to Preston. Back to where I belong.

PRESTON

I know what Sawyer's doing—he's trying to distract me, to calm me down. And it's working. I can't remember my parents' names, never mind string together a coherent sentence. All I can focus on is getting Sawyer's dick inside me.

I flip onto my hands and knees while Sawyer grabs the lube, but when he comes back, he flips me over again.

"I want to watch your face as I open you up," he explains at my questioning look.

He takes my knees, pushing them up toward my face. "Grab those."

I suck in a gasp as a shiver of perverse pleasure ripples through me. My feet are sticking up in the air, my knees are spread wide. My buttocks are lifted off the bed, ass, balls, and dick on full display. Sawyer kneels in front of me, his hand pets the back of my thigh, and his eyes devour me. He's eating me up, consuming me.

"You're so gorgeous, Preston," he says in a hushed

voice. I don't need to understand social cues to hear the awe and reverence in his tone. Awe and reverence for me —me.

A few months ago, I wouldn't have believed it. I would've written it off as some weird unspoken communication thing I didn't understand. There are still moments when I have my doubts, but over the past weeks and months, Sawyer's been training me to accept the truth: he loves me, all of me, unconditionally. And I've been doing my best to be worthy of that love.

Even so, Sawyer's the truly gorgeous one. Rounded pectorals that make the perfect pillows for my head. Neatly stacked abdominal muscles that are visible even when he's relaxed. Those two deep lines at his hips that form an enticing V. Wide shoulders. Narrow hips. There isn't a single thing about him I would change.

A sound escapes my throat, a mix between a moan, a whimper, and a choke. I don't know what it means or what message I'm trying to convey. I just... want. Need. The urge is this sentient thing, it lives inside me and yet it has a mind of its own. It knows things I don't know. It understands things I don't understand.

The urge grows underneath my sternum, expanding through my chest and up toward my throat. It gets so big I can't contain it and it comes out as that indecipherable sound.

But Sawyer seems to understand exactly what it means. He squirts a generous amount of lube onto his fingers, then rubs them together to heat up the viscous fluid. There's no shock of cold when he touches my hole, just lovely, soothing warmth.

With a look of utter concentration, Sawyer draws circles around my hole before pushing one digit inside. I push out the way he's taught me and his finger sinks in. He doesn't stop until his knuckles bump up against my flesh and another one of those sounds escapes from me again.

Sawyer's gaze locks with mine, and I'm enraptured by it. The heat. The desire. The unwavering focus, trained exclusively on me. That urge inside me grows under his scrutiny, compressing my lungs, blocking my airway. My heart thuds heavily against it, the reverberations echoing through my body.

My fingers dig into the backs of my knees, keeping myself open and exposed to him. I'm helpless, defenseless, completely at his mercy, and I wouldn't want it any other way.

Sawyer pushes another finger into me. He's so gentle there's no burn, no pain whatsoever. Just a pleasant fullness that I love. I adore having him inside me. His tongue, his dick, his fingers. It doesn't matter what. Just the knowledge that a piece of him is in my body sends a thrill to the very core of my being. I want to keep him there always and forever. I want to carry a piece of him with me wherever I go.

Sawyer penetrates me with his fingers, his eyes flicking from my face to my ass and back again like he can't decide what he wants to watch more. He twists his fingers around, rotates, and scissors them. He finds my prostate and gives it a light massage. Pleasure shoots through me, waves of it that set fire to my insides. I can feel the heat rising from my skin, making the air around us thick and heavy.

"Sawyer," I manage to get out between my unintelligible grunts and groans. "Please."

His eyes swirl blue and green as he takes a shuddering breath. With his fingers still inside me, he slicks up his erection.

"Please, Sawyer, please."

He pulls his fingers from me and immediately replaces them with his dick. The rounded head pushes against my hole. I bear down and he slides in, steady and unrelenting, until he's fully sheathed inside my body.

"Yes, yes, yes." He fits me so well and fills me so perfectly. I clench around him, loving how deep he goes, how he stretches me.

Sawyer takes my nipples between his fingers, pulling, pinching, twisting, rubbing. They're already so tender from before, and now, as he works them over, the pleasure tips closer to pain.

But my dick doesn't seem to mind. It pulses and releases pre-cum with every pull, pinch, twist, and rub. Then Sawyer starts to move, thrusting into my ass while turning the dials on my nipples. I'm still clutching the backs of my knees, holding myself open for the dual assault on my body.

Ass to nipples. Nipples to ass. Sawyer handles me like I'm a piece of gym equipment that needs to be aligned just right. And all I can do is lay there and take it, absorb the sensations, suffer the onslaught.

"Sawyer," I sob. "Sawyer, please!"

"Shh," he admonishes. "Don't make me gag you."

I gasp at the suggestion, back arching, ass clamping down hard around him.

Sawyer cocks an eyebrow. "Or maybe you want me to gag you? Hmm? Would you like that, Pres?"

I don't know. I've never been gagged. It's not something I've ever had to consider and I have no clue whether I'll like it. But the way Sawyer says it, so casually, like it's something he does every day… I want it. I want to try it at least. And yet, all that comes out of my mouth is one of those animalistic sounds.

"Fuck, Preston." Sawyer's wild gaze darts around us and lands on my underwear still tucked into my pajama pants. He pulls it free and balls it up in his fist. "Open up."

I tentatively open my mouth and Sawyer gently pushes my own underwear past my lips. I cry out at the unfamiliar sensation of fabric on my tongue, between my teeth. I can smell the scent of my own pre-cum, the musky aroma of my own arousal. There isn't so much fabric that my jaw is uncomfortably wide, but there's absolutely no denying I'm properly gagged. My cry is muffled.

I cry out again, louder this time—still muffled.

"That's it, babe. Let it all out. Be as loud as you want." Sawyer's fingers go back to my nipples and when he touches them this time, I scream. "Fuck." He pulls back and slams into me. "You look so fucking hot, Pres. You have no idea. Fuck."

I can barely hear what he's saying. My brain is too preoccupied with other inputs—the pounding against my glutes, the pain at my nipples, my own voice, directed back at me through the underwear gag.

Sawyer pinches lines up and down my torso, then rakes his nails over the tortured flesh. Once my front is completely red from his attention, he moves to the backs of my thighs, my calves, every inch of me he can reach. And all the while, his hips set a steady pace, and his dick pistons in and out of my hole.

"Fuck, Preston, fuck, I'm so close." Sawyer grabs my ankles and pulls them toward him. My knees slip out of my grasp as he straightens my legs and drapes them up his body. My calves are on his shoulders and Sawyer turns to sink his teeth into one.

I scream again, scrabbling for something to hold on to, something to anchor me. Above my head, I latch onto the wooden headboard and I hang on for dear life.

"Yes, that's it. Keep your hands there. God, you're so fucking gorgeous." Sawyer bites my other calf, hard enough that he leaves marks. He grabs the tops of my thighs, pulling me into the thrust of his hips.

"Are you close, babe? Are you going to come? Because I'm going to come. I'm going to flood you with my cum. You like that, don't you? When your hole is all sloppy and wet with my cum."

I cry into my gag and nod frantically. I do love it when Sawyer comes deep inside my ass. I love trying to keep his cum inside me as long as I can. I love the slick, slimy feeling as it leaks out of me.

"You going to come for me, babe? Can you come hands-free?"

We both turn our gaze to my erection, so engorged with blood the head is angry and red. My belly button is full of pre-cum and even more has trailed down my sides, wetting the sheets under me.

"Fuck, you look like you're about to burst."

I feel like it too. My orgasm hovers just outside my reach. I can brush it with my fingertips, but I can't quite grasp it. I sob desperately, thrashing around as I strain for it.

"Need a little help?" Sawyer bites my calves again. Left and right, up to my ankles, down toward my knees.

I nod, pleading with my eyes. I want to come, so badly. I want Sawyer to make me come. I want to give him my orgasm. I want every orgasm to be his.

"I've got you, babe. I'll help you come. I've always got you, babe. Always." He reaches between my legs but completely bypasses my dick and balls. Instead, he goes for my perineum. He pinches the flesh, twists it, and presses down.

Sharp pain shoots straight to my prostate and quickly metamorphosizes into exploding pleasure. White. Blinding. Fire. Muscles so taut they spasm. Lungs burning. Heart stuttering to a stop. Static in my ears.

It goes on and on, pulse after pulse, radiating from my prostate, rupturing every cell, frying every nerve ending. Tears pour from my eyes, snot from my nose.

It only stops when Sawyer's hips falter and lava pours into me. It's hot, scorching—the perfect antidote to the painful pleasure wracking my body.

I'm barely conscious when Sawyer lowers my legs. I instinctively wrap them around his waist, locking him into place. I don't want him pulling out yet. I want to keep him inside me.

My hands are stiff when I force them to release the headboard and my shoulders ache when I reach for Sawyer. He lowers himself onto me, his weight comforting and familiar.

He tugs the underwear from my mouth and I wiggle my jaw side-to-side.

"Sore?" He rubs gently at the joints.

I shake my head and hum happily.

Sawyer nuzzles behind my ear, then buries his face into the crook of my neck. His breathing slows gradually, hot breaths over my skin.

I never knew it was possible to have something like this. That two people could be so close and feel so right together. Like we were made for each other. Like we were meant to be.

Whatever happens tomorrow with my parents, no matter how they react. I'll always have Sawyer, and he'll always be more than enough.

SAWYER

The next morning, I'm trying to coax some food into Preston when Mrs. Boyer waltzes into the dining room. She pauses to adjust the placement of a silver ornament on the white Christmas tree in the corner, then straightens one of the flower arrangements on the dining table before turning to us.

"Preston, so sorry we weren't here to welcome you when you arrived yesterday." She leans into him for air kisses on each cheek. "I trust you had a good flight?"

"Yes, Mom. It was fine."

"Good morning, Mrs. Boyer." I stand from my seat to let her give me an elbow-clasping hug and more air kisses. "How was the Christmas party you and Mr. Boyer went to last night?"

Mrs. Boyer waves her hand dismissively. "Oh, it was some half-baked thing. A waste of our time really, but Jim needed to be there for business. Tomorrow's soiree, now that will be the real party."

One of the house staff brings in a plate of breakfast and a cup of coffee for Mrs. Boyer as she takes her usual seat at one end of the table.

"Now, boys, what are your plans for the day?" she asks, taking a sip of her coffee. Her words and tone are friendly and cheerful, but something about her demeanor makes it sound flat.

I don't answer right away, giving Preston room to take the lead, but when he shrinks in on himself, I jump in. "We're going to my mom's place a bit later. She's working tomorrow, so today's the only time we have to spend with her."

"We?" Mrs. Boyer looks from me to Preston with a sharpness in her gaze.

"Uh, yes," I say when Preston doesn't respond. "Mom wanted me to bring Preston this year."

"I see."

And I wonder what exactly she sees. As far as I know, Mr. and Mrs. Boyer don't know about me and Preston yet. Preston barely talks to them, and I certainly haven't said anything. There's no way she could know… could she?

Under the table, I nudge Preston's knee, urging him to take control of the conversation. He's spent the last several weeks gearing up for this moment, and now it's finally here. His hand lands on my thigh, and I grip it, sending as much strength and courage as I can through the connection.

Preston tries to speak, but the only sound that comes out is a squeak. Mrs. Boyer cocks an eyebrow at him.

"Yes, Preston? Did you want to say something?"

Preston swallows and sucks in a deep breath. "I need to talk to you and Dad."

Yes! That's it, babe!

Mrs. Boyer narrows her eyes. "About what?"

"Uh, about…" He clears his throat, pulls himself up to his full height, and squeezes my hand so hard he might break some fingers. "About my future." It doesn't come out quite as solid as he might have liked, but it's clear and he's looking Mrs. Boyer directly in the eyes.

She sets down her coffee mug and folds her hands in her lap. "I see."

And this time I know she definitely does.

"When would you like to speak with us?" she asks, her voice now decidedly frosty.

"N-now?" Preston shrinks back a fraction.

Mrs. Boyer turns her icy gaze to me. "And would you like to speak with Mr. Boyer and myself as well?"

"Oh, no—" I start to say. This is Preston's show and besides, I don't think Mr. and Mrs. Boyer would appreciate me barging in on what they would surely consider a private family matter.

But Preston cuts me off with a, "Yes, he does. We both do."

Oh, shit. I hadn't realized Preston wanted me in the room with him. I assumed I'd be waiting somewhere, ready to comfort him when he finished. But the way he's gripping my hand now, sandwiched between both of his, the jaws of life couldn't pry him away from me.

Mrs. Boyer's eyes are so narrow, they're practically slits. Her lips are tightly pursed and I'm sure if she exhales, the entire room will freeze.

"In that case, I'll go see if your father is available." She pushes away from the table and stands with so much grace and elegance I want to bow as she floats past. She's halfway out the door when she pauses and calls over her shoulder. "Come along, boys."

Preston and I scramble after her, our chairs scraping loudly against the floor. Preston almost trips over his feet but manages to stay upright only because he's still clutching my hand.

We follow Mrs. Boyer down the hall toward Mr. Boyer's office like two schoolboys being sent to the headmaster's office. I feel like one too, heart racing and palms clammy, certain I'm going to be expelled.

The door to Mr. Boyer's office stands open and Mrs. Boyer gives it a perfunctory knock.

"What is it? I'm busy," comes the growled answer from inside.

"Jim, dear, your son would like a moment of your time."

"Preston?" Mr. Boyer says, like he's not sure who his son is. "What does he want?"

Mrs. Boyer steps to the side and ushers us in.

Mr. Boyer's office looks like a cross between an old school library and some sort of homage to himself. One wall is covered from floor to ceiling with books. Another holds awards, trophies, and pictures of Mr. Boyer posing with important people. He's sitting in a leather-bound executive office chair, behind an absolute monstrosity of a desk. He couldn't look more intimidating if he tried.

Preston shrinks into me, but I nudge him forward. This is it. This is his moment to shine. He can't back out now.

"Preston would like to speak with us about his future."

Mr. Boyer scowls. "His future? What is there to talk about?"

Mrs. Boyer turns to Preston with raised eyebrows, but Preston seems to have lost his voice.

"Why don't we all take a seat?" Mrs. Boyer gestures to the sitting area surrounding a large wood-burning fireplace. The dark brown leather couch, loveseat, and armchairs are all plush and oversized.

"Really, Yvette, I don't have time for this." Mr. Boyer makes to turn back to his work, but Mrs. Boyer stops him with a single word.

"Jim."

Jesus Christ. If Mrs. Boyer said my name like that, I might shrivel up and die. As it is, Mr. Boyer looks annoyed, but he obediently stands and comes around the side of his desk.

"Please, let's all sit." Mrs. Boyer points me and Preston to the loveseat, while she arranges herself and her husband in the armchairs across from us.

A low wooden coffee table sits in between, and for some reason I feel better with it there. Not that things will turn physical—god, I hope not—but separation is good, some distance is good.

"Alright, let's get this over with. Whatever it is, just spit it out." Mr. Boyer sprawls in his armchair and Mrs. Boyer sits primly in hers.

Preston and I are huddled together on the loveseat. We couldn't get any closer without him climbing into my lap. He's still holding my hand like I'm the single lifeline keeping him from drowning.

Mrs. Boyer's noticed, of course, and her eyes are zeroed in on our hands.

"Well?" Mr. Boyer calls out when no one speaks.

I try to poke Preston with my elbow, but he doesn't react.

Mrs. Boyer seems to take pity on him, thank god. "Why don't you start with that?" She nods to our hands.

Preston looks down like he hadn't realized he was clutching me so tightly. Then he glances up at me, fear shining from his eyes, pouring off him in waves. I could do this for him, just say it and get it out there. Preston and I are a couple. We love each other and we're going to spend the rest of our lives together.

But I can't do that. I can't take this opportunity away from Preston. He's been so intent on having this conversation with his parents it wouldn't be right for me to barge in and save the day. I've always wanted to take care of him, to protect him, and right now, the best way for me to do that is to let him fight for himself.

I nod and whisper, "You can do it," not caring if his parents can hear me.

"I love you," Preston blurts out. Which isn't exactly how I thought he'd broach the subject, but it seems to do that trick.

"What?" Mr. Boyer's expression is mostly confused but I think I detect a hint of disgust.

"I love him." Preston turns to his parents now. "I love Sawyer—romantically. I love him, and—and we have sex—"

"Oh god," I mutter, squeezing my eyes shut.

"He's my boyfriend, and we're together. A couple."

Mrs. Boyer hasn't moved an inch, not a single muscle twitch, and I can't tell whether that's because she already knew, or if we've shocked her into paralysis.

Mr. Boyer, though, has no trouble expressing himself.

"What?" He sits forward, one hand braced against the arm of the chair like he might launch himself at us. A flush inches rapidly up his neck, making his skin all mottled and splotchy. "Are you fucking with us? You and *him*?"

I recoil at the way he says "him" like I'm the most revolting thing in the world.

"Jim."

"No, Yvette, Preston needs to explain himself. I get that you two are…" He waves vaguely at us. "… whatever. But he doesn't bring anything to the table. He's just some college drop-out."

"I believe Sawyer is still enrolled in college," Mrs. Boyer corrects him, but he's beyond stopping at this point.

"Whatever. Doesn't matter. What matters is he's a nobody, a nothing. His name doesn't open any doors. He barely has a family. What kind of advantage would he bring to the relationship?"

Every word Mr. Boyer utters feels like a sword straight through my gut. So it isn't the gay thing he objects to. He couldn't care less that I have a dick. He's more concerned about what kind of political, social or business value I can lend to the Boyer family. Which is nothing—he's right.

I was a scholarship kid at the prestigious high school, raised by a single mom. I man the front desk at a gym and I don't even have an undergraduate degree. I don't know any influential people. I don't have connections in high places. I'm a nobody.

"Listen, you want to have a side piece, fine. Go ahead. But you need to have someone reasonable in public. Someone who you won't be ashamed to stand next to."

"No!" Preston roars as he jumps to his feet, surprising everyone in the room, including him. But he's standing now, and he's got no intention of sitting back down. He stomps his foot and shouts again, "No!"

Mrs. Boyer's eyes are wide with shock. Mr. Boyer flies back into his chair. I feel like I'm bleeding out on the couch.

"You're wrong. Sawyer's not nothing. He's everything!"

PRESTON

"You're wrong! Sawyer's not nothing! He's everything!" Words are coming out of my mouth, but the voice doesn't sound like my own. It sounds commanding, intimidating, fierce. It sounds like Dad's voice—but it's mine.

Dad has said a lot of shitty things about me over the years, about my decision to go into academia, about my inability to live up to his expectations and be the son he's always wanted. It hurts, but I bear it because it's easier to let it wash over me than try to confront him. This time, though, he's gone too far and I can't let it go unchallenged. I won't let him say all those awful things about Sawyer. I won't.

"Sawyer's kind and thoughtful. He's smart and strong and funny. He's responsible and compassionate and never complains. He's the best person I know."

Mom's eyes are wide with shock and Dad's jaw is practically on the floor. I'm just as surprised, but for the first time in my life, I don't have to struggle for words. They flow out of me like new neuropathways have suddenly flickered to life in my brain.

"He takes care of me. He makes sure I don't work too hard. He protects me and never lets me down. Everyone loves him and wants to be friends with him, and he's fucking hot!"

Dad's jaw snaps shut as he grows red with anger. Mom closes her eyes like she's trying to calm herself.

"He's amazing and I'm not ashamed of him. I love him. I'm going to stand next to him everywhere, every day, for the rest of my life, whether you like it or not!" I stop long enough to suck in more oxygen. "And not only that! I'm not working for you. Not when I graduate. Not ever. I'm staying in academia. I'm going to be a professor, and you can't stop me."

Dad jumps to his feet to stare me down, his face so red it might explode. For a split second, I cower, a trained response to his temper. But then I steel myself and stare back at him. He tried to attack Sawyer's character. He tried to denigrate him. I won't sit by and let him get away with it. I take a step forward, putting myself in front of Sawyer.

"No, you are not. You are my son and if I say you're working for me, then you're going to damn well work for me. My father built this company out of nothing and he passed it on to me with very specific instructions. It is your duty as a Boyer to take over when I step down and that is non-negotiable."

"Then I won't be a Boyer anymore!" I have no idea where that comes from, but once it leaves my tongue, I know it's the best idea I've ever had. "I'll be a Paige!"

Dad really looks like he's going to have an aneurysm, but I can't bring myself to care.

"I don't need your name. I don't need your money. I have a trust fund. I can take care of myself."

Mom rises slowly to her feet and places a hand on Dad's arm.

"I think we've had enough yelling for one morning," she says, voice calm and soothing. "Preston, perhaps you and Sawyer can go cool off somewhere else."

When she looks at me, there's something surprisingly soft in her eyes. Mom is so perceptive, so shrewd. She can dissect me with nothing more than a single glance, crack open my skull and analyze every awkward, uncomfortable part of me. She always sees more than I want to reveal, but I've never felt truly seen by her until this moment.

She gives me a minuscule nod that seems to speak volumes. I think she understands. I think she's trying to be reassuring.

Sawyer tugs on my hand and I follow him out of Dad's office. Mom closes the door behind us. We don't stop until we're up in Sawyer's bedroom again, and he collapses into the armchair by the window. He hunches forward, shoulders slumped, head bowed. He looks so defeated, so devastated.

No, that's not okay. Sawyer's not supposed to be crushed. He's supposed to be resilient and confident and self-assured. I drop to my knees in front of him.

"Don't listen to him," I say, pressing my forehead against his. "Dad doesn't know what he's talking about. And besides, I don't care about any of that. I only care about you."

Sawyer chuckles softly, but it sounds a little pained. "I know you don't care about that stuff, Pres. But it's still hard to hear it laid out so plainly."

"Well, Dad can… go fuck himself."

This gets a genuine chuckle from Sawyer. He pulls back to look at me. He's got such beautiful eyes. Blue and green swirls that dance in the mid-morning sun streaming through the window.

"I love you, Pres."

"I love you too, Sawyer."

"You weren't serious about changing your name, were you?" He quirks his lips at the suggestion.

I shrug as I turn the idea around in my mind. "I kind of like the sound of Preston Paige. The alliteration is nice."

Sawyer's teasing smile dims and he's silent for long enough that I second-guess myself.

"Unless you don't like it. I just spat out the idea without really thinking. I don't actually have to change my name."

Sawyer smiles again and this time I feel the love shining through his eyes just as potently as I feel the sun on my skin.

"I like the sound of Preston Paige too. Maybe we can come back to it at some point." He straightens then, taking a deep breath. "How about we go to my mom's? I think we'll both be more comfortable there."

Mom's in the foyer when Sawyer and I get downstairs with our bags. "Going to your mother's?"

"Yes, she's expecting us," Sawyer says.

"I understand." The smile Mom flashes at us is filled with resignation and sadness. "I'm sorry things unfolded the way they did. Your father… well, in the long run, I think this was for the best."

Mom pulls me into a hug. Not the ones she usually

gives where she holds my elbows and gives me air kisses. This one is a real hug with full-body contact.

"Give him time, Preston. He'll come around."

And suddenly my eyes are prickling with tears.

Mom steps back, her eyes also not entirely dry. "In case I don't see you, have a wonderful Christmas." She picks up a bag I hadn't noticed sitting next to the door. "For you both, and your mother, Sawyer." Then she leaves us to see ourselves out.

"That was… unexpected," Sawyer says when she's out of earshot. "I think she's on our side."

"Yeah, I think she might be too."

———

I've never been to Mrs. Paige's apartment before. She's always come to my parents' house or visited Sawyer in New York. But after the confrontation with Dad, I have a feeling I'm going to love her place.

The snow starts falling during the drive and by the time we arrive, there's already some decent accumulation on the ground.

"The snow will be a good excuse to stay here for the night," Sawyer says as he leads me from the car to the building. "Mom's got a pull-out couch."

Mrs. Paige flings open her door before we even manage to knock. "Merry Christmas, sweetheart!" She gives Sawyer a bone-crushing hug before turning to give me one as well. "And merry Christmas to you too, Preston!"

"Merry Christmas, Mrs. Paige."

She ushers us into her cozy one-bedroom apartment

with the same type of enthusiasm I'm used to from Sawyer.

"Okay, you two get comfortable. I'm making hot cocoa for us." She disappears into the little alcove kitchen and Sawyer leads me farther inside.

The place is small with a single space for living and dining. Windows line the far wall, with a door leading out to a balcony. Two more doors are tucked into a mini-hallway—one stands open, revealing a bathroom, so the other must be Mrs. Paige's bedroom. The walls are lined with photos, the furniture is well-loved, and there's a warmth that makes me feel like I'm walking into a hug.

Beside the window is a large fake tree, already strung with lights, and a few wrapped presents sitting underneath. Sawyer crouches down, unzipping the bag with the presents we brought from New York. He adds them to the pile, along with the random ones Mom unexpectedly handed to us on our way out.

"Do you think she'll like what I got her?" I ask in a whisper. I'm terrible at picking out gifts and Madison usually takes care of it for me. But this time, I wanted to choose something myself for Mrs. Paige.

Sawyer chuckles. "For the millionth time, yes. She'll love it. You probably got her too much, to be honest. You're going to make me look bad."

"They can be from the both of us."

Sawyer pauses, turning to look up at me from the floor. The love shining from his eyes makes the love in my heart swell in response. I'm still jittery from the confrontation with Dad, but as Sawyer takes my hand to plant a kiss on my palm, much of the tension melts away. I'm safe here. I'm loved here. This is the only place I want to be.

"Hot cocoa!" Mrs. Paige announces as she brings in a tray with three giant mugs on it. There's also a plate with several different kinds of cookies.

"Thanks, Mom." Sawyer stands and takes one of the mugs, handing it to me before grabbing a second one for himself.

I wrap my fingers around the warm ceramic and bring it to my nose. It smells chocolatey and sweet, the top covered in a layer of mini marshmallows.

A picture on the wall catches my attention and I wander over to take a closer look. It's an old photograph of a young Mrs. Paige and a man who bears a striking resemblance to Sawyer. In her arms, she's holding a baby, bundled up in blankets.

"That's the day we brought Sawyer home from the hospital," Mrs. Paige says quietly.

"And that's Mr. Paige?" Sawyer's dad died when he was still a baby and he doesn't really remember him. But it looks like Mrs. Paige has tried to keep his memory alive.

"It is. Sawyer's a spitting image, isn't he?"

I nod in agreement, then drift to the adjacent photo. This is one of Sawyer as a kid, on a tricycle, ribbons streaming from the ends of the handlebars.

"Oh god, please don't look at those." Sawyer groans from behind me.

"Do you want me to pull out the photo albums instead?" Mrs. Paige asks.

"No! No, that's okay. The wall pictures are more than enough."

"That's what I thought."

A smile tugs at my lips at their easy exchange. I've always enjoyed listening to Sawyer talk with his mom, and the teasing and banter that only comes with familiarity. I've never had anything close to that with my parents. I've only had tense, awkward exchanges and then... this morning.

There are more pictures of Sawyer as a child. He's playing a sport in most of them—soccer, basketball, baseball. Then him in his rugby uniform from Westbourne. He's got his arm around Mrs. Paige. It must be from one of the tournaments they won because he's got a medal around his neck.

Then I glance at the next picture and gasp. Sawyer's still in his rugby clothes, but this time he's got his arm around me. I'm tucked into his side, with my face upturned to admire him. He's returning look is doting and we're both sporting wide grins.

This must have been taken in high school. But the way we're looking at each other... there's so much love. The camera has captured all of it. It's so obvious, even to me. How did it take us more than a decade to realize what was between us?

Big, strong hands settle on my hips and I lean back against Sawyer's broad chest. He kisses my temple.

"I forgot about that picture," he says.

"I don't remember it being taken."

"We look good in it."

I nod.

After a moment, Sawyer reaches up and takes the picture off the wall.

"What are you doing?" I ask, alarmed at him so casually removing the photo.

"I'm stealing it from Mom." He shrugs and goes to stash the picture, frame and all, into his bag.

"Are we allowed?" I glance over my shoulder, but Mrs. Paige isn't in the room with us.

Sawyer snorts. "Why wouldn't we be allowed? It's a picture of us."

"But what about?" I wave at the empty spot on the wall.

"She'll fill it with something else."

"Fill what with something else?" Mrs. Paige comes back, carrying a large plastic container. She sets the container down on the floor and plants her hands on her hips.

"I'm stealing a picture of me and Preston." Sawyer pulls the photo out to show her.

Mrs. Paige puts both hands over her heart. "I love that photo. And yes, you guys should definitely have it. It's so lovely."

"Thank you, Mrs. Paige."

"You're very welcome, dear." She claps and rubs her hands together. "Ready to decorate the tree?"

She pops the lid off the container to reveal brightly colored ornaments in all shapes and sizes.

"Yes!" Sawyer jumps to his feet and rushes over. "Come here, Pres. You're going to love this."

He picks up a square frame made of popsicle sticks and decorated with little foam snowflakes. In the middle of the frame is a child's scrawl that reads, "Merry Christmas!"

"I made this when I was, what… five? Six?" Sawyer asks his mom.

"Something like that."

Sawyer holds it up for me to take. "Go on, you can put the first ornament on the tree."

"Are you sure?" I stare at the square spinning on the string loop.

Sawyer gives me a lopsided smile. "How about we do it together, then?" he offers instead.

We turn to the tree and I gingerly take hold of the string. Together, we loop it over a prickly branch. It's so simple, putting an old ornament on a tree with Sawyer. There's no real meaning behind it. It's not a tradition or ceremony in any way. And yet, it's special.

"I love you," I say, leaning into him.

He wraps his arms around me. "I love you too."

SAWYER

Mom's apartment feels like a spa or a church or something equally safe and soothing compared to the Boyers' house. It's a fraction of the size, decades older, and yet I would rather spend an evening here any day of the week.

I like seeing Preston here too. He's relaxed, at ease. None of that frenetic tension he always gets at his parents' place. Preston should always be in spaces like this—homey, comfortable, warm.

The box Mom brought out contains our holiday decorations. All the ornaments I made as a kid, all the cheesy ones we've collected over the years, and the antique star Mom says has been in Dad's family for generations.

I pull up my Christmas playlist on my phone and we listen to Mariah Carey tell us what she wants for Christmas while transferring each ornament from the box to the tree.

Mom and I let Preston do most of the hanging since

he's never really had the chance to do anything like this before. The trees at his parents' house are professionally decorated with brand-new crystal ornaments each year.

He takes the job very seriously, considering the placement of each one like he's running an algorithm in that big, beautiful brain of his. This one is round, so it can't go next to that other round one. This one is blue, so it can't be next to that other blue one. The whole process is a lot slower than what Mom and I usually manage, but I love it. I love watching Preston nibble on his lip as he finds the perfect branch for each ornament.

Mom eventually leaves us to it while she finishes cooking dinner. When the last ornament has been placed, I drag Preston to the couch for cuddles. He snuggles in beside me as I turn on the TV, searching for a holiday movie to play in the background.

"Having fun?" I ask, leaning my head against his.

He nods. "So much better than my parents' house."

"Yeah," I agree with a touch of regret. Not that I regret Preston finally standing up to his dad. But I wish it hadn't turned quite so ugly. There was a moment there when I really thought punches would start flying.

"Do you think your mom's right?" I ask. "That your dad will come around?"

Preston shrugs. "I wouldn't have thought so, but… Your mom told me something at Thanksgiving. She said my parents just want me to be happy. I hope she's right."

I chuckle. "If Mom said it, it's most likely right. She's rarely wrong."

"Correction: I'm never wrong," Mom says, coming out of the kitchen. "Dinner's ready. Come help set the table, Sawyer."

Dinner at Mom's is nowhere near as fancy as dinner at the Boyers'. I move the poinsettia to the corner of the table so there's room for the ham she's roasted. Plus creamy mashed sweet potatoes, crispy green beans, and crunchy asparagus. She hands me the pack of Christmas-themed paper napkins I'm pretty sure we've had since I was in high school.

When we sit down, Mom holds her hands out to both of us. Preston shoots me an uncertain look and I give him a reassuring nod as I take Mom's hand.

"We're not a religious household or anything, but on days like today, there's something special about stopping to acknowledge and give thanks for the things we have." Mom looks at Preston. "I'm really glad you're here with us, sweetheart."

Preston blinks at the endearment.

"I've watched you and Sawyer grow up together, turning into the men you are today. In some ways, you're like a second son to me." She rolls her eyes when I make a choking sound. "Not in a gross way, obviously. I want you to know, Preston, that you're always welcome here. My apartment might be modest, but you can consider it your home."

Preston's eyes are a little glassy with unshed tears. My own throat gets tight with emotion. I haven't told Mom about the whole thing with Preston's parents, but her mother's intuition seems to have picked up that something happened.

"Okay, enough of this sentimental stuff." I cut the ham and make sure Preston gets a nice thick slice. Then I pile on the sweet potatoes, green beans, and asparagus.

Preston looks at the small spread like it's the most

decadent meal he's ever laid eyes on. We tear through Mom's cooking, which is just as good as—if not better than—any of the five-star Michelin chef stuff that Preston's parents get catered at their events. Not that I'm biased or anything.

After dinner, Mom brings out the pecan pie she left warming in the oven, and by the time we're done, I'm about to keel over from my food coma. Preston actually winces in discomfort as he leans back and tugs at the waistband of his pants, trying to give his stomach extra room to expand.

Mom laughs at us as she sips her coffee.

"How can you even drink that?" I groan. "I think my stomach will burst if I swallow my spit."

She shakes her head at me. "You need to know when to stop."

I drop my head back and do my best imitation of a dying goose. Preston shifts, making a pained noise.

"Preston, why don't you change into something more comfortable?" Mom suggests.

Preston goes to change while I help Mom clear the table and pack up the food in containers.

"How are things with Preston's parents?" Mom asks quietly as we move around the tiny kitchen together.

I chuckle softly. "How did you know?"

She scoffs. "Give me a little more credit than that. I've watched you boys grow up. I know."

I take a second to glance toward the bathroom where the fan is running loud enough to drown out our conversation. "Well, there's a reason we brought all our things with us."

Mom shakes her head and sighs. "The Boyers are stubborn and entitled, but they're still parents. I think they'll come around." She pops a lid onto a container of green beans. "I'm just glad you and Preston have finally gotten yourselves sorted out."

The smile that grows on my lips comes from the very depths of my soul. "Me too."

Once the food is put away and we've all changed into our pajamas—with Preston wearing one of my old t-shirts —the three of us gather around the tree.

"Merry Christmas, boys," Mom says as she hands each of us a present.

I know what they are the moment I hold mine in my hand. It's soft underneath the wrapping paper and just the right size and shape too. I rip into it, revealing a yellow and orange hand-knit scarf. She makes me one every couple years, just as the one before starts growing tattered.

I wrap it around my neck and strike a pose. "How do I look?" I ask.

Mom rolls her eyes and Preston snickers under his breath.

I poke at his present. "Go on, open it."

He's a lot more meticulous than I am, carefully peeling back the tape like this is the most precious gift he's ever received. He gasps as he pulls out a matching scarf, except his is in varying shades of blue.

"It's just like yours," Preston exclaims, and I help him drape it around his shoulders.

I don't know how Mom did it, but she's managed to capture the blue of Preston's eyes perfectly in the vibrant colors of the scarf. They make Preston's eyes brighter, almost glowing in the lights of the Christmas tree.

"How do I look?" he asks, cheeks turning slightly pink as he tries to copy my pose.

"Breathtaking," I whisper, and his cheeks grow a little rosier.

"Thank you, Mrs. Paige," Preston says as he buries his fingers into the soft ends of the scarf.

"Yeah, thanks, Mom." I get up to give her a hug and a kiss on the cheek.

Preston's ready with her gifts in hand when I sit back down.

"Mine first," I say, taking the package from Preston and passing it to Mom. "I don't want Preston to upstage me."

Mom snorts and shoots me a teasing smile. "Too late."

"Hey!" I protest with a laugh.

She quickly opens the Alexa I got her and stares dumbfoundedly at it. "What is it?"

"It's a smart speaker!" I throw my hands in the air as Preston giggles next to me. "You can tell it to do things, like play music or podcasts or audiobooks. You said you like listening to audiobooks now, right?"

"Yeah, I just do that on my phone. Why do I need this?"

I give her an exaggerated eye roll. "Because you do. Trust me." I make a gimme motion with my hands. "I'll help you set it up before we leave."

Mom hands it over with a shrug.

When Preston holds up his gift, though, she takes the slim envelope with something close to reverence.

"Thank you, Preston." She holds it close to her chest.

"You don't even know what it is yet," I harrumph, crossing my arms.

"Doesn't matter. I can tell I'm going to like it." She

breaks the seal on the back of the envelope and pulls out two cards. One is a gift certificate for a fancy spa Madison recommended—a one-day pass, complete with a massage, mani-pedi, and facial. The other is an all-expenses paid trip to Paris.

Mom gasps, hand over her mouth, as she reads the cards. "Oh, Preston!" she says with tears in her eyes. "This is so lovely! Thank you so much!"

Despite my feigned grumpiness, I'm thrilled Mom likes Preston's gift. She deserves to be pampered and catered to.

"Merry Christmas, Mrs. Paige," Preston says right before Mom descends on him with a bone-crushing hug. He gives me a startled look from over her shoulder, but I just grin as he gets the full Mom treatment—he deserves that too.

Later, after we've pulled the sofa out into a double bed and Mom has bid us goodnight, Preston and I crawl in under the covers. The bed is a lot smaller than our king-sized one at home, but we're used to sleeping on top of each other. I tug Preston to me so I can spoon him from behind. He wiggles his ass into my crotch and I growl in his ear.

"Pres, we're in my mom's living room."

"I know," he says and I can hear the laughter in his voice. "I just like how it feels."

"What? My hard dick nestled against your ass?"

He sighs like I'm whispering sweet nothings to him. "It's nice."

I cant my hips to press myself a little more snugly into him. "It is nice," I agree.

"I like spending Christmas with your mom."

I kiss the beauty mark behind his ear. "I'm glad you had a good time."

"I always have a good time when I'm with you." His voice grows a little slurred with sleep.

"I love you, Preston," I murmur, nose buried in his hair.

"I love you too, Sawyer."

PRESTON

We wake up to a winter wonderland. The streets, rooftops, and trees are blanketed with sparkling white snow and the sun is out in full force, lighting everything up.

"It'll take a while for the streets to get cleared," Sawyer says as he surveys the snow from the window.

"Do we have to go?" I ask, feeling pouty.

"Madison will kill us if we don't show up."

"But my parents will be there," I object, now actually pouting.

"I know, babe, but it's a big party. We'll find a way to avoid them."

Mrs. Paige makes us pancakes for breakfast, then we get ready to leave. I don't want to go. I don't want to leave the safety and warmth of Mrs. Paige's apartment. I want to hold onto that joyful, lighthearted feeling, and pretend the whole situation with my dad doesn't exist. I want to live in this little bubble with Sawyer forever.

Since it's nearly noon by the time we leave Mrs.

Paige's, we go straight to Madison's parents' house. The mansion is already full of guests when we arrive, with no one manning the door to greet newcomers. Sawyer and I hand our coats and bags off to a staff member, and I give my new scarf an extra pat before letting it go.

A part of me wants to keep it on while in the house, as a sort of armor in case we run into my parents. As if a few yards of yarn, woven together by Mrs. Paige's talented hands can somehow protect me from Dad's wrath.

"Ready?" Sawyer takes my hand and kisses the back.

When I give him a nod, he leads us farther into the house. We don't make it far before there's a shout.

"Finally!" Madison comes striding up to us like she's on a mission. "Where the hell have you guys been?"

"It took a while for the snowplows to get to my mom's neighborhood," Sawyer explains with a touch of indignation.

Madison ignores him and zeros in on me instead. "Your parents are…" She seems to be at a loss for words. "… acting weird."

"Weird how?" Sawyer takes a half-step forward, pulling himself to his full height.

"I don't know." Madison throws her hands in the air. "Just weird. They're still schmoozing and all that, but it's different. I can't explain it. What happened with them? You didn't give me an update!"

Oops.

Sawyer looks at me, giving me a chance to tell her myself.

"It didn't go well." Then I reconsider. "But it could've been worse?"

Madison gives me an exasperated look. "What the hell is that supposed to mean?"

Sawyer sighs. "There was yelling. There was name-calling. But in the end, you got your message through."

"Yeah, that." I huddle in a little closer to Sawyer.

"And? Now what?" Madison asks.

Sawyer and I exchange a glance and the gesture makes me feel all warm inside. I'm not usually able to communicate with nothing more than a look. But I can do that with Sawyer now. I can tell what he's thinking.

"I'm not sure," I answer. "My mom thinks it'll be okay eventually."

Madison considers that for a moment, then her expression turns sympathetic. "I hope so. Come on. Party's this way."

As we follow Madison toward the party, the hum of conversation grows louder. A warm, crooning voice sings Christmas songs over a live jazz band. Madison makes a beeline for the bar first and orders all three of us drinks: glasses of wine for me and her, and a beer for Sawyer. We try to find an out-of-the-way corner to loiter in, but any hope of avoiding my parents is dashed almost immediately.

"Preston!"

"Fuck," Sawyer mutters at the same time Madison says, "Oh god."

Dad's large hand comes clapping down on my shoulder before any of us have time to react, squeezing hard enough that I wince. What is he doing? Didn't he hear anything I said yesterday? I'm not going to play along with him anymore.

On my other side, Sawyer tenses like he's about to

push Dad away. But he stops himself when I give him a small shake of the head. His jaw is set, his whole body primed to act the second I give him the slightest signal. I love him for it, but I need to get used to dealing with Dad myself.

"Gentlemen!" He drags me over to a group of men, never taking his hand off my shoulder like he's afraid I'll slip away if he does. "I believe most of you have met my son, Preston."

I try my best to smile and not wilt under the weight of all their scrutiny. One of them extends a hand and I shake it automatically.

"Preston's finishing up his PhD in neurobiology at Grantham University down in New York," Dad says and my gaze snaps to him in shock.

He's never started his spiel with that before. He usually launches straight into what I'm going to do at Boyer Pharmaceuticals.

"He's doing some of the most cutting-edge research in his field. Why don't you tell us about it, Preston?" He looks at me with the same old overbearing expression, and he doesn't take his hand off my shoulder. But he's also never asked me to talk about my research before.

"I, uh, it's, um…"

"An AI?" Dad prompts.

"Yeah, an AI." Did Dad get a brain transplant? This is so unlike him. "It takes data from brain scans and tries to reproduce the image the subject was looking at when they were scanned."

"That's fascinating," one of the men says. "I can think of so many practical applications for that kind of technology. Is your school looking for any industry partners?"

"Uh…" I peek at Dad to make sure it's okay for me to respond. He stares at me expectantly, like he's curious about the answer too. "I'm not sure, but I guess I can ask."

"Grantham would be an excellent institution to partner with," Dad says like this is some presentation we've rehearsed. "It would be a smart investment."

The man holds out a business card to me. "Talk to whoever is in charge in your department and have them give me a call if they're interested."

I take the card, dumbfounded. "Uh, okay."

Then as quickly as I got sucked into Dad's vortex, I'm spit back out again, and Dad's entourage disappears into the crowd.

"What the hell was that?" Madison says, closing in on me.

"Seriously, what the fuck?" Sawyer's still staring at Dad's back in disbelief.

"We had a long talk after you left yesterday."

I spin around to find Mom standing behind me. She's got that soft look in her eyes again.

"Your father and I had an honest conversation about the expectations we've had of you, and came to the conclusion that we've been a tad unrealistic."

My jaw hangs open and my brain throws up flashing error messages. She can't possibly mean what I think she means.

"We won't force you to join Boyer Pharmaceuticals." Then she mutters under her breath, "God knows that would've turned into a disaster," before continuing. "But we do still expect you to put in appearances now and then. You might not be an executive, but a world-renowned professor has his own kind of clout."

Mom glances briefly at Sawyer before turning back to me. "Merry Christmas, Preston." Then she walks away.

"Wow." Madison looks impressed.

"Shit." Sawyer looks dazed.

I don't know what to say.

"So, I guess that means everything's going to work out?" Madison says, cheeky and hopeful.

"I think it does," Sawyer agrees. "How do you feel?"

I take a moment to assess before answering. "Good," I say, entirely sincere. I step closer to Sawyer and let him pull me into his arms. "I'm good."

Later that evening, when most of the guests have left, Sawyer and I stand in front of a Christmas tree. The room's lights have been dimmed, leaving the tree glowing in the darkness.

"Fitz isn't so bad," I say.

Sawyer chokes out a, "What? Why are you thinking about Fitz?"

I gaze up at him. "Because he brought us together."

Sawyer smiles down at me. "No, he didn't. We were always meant to be together."

SAWYER

Graduation speeches are the most boring things in the entire world. I know they're supposed to be all inspirational and everything, but all I really care about is when Preston walks across that stage and gets hooded.

My own graduation ceremony was the day before, and he was there in the audience with Mom. She let out an ear-splitting whistle when I did my walk and Preston jumped up and down, waving his hands in the air.

But I just got a measly undergraduate degree. Preston's becoming a doctor.

It takes forever, but eventually, it's Preston's turn. They call his name, he walks to the center of the stage, and kneels in front of his academic advisor. Then Professor Graves places the red and gold hood around his shoulders.

I rush onto the stage, ignoring all the surprised and annoyed looks I get along the way. By the time Preston stands up and turns around, I'm there, on my knees, velvet ring box in hand.

"Sawyer?" Preston blinks at me. "What are you doing here?"

"Preston Boyer, would you like to change your name to Preston Paige?" It's not the most romantic proposal in the world, but I say those pretty words to him all the time. He knows how I feel about him. He knows how much I love him. What he needs to know now is I want to marry him. I want to give him my name.

Which he hasn't said yes to—yet. I know he will. There's no question about it. But my heart is still hammering against my chest as I wait for his mouth to catch up with his beautiful brain.

He stares at the simple gold band nestled inside black velvet. There are no jewels or gemstones embedded in the ring, but rather, it's engraved with a single oscillating line.

Preston bends forward to study it closer. "Is that a brain wave?"

I nearly drop the box. Of course he'd zero in on the engraving instead of answering my damn question. "Yes, babe, it's a brain wave. My brain wave, to be exact. Fitz said it's the alpha frequency, whatever that means. But you're kind of leaving me hanging here..."

"Did Fitz scan your brain?" he asks, almost accusingly. "How come you didn't ask *me* to scan your brain?"

"Preston, put the man out of his misery and answer his question!" This comes from Professor Graves who is hovering behind him.

"What? Oh, sorry, what was the question?" Preston's cheeks turn a little pink when he realizes he's still standing in the middle of the stage with hundreds of people staring at him.

"Preston Boyer, will you marry me?" I say, opting for the direct route rather than the witty inside joke.

He smiles so brightly, he could rival the sun. "Yes, yes, I'll marry you."

He throws himself at me and I barely manage to catch him without ending up sprawled on the floor.

"I can't believe you asked Fitz to scan your brain," he murmurs against my lips in between kisses.

"I couldn't ask you," I murmur back. "It would've ruined the surprise."

I disentangle Preston from me long enough to slip the ring onto his finger and he immediately brings it to his face to study the engraving. I can't wait to hear what he thinks about my brainwave.

We're ushered off stage—or more like shooed—and Madison is there, waiting for us. She squeals before enveloping Preston in a hug.

"Congrats, babe!"

"Thanks, Mads."

Behind Madison are Mr. and Mrs. Boyer, looking collected and reserved. If they're proud of their son earning a PhD, you'd never be able to tell. But Mrs. Boyer is holding what I expect is a very expensive bottle of wine.

"Congratulations, Preston," she says coolly as she hands the bottle over. "On your doctorate and on getting engaged."

Mr. Boyer shakes Preston's hand. "Good job."

I bite my tongue. Things are still strained between Preston and his parents, but they've managed to respect his wishes so far. There's been no mention of joining Boyer Pharmaceuticals, even though I got a distinctly icy welcome from Mr. Boyer at Easter. That's fine—I can deal with icy welcomes and cold shoulders. The important thing is Preston is free to do what he wants with his life.

"You'll be staying at Grantham?" Mrs. Boyer asks.

"Yes," Preston answers. "They offered me the new post-doctorate position."

"That's lovely." Then she turns to me. "And you, Sawyer?"

"Still at the gym," I chirp because I'm not ashamed of my job. Especially not since Beau and Gavin approached me about creating custom dietary plans for our members.

Mr. Boyer clears his throat, and then pointedly checks his watch. "We should get going."

Mrs. Boyer presses her lips into a thin line, but she doesn't object. "Yes, we should. It was wonderful to see you all. Preston, we'll be in touch."

"That wasn't so bad," Madison says after Mr. and Mrs. Boyer disappear into the crowd.

"Definitely could've been worse," I agree.

Preston turns to face us and shrugs more nonchalantly than I'm used to from him. "It doesn't matter." He holds up his hand, the gold ring glinting in the sunlight. "I'm going to be a Paige."

BONUS SCENE

Everyone keeps asking if I'm nervous, and I don't know why. Why would I be nervous? I'm marrying my best friend. I've known him for years. He's the best person I know. It's not like I'm marrying a stranger.

Madison accuses me of being unromantic, and maybe I am. After all, it's just a piece of paper we sign and file with city hall. The part I'm most excited about is getting to change my name after. I've already started thinking of myself as Preston Paige and I like it so much better than the original.

But Sawyer is a romantic, so I acquiesced to a small wedding…

To read the rest of the bonus scene, sign up for Linden Bell's Very Important Reader newsletter here: bit.ly/stackedbonus.

PUMPED

Brothers-in-law, Everest and Owen, hate each other's guts, but now they're forced to work together to raise their orphaned niece in the next Mars Fitness book, *PUMPED*.

THANK YOU

If you've enjoyed *STACKED*, please consider recommending it to your friends. Leave a review for *STACKED* on social media, your own blog, Amazon, or Goodreads so other MM romance lovers can get to know Sawyer and Preston too.

If you would like to stay up to date on future Linden Bell books, join the Very Important Reader mailing list and also receive the exclusive bonus scene! bit.ly/stackedbonus

You can also follow me on:
Facebook - facebook.com/authorlindenbell
Instagram - instagram.com/authorlindenbell
Amazon - amazon.com/author/lindenbell
Goodreads - goodreads.com/authorlindenbell
Bookbub - bookbub.com/authors/linden-bell

ABOUT LINDEN BELL

Linden Bell writes romances that heat you up and make you smile. Her books are low angst, feel-good reads, with no third-act breakups!

For a reading guide to Linden Bell books, check out lindenbell.com/books.

facebook.com/authorlindenbell

instagram.com/authorlindenbell

amazon.com/author/lindenbell

goodreads.com/authorlindenbell

bookbub.com/authors/linden-bell